The Great Big Demon of
Flint Hall

(Spencer & Bart:2)

by

Peter Oxley

Burning Chair Limited, Trading As Burning Chair Publishing
61 Bridge Street, Kington HR5 3DJ

www.burningchairpublishing.com

By Peter Oxley
Edited by Simon Finnie
Cover by Burning Chair

First published by Burning Chair Publishing, 2024

ISBN: 978-1-912946-39-6

Also by Peter Oxley

The Great Big Demon Hunting Agency

The Infernal Aether Series:
  The Infernal Aether
  A Christmas Aether
  The Demon Inside
  Beyond the Aether

Plague: The Old Lady of the Skies Episode 1

The Wedding Speech Manual – The Complete Guide to Preparing, Writing and Performing Your Wedding Speech

Chapter One

The wall exploded in a shower of bricks and mortar.

Spencer ducked down to avoid the shards flying his way and let out a string of curses. He looked over at his friend and yelled, "Bart, you bloody idiot! What the hell are you doing??"

Bart, a mountain of a man with an immense unkempt beard and perfectly bald head, turned and shrugged. "You said you wanted me to get its attention."

Spencer shook his head and tried to brush the dust from his clothes. "Only had this jacket a few days," he muttered. "Tess'll kill me if she sees the state of it." He peered round the corner of his hiding place and then quickly darted back to safety. "If that thing don't kill me first."

"So what's our plan?" Bart asked.

An almighty roar echoed from the street behind them, a bloodcurdling sound which made the ground rattle. Spencer flinched. "All right, Spencer," he muttered to himself. "Think."

"Come on," said Bart. "Could do with that plan. What is it?"

"I'm trying to think," Spencer said through gritted teeth.

"About what?"

"Trying to come up with a plan. Which is pretty bloody hard if I've got you nagging me while I'm trying to think."

Bart stared at him. "I thought you already had a plan? You're always the one with the plan."

"I did. But it involved that big thing back there thinking we were over there," he pointed vaguely towards the other side of the street, "not over here. It's a bit hard to do a sneak attack if the thing you're trying to surprise knows exactly where you are, don't you think?"

Bart grunted, scratching his head. "Suppose so. Why didn't you think of that before you told me to get it looking over here?"

"I didn't—" began Spencer, then shook his head. "Never mind. Get your axe ready; we're going to have to do this the hard way."

There was another roar and another shower of dust, and then a short, lithe figure threw herself to the ground in between them.

"Afternoon boys," said Tess. "What are you doing sitting around back here?" She was wearing riding breeches and a short coat, looking for all the world as though she were about to go out for a bit of horse-riding in the country.

Spencer gaped at her, while Bart broke into a broad grin.

"We're hiding from that bloody great big thing back there," snapped Spencer. "What do you think we're doing? More to the point, what are you doing here?"

"You seemed to have managed to get yourselves boxed in," she said. "I thought I would come and lend a hand."

"Welcome on board," grinned Bart.

Spencer groaned. "So now, rather than just the two of us, we're now three idiots trapped by that great big demon. Brilliant."

Tess tutted. "Always so negative. Look, I brought some things to help." She held up a long brass tube with a box attached to its midsection. Two large dials were set on the front of the box, with a large lever on top.

"What's that?" asked Bart. "Some sort of gun?"

"Of sorts," she said. "I have been itching for an opportunity to test it; now seems like an opportune time, do you not think?"

"I suppose," said Spencer, eyeing it suspiciously. "Where'd you get that from?"

"I have been corresponding with a scientist, an immensely clever chap who has…"

Her words were drowned out by another bellow from the

demon.

"Maybe save the story for later, eh?" asked Spencer. "So what does it do?"

She beamed at him. "That is why I am so keen to test it. I have absolutely no idea!"

Spencer groaned. "All right. Give it here."

She snatched it away from his outstretched hands. "No. This one's mine. I brought something else for you." She reached into her jacket and produced another device, this one about the same size and shape as a box of matches, although slightly bulkier and with a large button on one side. A series of wires snaked around the button, and a tube ran around the device's edge. The whole thing was smoking slightly.

Spencer stared at it. "Suppose you don't know what that does either, do you?"

"Oh I do," she smiles proudly. "Press that button and count to five. Then it will explode, very messily."

"Why five?" asked Bart.

"What do you mean?" asked Tess.

"It's just it's more normal to say count to three, ain't it? One, two, three, go. That'd make more sense."

"But that's just what the person who made it..."

"What if," Bart's eyes gleamed in inspiration, "you count to three but a bit slower. That'd be the same, right?"

"Yes," said Tess. "Well done." As Bart grinned proudly, she handed the device to Spencer, mouthing the word "five", and then added, "Best to make sure you're as far away from it as possible when it explodes."

"Right," Spencer said, holding it as gingerly as he could without dropping it. "Don't suppose you happened to see what that demon was doing when you threw yourself in here?"

"It was stomping around, smashing things to pieces over that way. It did not seem to have figured out exactly where you are. Not yet, anyway."

"All right," said Spencer. "So it's more stupid than us.

Amazingly. That is something we can work with."

"Indeed," said Tess. "I was thinking that you could run over and throw that device at it, in the hope of not only distracting it but maybe also wounding it. I will then, once you are clear, test out this thing," she said, holding up her weapon. "And then Bart can finish it off."

Bart grinned, holding up his weapon. "With me bloody big axe."

Spencer looked from the axe, to Tess's intricate weapon, to his own much less imposing-looking one. "Sounds like a plan," he muttered. "Although not sure why I have the smallest one."

Bart laughed. "It's the smallest, 'coz you are too!" He then blinked. "No offence, mate..."

Spencer glared at him but, before he could respond, Tess spoke up. "It is nothing to do with size. But you are far and away the quickest and nimblest of us; I just thought that you would stand the best chance to use it most effectively."

"I suppose..." he muttered.

"And," added Tess, flashing him a smile, "I think you will be pleasantly surprised by how effective it is, for such a small thing."

They all winced at another almighty crash from the street behind them.

"All right," said Spencer, raising himself to his haunches, ready to run. "Let's get this over with. You both all set?"

They nodded. "Yup," grunted Bart.

Spencer took three quick breaths as he bent forward in a crouch. "Can't believe I keep getting myself in these stupid situations. One day..." Then he sprinted out of their cover.

Tess watched him go, wincing. "Do you think he will be all right?"

"Oh yeah," said Bart. "Well, maybe. Probably. Yeah." He frowned, straining to hear. "I should maybe go out there and..." He straightened up and lumbered out, the axe above his head.

Standing in the middle of the street, he looked around, blinking in the dusty street. There, at the far end, stood the demon. It must have been at least seven feet tall, and its arms and legs were thicker than Bart's entire body. He gulped and looked down at his axe, which suddenly felt nowhere near big enough for what was needed.

He turned at the sound of someone hissing from somewhere to his side.

Spencer had hidden behind the nearest pile of rubble, waiting for a safe moment to sprint out, relieved that the marauding creature hadn't seen him. He had then watched with a resigned amazement as his friend had just sauntered out, in full view.

"What are you doing now?" Spencer asked as his friend lumbered over.

"Looking for you. I thought you were s'posed to be having a go at that?" Bart gestured at the demon, which had stopped tearing chunks out of a nearby building and was now advancing on them.

"I was waiting…"

"For what? If you wait too much longer, it'll be on us!"

Spencer opened his mouth to reply, then thought better of it. Gritting his teeth, he shook his head, then turned and ran out of the other side of his hiding place, taking him round and to the side of the advancing creature.

The demon paused for a moment, looking from one of them to the other before deciding that the larger of the two looked the tastiest. And anyway, that one wasn't moving, while the other looked too much like hard work to catch. It let out a loud roar, shattering the remaining intact panes of glass in the street, as it continued towards Bart.

Bart swung his axe as he ran in a circle around the demon, darting close to catch it with a glancing blow across its back before sprinting away as fast as he could. The demon roared and followed him, its size making it slower and more cumbersome than even Bart, who was usually not known for his speed and nimbleness. He stopped and looked back, mildly surprised to see that the creature was still not upon him.

"Could get used to this," he muttered to himself. "I don't think I've ever been able to dodge away from anyone before."

He ran at the demon, only to be caught a glancing blow by a clawed fist across his jaw. He flew back, landing against a wall and collapsing to the ground in a heap.

"You got carried away, didn't you?" Spencer said, helping him to his feet. "You thought you were quick enough to keep dodging it."

"Yeah, well," grumbled Bart. He pushed his friend to the side. "Watch out!"

The demon's fist swung through the space vacated by Spencer's body. "Ow!" Spencer shouted, hitting the floor, hard. He glared at Bart.

"I just saved you," Bart said. "This way," he yelled, picking his friend up and again pushing him away from the advancing creature.

They ran, splitting off into two different directions, forcing the demon to choose which one of them to follow.

Finding himself round the back of the demon, Spencer held up the device Tess had given him. "Push the button," he muttered, pressing it down. "Then count to... was it five or three?" He snarled a curse and then shrugged before throwing the device at the demon. He ran in the opposite direction as fast as he could.

The device arced through the air and bounced off the demon's scaley back, clattering to the ground where it failed to explode.

Tess looked out from her hiding place and let out a curse. "I shall be having words with Maxwell later," she said, before raising her weapon and taking careful aim. She remembered that the inventor had told her to make sure she had a good grip and was ready for a rather powerful recoil. Not that she believed that for a second; it was far too small.

She pulled the trigger, and then disappeared in a thick white cloud. A beam of energy thundered towards the demon, which staggered back beneath the impact. It dropped to one knee, clearly injured.

Spencer grunted in appreciation from where he was hiding. "Bart! Now!" he yelled, when he saw his friend torn between checking on Tess and advancing on the demon.

Bart looked up and nodded, running at the creature with his axe raised. He swung and caught it in the shoulder, the weapon sticking firm in its armoured flesh. He strained to pull the axe free so he could deal a killing blow, but the demon swung an arm round, sending him flying across the street. The demon pulled the axe from its body and threw it away, roaring at the sky.

It was at that moment that the device which Spencer had thrown finally decided to explode.

It detonated with the sound of a hundred cannon, and almost as much force. Spencer pressed himself against the wall he was hiding behind as a mighty wind rushed past him, sending masonry and bits of demon flying through the air.

When the explosion had settled, Spencer sat up, his ears ringing and the world seeming to swim around him. Eventually, shapes formed into solid brick and mortar—or what was left of it—leaving him coughing as he looked around for his friends.

Bart's huge form emerged from under a pile of bricks. "I'm all right," he said as Spencer approached, then turned to look for Tess.

They found her lying on the ground, covered in dust. "How could such a small weapon exert anything like that amount of recoil? The physics just should not allow it." She held her gun in front of her face, examining it with awe, as Bart lifted her to her feet.

"Great," said Spencer. "We killed the demon, by the way."

She beamed at him. "I told you the device would do the trick."

"You could've got yourself killed," said Spencer.

"But I did not," she grinned. "All is fine; we saved the day once more." She started to walk away.

Spencer turned to Bart. "She got a death wish or something?"

"She's just doing her bit," said Bart.

"Yeah, but—"

They were interrupted by the sound of a whistle and running feet. Two police constables ran round the corner, accompanied by a man in a long dark greatcoat. "What's going on here?" bellowed one of the constables.

"Demon," said Bart. "Bloody big demon. We stopped it."

They looked around. "What demon? Where?"

Spencer gestured at the walls and floor. "It's kind've spread all over the place. Not much left. Hang on: there's one of its hands. And I think that's its head over there."

"Nah," said Bart. "I think that's a foot."

"Strange shaped foot. Got to be a head."

"Look, it's got claws on it. Never known a demon to have claws on its head. Have you?"

"Really? Oh yeah. Me eyes must be fading; it'll be that explosion. Damn near knocked the stuffing out of me. Reckon I'll be seeing stars for days…"

The man in the greatcoat cleared his throat. "If you've quite finished?" Behind him, one of the constables had made the mistake of bending down to examine the debris at his feet, and was now in the process of throwing up.

"Yeah. Sorry, officer," said Spencer. "Hang on, don't I know you?"

"You do. We crossed swords a little while ago. When I warned you to keep out of trouble." He turned to Tess and held out his hand in greeting. "Inspector Jones, ma'am. I trust these men are not bothering you?"

"Not at all," said Tess. "Far from it; we are, in fact, colleagues."

"Colleagues." Inspector Jones glared at the two men. "Is this another one of your scams?"

"Not at all," said Spencer. "We're totally legit, just like you told us to be. Ain't that right, Bart?"

"'S'right."

"But you weren't an inspector when we saw you last,"

continued Spencer. "You was in uniform, if I ain't mistaken."

"I have been promoted," he said. "I am now part of the detective force."

"Does that mean you aren't plodding the streets no more?"

"I will leave that to my colleagues. But that doesn't mean I'm still not interested in you. Especially if you've moved on to hoodwinking innocent ladies."

"Inspector, really," said Tess. "I can assure you—"

"Ma'am, these men are hardened criminals. I have followed them for many years, and I can assure you that they are very bad people." He turned to Spencer. "And what a surprise to see you in the midst of this destruction."

"It was a demon," said Spencer. "That's what we do now. We hunt and kill demons for clients. This one was a big menace, been trashing the area, driving out folk, destroying their livelihoods. We'd been tracking it for days!"

Inspector Jones stared at him. "Tracking it. A creature that destroys whole streets," he deadpanned. "Hard job, was it, tracking it down? Require lots of skill to locate such a ghost-like figure?"

"It wasn't being a nuisance all the time," said Spencer. "Sometimes it slept."

"Yeah," added Bart. "And ate. It was quiet when it ate."

"It ate people," said Inspector Jones. "Didn't you think to just follow the bodies?" He rolled his eyes. "If you really are demon hunters, you're particularly bad at your jobs. Which just makes me even more convinced that you're up to no good. What better way to extract money from innocent businesses than to let a demon loose, and then wait until they are desperate enough to pay any price to get rid of it. That, boys, is extortion; and that is enough to see you back in the clink."

"That is quite enough, inspector," snapped Tess. "I do not know the source of your prejudice against these gentlemen, and to be frank I do not care." She ignored his spluttering as she continued. "These men are my business partners, and very dear friends. We are respectable businesspeople, doing honest work. In fact, if the police did your jobs and kept the streets safe from the demons, there would be no need for our services. You should be thanking us for helping keep this neighbourhood safe and well."

Inspector Jones looked around at the smouldering ruins of what remained of the neighbourhood. "Indeed," he said. "Ma'am, I have no reason to doubt your word, although I would ask that you give careful thought to the company you keep."

She glared at him. "I will be the judge of what company I keep, sir. And I would thank you to keep your opinions to yourself. As for your allegations against these men… If you are accusing them, you are also accusing me. In which case, I would like to see what evidence you have to back up what you say."

Jones cleared his throat, his cheeks reddening under the force of her scrutiny. He looked around at the constables, who shrugged back at him. "Very well, ma'am. You are all free to go. I would, though, insist that you let me know the address of your lodgings. In case we need to speak to you about…" He gestured vaguely at the destruction around them. "This."

"Of course," said Tess, gesturing to Spencer, who produced a business card with a flourish, handing it to the officer with a sly grin.

"Just in case you need any help disposing of any other demons," said Tess. "I think you'll find our rates very reasonable."

Chapter Two

"That was fun," chuckled Spencer as they walked away. "We should do that more often."

"What?" asked Tess. "Nearly get killed by an out-of-control demon?"

"No. Getting one over the Bobbies. Did you see his face? Never seen anything so funny."

"I did not like the way he was talking to you."

"Happens all the time," said Bart. "You get used to it." He stopped as he saw a wagon selling pies. "I've got a hunger on me. Wait while I get something? You want any?"

Tess eyed the rudimentary wooden stall and the scruffy man standing behind it. She shuddered as she watched the vendor pick his nose and wipe it on his trousers. "No," she said. "I will be fine, thank you."

"Suit yourself. Spencer?"

"Yeah. Get me a meat one. Ta."

"No problem; I've got the cash." He grinned at them. "Never get tired of saying that!"

They chuckled as they watched him lumber off. "He is a funny one," said Tess.

"He's a good lad," agreed Spencer. "And he's still very taken with you. When're you going to let him down, tell him you're not interested?"

"I will," she squirmed. "Just... maybe not right now..."

"He's convinced himself you two've got some sort of future. You know, romantic like. I won't have you hurting his feelings any more than you will already, you know?'

"I know." She looked around. "Anyway, I should be going. I have an appointment. See you back at the office." She ran away before he could reply, hailing a cab and jumping in.

"Where'd she go?" asked Bart as he returned with their food.

"Don't know. Said something about an appointment. Must be something personal; don't remember any work stuff coming up."

They grabbed a couple of pots of beer to wash down their pies and then sat on a nearby wall to eat, watching the crowded streets in companionable silence.

"You reckon she's all right?" Spencer asked.

"Who?"

"Tess."

"Yeah. Why?"

"It's just... she seems a bit too keen to get stuck in, you know?"

"She wants to do her bit; got to respect that, no?"

Spencer shrugged. "I guess. It's just... Remember last week, with that demon out the West End? We'd got it trapped, it was done for, and she kept on whacking it with that device of hers."

"Well, yeah, we had to stop her..."

"And just now, the look in her eyes. If we weren't there, I reckon she'd've happily pounded the demon's remains and danced on his guts."

"Well it did take too long to stop," said Bart. "I was pretty frustrated myself."

"Yeah. Look, don't get me wrong; I like killing demons as much as the next bloke, but she sometimes takes it to another level, you know?"

Bart chuckled. "She's not like other girls, I'll give you that. And definitely not like the other ladies like where she's from. But a girl can have a hobby, right? Just 'cause she's a bird, doesn't mean she can't have fun when she works."

Spencer grunted noncommittally.

"All right," said Bart. "Know what? Let's keep an eye on her.

But I don't think there's any harm in her being a bit hard on the demons, not given the line of work we're in, right?"

The door to a nearby pub swung open and they watched as a hulking demon walked out, carrying two huge barrels of ale. The landlord directed it down to the cellar, wincing as the creature left a trail of upturned tables and broken glasses in its wake.

"Still can't get used to seeing them working in normal places," said Bart.

Spencer shrugged. "Guess we'd better. They ain't going anywhere soon, and they're pretty handy at doing heavy work and other stuff that's a bit tricky for us mere humans."

"Them that behave themselves," pointed out Bart.

"Yeah. But the ones that don't, they provide the likes of us with work, right?"

"I'll drink to that!"

*

As they were finishing their food, a tall shadow fell over them. Spencer looked up. "Oh. It's you. I thought we'd seen the last of you for today."

Inspector Jones shook his head. "No such luck, boys. Now that your bodyguard lady has deserted you, let's talk."

"We've got nothing to talk to you about," said Spencer, pulling himself to his feet.

"You'll talk to me here and now, or we can go down to the station and talk there. Maybe after you've spent a few nights in the cells." He turned to Bart. "And don't think you can intimidate me; I've dealt with worse than you."

Bart frowned. "Intimidate? I was just sitting here."

Spencer thought for a moment and then shrugged. "All right. We're law-abiding citizens these days, so we'll gladly help the law if we can."

"We will?" asked Bart.

"Yes. If he had something to pin on us, he'd already be

arresting us," hissed Spencer in reply. He turned to Jones. "So what do you want to talk about?"

"I want to know what you two are up to. We've interviewed the witnesses in that street, and they back up your version of events: that you came to help get rid of the demon."

"Thank you," grinned Spencer.

"Whether you did so in the best way, with regard to safeguarding property and others around you… That is another question."

"You ever tried to get rid of a great big demon without there being a bit of mess?" asked Bart. "And anyway, the demon made most of the mess before we even had a chance to blow it up."

"And in doing so you blew up half of the neighbourhood as well," pointed out Jones. "Have you any idea how much damage you caused?"

"Yeah, well… No more demon though, is there?"

"Indeed." Inspector Jones stared at them.

"So you're not going to arrest us, we're not in trouble… What are you doing here?" asked Spencer.

"Don't try to be funny," said Jones. "I am here to warn you both. I don't know what you're up to, but I know what sort of people you are, so whatever you are up to, it can't be any good."

"We're law-abidin'…"

"Don't," snapped Jones. "I know your type. I know what you've always been, and I know that you'll never change. I don't know how you've managed to hoodwink that poor lady you are now hanging around with, but I will get to the bottom of this and I will put a stop to whatever scheme you're carrying out."

"It's not a scheme," protested Spencer. "We've genuinely gone straight. We're working with Tess; we started a demon hunting agency and she's joined us."

"Yeah," said Bart. "She's set us up with an office and money and stuff and we—"

"I knew you'd be scamming her for cash," said Jones with a satisfied smile.

"No," Spencer glared at Bart, who held up his hands in confusion. "It's not like that. There's no scam here, and she'd back us up in that. It's a legit business and she's our business partner. You saw back there; she's as involved as we are."

"Even more than us sometimes," said Bart. "She's the brains in the partnership."

"Well, one of the brains," said Spencer.

"Yeah, you come up with some good plans, mate, don't get me wrong. But she's got all the good ideas when it comes to science and stuff. She's got some great inventor mates. How'd you think we managed to make such a big explosion back there, eh?"

"Thank you for reminding me again about the damage you caused," said Jones. "I am sure there are plenty of people who will be interested in getting hold of you, to understand how you will be paying for the repairs."

"Wait, what?" asked Spencer. "We was doing them a favour! They paid us to get rid of the demon, to make their neighbourhood safe!"

"Yes, but they probably intended that there would be some sort of neighbourhood at the end of the process, rather than the pile of rubble you've left behind."

"That was the demon," protested Spencer.

"Yeah," said Bart. "It did the start of it. We only did the big explosion at the end."

Spencer turned to him. "Mate, you know when you think you're helping? Sometimes, you're really not…"

Jones chuckled. "Don't worry boys, I know exactly where to find you." He held up the business card they gave him earlier and walked away, whistling.

Bart frowned. "What does that all mean?"

"It means," groaned Spencer, "that he's going to try and make our lives a misery. Again."

Chapter Three

Tess pulled up outside Number 42 Jermyn Street, opened the door next to the window of the busy tailor's shop, and walked up the stairs to the rooms she shared with her business partners. Inside, all was quiet; Mrs Dawson, the housekeeper, had clearly finished for the day. The curtains were pulled open, allowing the meagre light from outside to filter in and allow her to see through to the staircase to the upper floors. She glanced at the grimy windows, her daily reminder that they really should arrange for them to be cleaned at some point. When they could afford it.

She made her way past their offices and the rooms set aside for Spencer and Bart, and up to her own rooms, at the top of the house. She shrugged off her shawl and, turning to place it on a chair, saw a dark figure sat in the corner.

She screamed.

Grabbing the nearest thing to hand which could be used as a weapon—a poker from the fireplace—she brandished it at the figure, which had risen from the chair, hands held out in an attempt at reassuring surrender.

"It is I, Thaddeus," said the dark figure.

She lowered the poker very slightly and glared at him, her heart beating far too hard in her chest. "What are you doing here?"

"You agreed to meet with me," he replied. "I was waiting for you to return."

"And what made you think that here was a suitable place to

wait for me? In my bedchamber? And how did you get in here anyway?"

"I…"

"Never mind." She needed him out of her room, so she could gather her senses together and calm herself down. "Wait for me downstairs. In the sitting room."

He nodded and turned to go.

Tess let out a slow, shaky breath. "Oh, and Thaddeus?" she said, causing him to pause as he walked out the door. "If you ever trespass in my bedchamber uninvited again, I will insert this poker in a place where it will hurt. No matter how magical you really are. Understand?"

He grunted in reply and then left the room.

*

Tess took her time getting changed, partly to prove a point to her unwanted guest but also to make sure she had fully removed all pieces of exploded demon from her hair and clothes. She found Thaddeus in the living room, sat in the furthest chair from the windows and door, staring into space.

Even though they had met a couple of times, he remained as much an enigma as ever. She knew from Spencer and Bart that he was a magician of not inconsiderable power; they had clearly witnessed some display of his powers to cause them to be afraid of him, or at least be very wary of him. Although whenever she had pressed them on what exactly they had seen him do, neither of them would tell her, no matter how much she pestered them.

Sat there in her apartment he was darkly compelling, his long brown hair and elegant suit lending an other-worldly aspect to his appearance which made her wonder whether he was actually much, much older than his smooth face made him seem.

He seemed to snap back into the room, his eyes focusing on her. They had a sharp, piercing and yet also brooding quality which drew her in, making her almost forget that he had invaded her private quarters just a few minutes earlier.

"Finally," he said. "I have been waiting for you for some time. What have you been up to?"

"I had to freshen myself up. You may not have noticed, but I was rather dirty and needed to remove dust and gore from my hair and clothes. And anyway," she bristled, "I do not need to justify myself to you. I cannot believe you broke into my bedchamber!"

"It was the most obvious place to wait for you, being the room you were most likely to go to."

"I…" she stared at him for a moment. "Just stay out of my private rooms in future. Understand? Anyway, Mrs Dawson should never have let you in without giving you clear instructions."

"Oh, she did not let me in," he replied. "I entered of my own accord."

"You…? But…!"

"I would not want to get your Mrs Dawson in trouble," he explained.

"So there is another rule: no picking of locks on my house. Ever."

"Oh, I did not need to pick any locks." When she stared at him questioningly, he held out his hands. "I have a particular set of talents, meaning there are very few places that are truly closed off to me."

She shuddered. "Was that meant to reassure me? You…! Just… No more breaking into my property. Understood?"

He shrugged and nodded.

Tess pursed her lips, realising there was little point in labouring the point any further. "Why are you here?"

"You will recall that I was instrumental in freeing you from the demonic possession inflicted on you by your late husband and his associate, Mr Emerson."

"So I understand."

"Your associates may have told you that I am somewhat of a

student of occult matters."

"Like the activities of our agency? Hunting demons?"

He cleared his throat. "Not quite. My interest is more in the arcane. What you may refer to as 'magic'."

She snorted with laughter, cutting herself short when she noticed the look on his face. "Oh, you are serious," she said.

"Of course," he frowned. "What do you find so amusing?"

"I just... Well, magic... It's..."

"I am not talking about illusions and cheap conjuring tricks."

"I know," she said. "I do not mean to cause any offence, but I prefer to deal in more... rational things."

"After all that has gone on in the world over the past few years, with demons invading from the Aether and now colonising our world, with you yourself having been possessed by a demon... And yet you insist on turning your nose up at the thought of magical powers." He shook his head. "In any case, I did not come here to enter into a debate on matters which are frankly self-evident—"

"To you."

"Granted. Self-evident to me. But to get to the point, I wish to discuss your experiences; those leading up to and including your possession and subsequent exorcism. It is not often that an opportunity arises to speak to someone who has been through and survived such an..."

"Ordeal?" Tess shuddered.

He blinked. "If you will. But it would be illuminating to understand your experiences, from your point of view."

Tess stared at him for a long moment, unsure exactly how to respond. She had suspected such a conversation would come up at some point, although had not been quite ready for it at that moment.

She knew precious little about the man in front of her, save for what she had picked up from Spencer and Bart. When they met him, he had been working for Milton, one of London's most notorious gangsters. They had not really told her what it was that he had done for Milton, although the way they reacted when his name was mentioned told her that he was someone to be wary of.

She did know that Thaddeus had been instrumental in ridding her of the demonic possession which had been placed on her by her late husband and his colleague, the mysterious Mr Emerson. After that, Thaddeus had disappeared and her attempts to locate him to thank him for saving her life had run up a succession of dead ends. Spencer and Bart had refused to help her find him, warning her that he was someone she was best to keep clear of, while not actually telling her why.

Which showed how little they still knew her; treating her like a child in that way was guaranteed to ensure that she did everything she could to track down Thaddeus. Which was exactly what she had done.

She was actually quite proud of herself; the way she was able to follow the chain of people from the events of that fateful day all the way to Thaddeus, developing contacts along the way. It was this that had given her faith, finally, that she could play a part in some form of detective work, and could be an active member in their demon hunting agency.

She had tracked Thaddeus down to a nondescript coffee shop in the East End, where he had seemed to be whiling away his days studying a thick red book. He had at first been reluctant to speak to her, giving her approaches short shrift. But then, just a few days later, he had sent her a message requesting a meeting.

And so now she found herself face-to-face with him in her sitting room, being asked to relive one of the most terrifying ordeals of her life so far.

She found herself stammering, not only at the unexpected nature of the request—or rather demand—but also her own annoyance at not having expected this. "Why should I... I do not..."

"You initially approached me, remember?" Thaddeus pressed her. "The only connection we have is that particular incident, so it is logical that that is the one thing we would have to discuss."

She stared at him for a moment. It was true; she had approached him. But that was just to thank him, was it not? She was suddenly hit by the realisation: had she approached him for some other reason? The events of those days were still painfully fresh in her mind and, while she had done her best to push them away, she still wanted answers. To understand why her husband and Mr Emerson had done what they had to her, and indeed, to understand what exactly they had done to her.

Thaddeus had been watching her, and clearly saw the emotions play across her face. "If you wish, I will leave at once and you will never see me again." He rose to his feet.

"No, no…" Tess held up a hand. "Please stay. I was just rather surprised with the abruptness of your approach, how direct and to the point you are in terms of your questioning."

He sank down in his chair and cocked his head to one side. "I do not understand. If there is something to be said, why should I not just say it?"

She chuckled, in spite of herself. "You do not spend much time in company with others, do you?"

"Not if I can help it. You went to great efforts to track me down. Why?"

She frowned and played with a loose thread on her clothing. Could he read her thoughts?

"I suppose… I wished to understand what happened, when I was… when the incident occurred. My colleagues are rather vague on the matter."

"Colleagues?"

"Spencer and Bart. You know them, I believe."

"Ah yes." There was an amused twinkle in his eye. "You have a rather interesting choice in *colleagues*."

"I find people tend to underestimate them."

"It is very hard to *over*estimate them."

She stifled a grin. "That is unfair. They have a unique set of skills, and are very decent people. In any case, I wished to understand more about what happened, so that I can take steps to ensure it does not happen again."

"So it sounds like our intentions here are aligned. If I tell you what I know, will you in turn tell me how matters transpired from your point of view?"

"That sounds a fair trade. You start."

He nodded and then leant back, his hands steepled in front of his face. "I shall not bore you with chronologies and the like; your colleagues can provide that. However, what happened to you was a direct result of a group of individuals with more money than sense, who decided to dabble in matters way beyond their comprehension."

"You are referring to my former husband, I believe. A man who was murdered as a direct result of his actions."

"Yes." He shot her a glance. "But I am sure you are not going to try and pretend that you are in any way upset about his demise. I seem to remember that you were rather… instrumental in his murder."

"That was not me!"

"It certainly seemed to look like you. The creature that tore him limb from limb wore your face."

"But I was…"

"Possessed by a demon?"

"Yes. But going back to my husband… He was involved with the Thaumaturgical and Paranormal Research Society, which was headed by an individual known as Mr Emerson. These are the ones you referred to as 'dabbling in matters beyond their comprehension'?"

"Indeed. I am sure their intentions started innocently enough. I had precious little interest in them at first. After a while it became apparent that they were kidnapping and experimenting on individuals—mostly women—but that was a matter for the police, not me. They did, though, draw my attention when I found out that Emerson had got his hands on a very powerful magical demonic text."

"Some sort of magic spell book?"

Thaddeus ignored the note of amusement in her voice. "Of sorts. In many ways, it is the original of that type of text. In particular, it contains instructions on how to force a demonic possession on an unwilling person, and how to reverse that possession."

"So that was what he used…"

"To allow the demon to possess you. Yes. And which I used to exorcise the demon from you, once I had the book in my possession. Which was in turn thanks to your colleague, Spencer."

"I already know all of that. But why? If my husband had wanted to get rid of me, there were surely plenty of ways less likely to draw attention than inserting some sort of insane demon into me."

"Your husband, Lord Marchant, was not really the brains in this process. I think it is fair to say that he was simply invited to join because of his money."

"My family's money," Tess shot back.

Thaddeus shrugged, as though to say that that was not even vaguely of interest to him. "He also had something which Emerson wanted. You."

"Me? What do you mean?"

"Think about it. They could have chosen any woman for their experiment. In point of fact, they did: their offices were full of females who had been subjected to demonic possession. But for their grand finale, they chose you. Like it or not, you seem to have a sensitivity for the paranormal."

She scoffed, but then frowned. "That might explain the seance…"

Thaddeus leaned forward. "Seance?"

"Yes. My husband arranged a session with some lady who claimed to be a medium, a clairvoyant. Mr Emerson was there, along with lots of others who seemed to be connected to their little society. I recall finding it very off-putting the way that Emerson talked to me. That was usually the case, but especially at the seance, and afterwards."

"And what happened at the seance?"

She shook her head. "I assumed at the time that it was some form of elaborate prank they were all playing on me. She made us all link hands, like they always do, and then the lights dimmed and something shot towards me. Something... Aetheric, I suppose. It could have emanated from some hidden source, a machine perhaps."

"And it shot directly at you?"

"It meandered around the table for a few moments, I think. But then it seemed to be directed straight towards me, yes."

"It was a test," Thaddeus said. "A reasonably basic one, to identify whether you were a suitable subject for what they were planning."

"To have me possessed by a demon? But why?"

"Why do those sort of men do anything? For power. The process you were subjected to not only required a lot of power to undertake, but its outcome was to create a being of immense power. I saw with my own eyes what you were capable of, how you—"

"Yes, yes. You do not need to remind me. But there are plenty of demons in this world capable of doing great damage; indeed, just this very afternoon, my associates and I despatched one which was laying waste to a large part of the East End."

"Yes, I am aware. But the creature you mention was just a mindless weapon. That is the thing with demons; they tend to either be blunt instruments or highly independent-minded. It is possible, with great effort, to bind a demon to your will for a limited time and for limited purposes. But when the binding is lifted, the demon in question will often be very angry at the indignity of it all and will inevitably take it out on the spell-caster, with rather fatal results. The spell they used on you, on the other hand, would create a demon totally in thrall to the spell-caster. It would be a slave in every sense of the word."

"Then why was I not in thrall to them?"

"Because they were impatient. Or rushed into doing the spell before they were ready. Or both. Instead of executing the spell properly, they were forced to rely on amulets which had been inlaid with runic symbols. These amulets protected the wearer, effectively repelling any interest the demon may have in them. That was the main reason why your colleagues and I were able to remain unmolested while we performed the exorcism on you. We stole amulets from Emerson and his men." He produced a circular medallion from his robes and handed it to her.

She turned it round in her hands, examining it. It was made from some sort of metal—bronze by the look and feel of it—and was a couple of inches in diameter. On the face of it were a series of symbols and shapes which seemed to blur in front of her eyes. She blinked and they resolved themselves into runic-looking symbols, surrounding a demonic effigy in the centre.

Thaddeus watched her keenly as she examined the object. "Does it provoke any feelings or memories in you?"

She frowned. "Not so much. It is rather interesting-looking, I suppose. For a moment the images carved into it seemed to blur and shift, but I suppose you would say that is because they are imbued with some sort of magical powers that make them appear fluid to mortal eyes."

"That is exactly what I would say." He sounded almost affronted. "But, more to the point, do you feel any discomfort when holding and examining it?"

"None at all. Should I?"

"Not necessarily. It is interesting that there are no residual effects from the possession. Now, thinking back to the possession itself, what do you remember?"

She frowned. "I was strapped into a cage of some sort. A bit like a glass fishbowl. I remember seeing Spencer and Bart there, as well as my husband and Emerson and their lackeys. I was fearful of what they were planning. I remember my husband gloating at me, and then Emerson started chanting. The noises were somewhat distinct…"

She remembered the feeling, of being trapped, unable to move, almost suffocated by the helplessness of her situation. Everything around her had seemed to become liquid, the very air morphing and swimming so that she was disoriented, not knowing which way was up or down, or even where she was.

She had found herself in some sort of misty hellscape, a wispy land which seemed to stretch out into eternity. She had looked around, unsure how she had come to be in that place or why, not really comprehending anything, unaware of the fact that she was no longer bound or contained in her glass prison, or indeed that she no longer seemed to have a form at all.

A presence had slowly started to resolve itself through the mist in the distance, something unknowable which drew her towards it with a dark malevolence. She had found herself allowing her body... no, not her body, her... awareness pulled towards it. At the same time she realised that there was no fear, no emotion at all, in her mind. She just *was*, and that was fine. Just fine.

The *thing* which she was being pulled towards had seemed as old as time, and just as powerful. A power which throbbed through her soul, making everything seem to spin and throb. A distant part of her knew that she should feel fear, or repulsion, but all she could think was, again, that it was all fine. Nothing to worry about, just... fine.

It had sucked her in and enveloped her, a marriage of their essences into something more, something intoxicatingly powerful. And then...

And then there was rage.

All the world had seemed to be on fire, and she was at the centre of it: railing and cursing and fighting, and gnashing and wailing and tearing.

The fire was everything, something to be conquered. And the thing had whispered to her that, together, they could do it. Together they could achieve anything. She just needed to surrender everything.

She had thought she had already given everything, but then

she realised there was more, and she was willing to do so, but then…

Then the presence was wrenched away from her, a sudden jolt which made her realise that all was not as it should be. Some distant part of her had started to reassert itself, noticing that she needed to do something. But what?

And then the dark presence was pushed away from her further again, and the voice in her mind had become a scream, and she realised that she needed to get out of that place RIGHT NOW.

Back in her sitting room, she blinked and looked back at Thaddeus, surprised at the strength of feeling that the recollections had created in her. Her face felt wet; she put a finger to her cheek and realised that she had been crying whilst she had been recalling those memories.

"Interesting." Thaddeus was leant forward, studying her intently. "So from your perspective there was an almost physical element to the process, as though you were transported elsewhere."

"I genuinely was," she said. "I still have nightmares…"

He watched her, waiting for her to continue. When she did not, he said, "Tell me about the nightmares."

"I think I have told you enough for today."

"But we are only just getting started."

"No. I think we are finished."

"Really, Lady Marchant, if you want to—"

"Do not presume to tell me what I do or do not want to do." She surprised herself with the steely edge in her own voice.

He stood. "And do not presume to speak to me like I am some lackey. Have you any concept what I am capable of? I have chosen to extract the information I require from you by talking with you; I could of course be a lot more—"

"Are you threatening me?" she asked, half-laughing.

"Of course not. Threats are made by people who do not intend to follow through on their promises."

"So you are saying that you are no better than them—my

husband and Emerson, the monsters who did…. what they did to me."

"I am so much *better* than them," he snapped. "They were mere amateurs. They could not hope to be able to hold a candle to what I am capable of."

She laughed in amazement, partly to hide the rising fear she felt in her chest. "You *are* threatening me! You come into my home and—"

They were disturbed by the sound of the front door opening and then banging shut.

"You!" said Spencer, stepping into the room. "What're you doing here?"

"I do not think that is any of your business," Thaddeus replied.

"It's our business if you're bothering her," said Bart, elbowing past Spencer to stand in front of the magician. "And it looks to me like she's very much bothered."

"Bart, I…" Tess said, holding up a hand.

"I will leave." Thaddeus stood. "You would do well to move out of my way. You, of all people, know what I can do."

"And you know what I can do," Bart rumbled. He turned at a sound from Spencer and, looking from him to Tess, finally got the hint and stepped aside. "You stay away from her, right?"

Thaddeus snorted and barged out of the room.

Bart turned to Tess, taken aback as she stormed to her feet. "I do not need you two to fight all my battles for me," she snapped. "I invited him here."

"But why?" asked Spencer. "We told you—"

"Kindly remember what happened to the last man who deigned to try and order me around," she replied coldly. "I would not want you to suffer the same fate." She stormed out of the room and up the stairs. A few moments later the two men flinched at the sound of the door to her bedchambers slamming shut.

"Did she just threaten to turn into a demon and rip us to

bits?" asked Bart.

Spencer shrugged. "If she did, it'd be an interesting take on the whole demon hunting agency thing, right?"

Chapter Four

Breakfast the following morning was a frosty affair, with lots of stony silences and meaningful slamming of crockery.

Finally, Spencer could stand it no longer. "Look, I'm sorry if we upset you yesterday. We were just trying to look out for you."

Tess shot him a cold look. "What made you think that I needed to be looked out for?"

"We all need looking out for, now and again, right? That's what me and Bart do for each other. Ain't that right, Bart?"

Bart looked up reluctantly, shooting his friend a look that made it clear he'd rather be kept out of this particular conversation. "Yeah," he said after a moment. "We've always done that. That's what makes us a team, right?"

"A team," said Tess slowly. She picked up a piece of paper. "Do you know what this is?"

"Paper?" Bart said hopefully.

She handed it to Spencer, who read it slowly, his lips moving as he did so. "A bill for lodgings," he said. "That's quite a lot of money. Does it really…?"

"Yes, it does," she replied, snatching the paper from him. "Keeping us all with a roof over our heads and food and suchlike costs money. Money which I would hope our *team* would be able to cover through fee-paying work. Speaking of which, what potential clients do you have lined up at the moment?"

"Well, there was the job yesterday," said Spencer. "And we've got a lead we're talking to later, right Bart?"

"We do? Oh, um, yeah, of course. Yes, we do."

"Yeah, and…" Spencer looked at her, realisation dawning.

"Here, is that what that Thaddeus bloke was doing here yesterday? Are you lining up something with him? 'Cause I'd just warn you…"

Tess turned, her eyes wild. "Do you really want to start that conversation again?"

Spencer opened and closed his mouth, searching for an answer. A knock at the door saved him and he jumped to his feet. "I'll get that," he said, running out of the room.

Bart swallowed the lump of meat he had been chewing. "You know he means well, right? We look at you as one of our own, that's all. But if you want us to back off then we will."

"I know," she sighed. "And I am sorry if I am being a bit too harsh. I am just finding things rather challenging right now."

He shrugged. "I get it. But you prob'ly should tell him that yourself, you know?"

The door opened and Spencer led a young lady into the room, clearing his throat to get their attention. She was a young woman in her early twenties, with long blonde hair tied back in the current fashionable style. She had a round, pretty face and was wearing a fine dress which looked as though it cost as much as several months' rent on their rooms. She looked around the room with darting glances, as though expecting ambushes to descend on her from every corner. Her gaze settled on Tess, who stood up with a broad smile on her face.

"Emilia Beaumont!" she exclaimed. "It is so good to see you; it has been so long!"

"Tessie, I am pleased to see you. I was not sure if I had the right address, but your doorman here was insistent."

"I go by the name 'Tess' now," she said, walking over and hugging her friend. She caught sight of Spencer's indignant expression and, with a smile, added. "And I should correct you: he is not a doorman. This is Spencer, one of my associates. And here is Bart, our other associate."

Emilia looked from one to the other slowly, blinking in slow comprehension as they stood and shook her hand. She returned their greetings with a faint reluctance. "I had heard you had made some interesting new friends here in London," she said softly.

Tess smiled, ignoring the comment. "Emilia and I are old friends," she explained to the men. "We grew up together."

"What, like sisters?" asked Spencer.

They both chuckled. "Not quite," said Tess.

"Although we spent a lot of time together as girls," said Emilia. "We shared lessons with the same governess for a while. And we spent many happy days playing together in my house."

Tess giggled. "Teasing your little brother Calvin. Those were some of the funniest times. How is he?"

"As annoying as ever."

"So what brings you here?" asked Tess, ushering her to a seat and pouring her a cup of tea. She looked over at Spencer and Bart, who were stood uncertainly, glancing at each other.

Spencer cleared his throat. "You two are clearly in need of plenty of catching up, so we'll be on our ways. We'll see you later, Tess."

"No!" The severity of Emilia's response seemed to surprise even herself as she continued. "I mean, I have a case which I would like… I need assistance which…" She took a long sip of her drink and then cleared her throat. "What I meant to say is that I have a problem which I believe your agency—all of you—can assist me with."

Spencer and Bart looked at Tess and, when she inclined her head, sat down at the table. They smiled at Emilia while Tess sank down into her own seat. "So," said Tess. "How can we be of assistance?"

Emilia looked each of them in turn, checking that they were giving her their full attention. "I am here on behalf of my family. You remember my parents, Tess? They send their regards."

Tess smiled and inclined her head. She remembered Lord and Lady Beaumont well, although she very much doubted that they had sent her their regards. Nevertheless, she allowed the untruth to pass, in the interests of politeness. "How kind. Do continue."

"It is a rather delicate matter," Emilia said. "I trust we can rely on your utmost discretion?"

"But of course," said Tess. "We can guarantee that anything you confide in us will be kept completely confidential. We believe in nothing less when it comes to our clients."

"Ahem," coughed Spencer. "That's to say she's totally right. That's part of the service we offer to our *paying* clients. Right?" He stared at Tess meaningfully.

She frowned at him, then nodded, a faint smile on her lips as she turned to Emilia. "Of course. Discretion guaranteed, all as a part of any services you procure from us."

"Oh, yes, without question," said Emilia. "I would not dream of asking for charity." She cast a faintly withering glance around the sitting room before continuing. "You will appreciate that money is no object for my family. Especially when it comes to a matter as pressing and delicate as this one. If you would like to advise of your fee, I am happy to provide a downpayment now, if that will satisfy you?"

As Spencer started to lean in eagerly, Tess quickly cut across him. "That will not be necessary. Why do you not tell us what your matter is, and we can then discuss fees afterwards. Once we know the commitment required."

Emilia smiled and sat back. "Thank you. That sounds very reasonable. It pertains to a rather sticky problem which my family are suffering with." She cleared her throat and looked down. "I understand that you have experience in dealing with demons?"

Spencer again leant forward, but Tess held up a hand to calm him down. "We do. It is rather a speciality of ours, you could say."

Emilia let out an overly loud sigh of relief. "That is good. You see, over the past week or so we have been, at our home, plagued by at least one demon, which refuses to leave us alone."

"I see," said Tess, scribbling in her notepad. "Can you describe this demon for us?"

"It is… big. With horns and shining red eyes," Emilia said.

"Any other features?"

She shrugged.

"How big?" Spencer asked.

"I am not sure. Bigger than a man."

"What colour skin does it have?"

"I don't know. Green maybe?"

Spencer stared at her. "Gonna need you to be a bit more specific, love. Difficult for us if we don't know what we're up against."

Emilia glared indignantly back at him. "I have only ever really seen it at night, and from a distance. I have not felt the desire to go up close and inspect it."

"Of course," Tess said quickly. "Totally understandable. Maybe we can try a different tack. What sort of damage has it done?"

"Damage?" Emilia blinked at her.

"Yes, you know: destroyed any property, killed any animals or people, that sort of thing?"

"Well, not really…"

"Nothing at all?" Spencer asked.

"I believe it has trampled some trees and bushes. But no damage yet, thank goodness."

Tess and Spencer looked at each other with raised eyebrows.

"What *does* it do?" asked Bart, breaking the silence.

"Well… It causes a nuisance, for one thing. It keeps us awake at night, and…"

"No offence, love," said Spencer. "We like killing demons as much as the next man. But it tends to be if they're doing something really bad. If it's not doing any real harm, well…"

"Don't seem right to do it harm if it's just walking around and being a bit annoying," said Bart, nodding.

Emilia's eyes took on a frantic look. "It's not what it is doing, so much as what we believe it will do," she said.

"Meaning what, exactly?" asked Tess.

Emilia looked around, as though she were checking for any bystanders listening in on them. Spencer and Bart looked around as well, wondering what she was looking at.

"Have you heard," Emilia asked in a low voice, "of the Curse of Flint Hall?"

Tess frowned. "No. I cannot say that I have."

Emilia nodded. "Although you and your family of course hail from the same parish as us, my family has taken great pains over the years to keep the tale of the curse out of the public eye. I had been afraid that the local gossips may have been ahead of us, but I am pleased to note that that is not the case.

"It all began in 1572. The original occupants of Flint Hall—and my ancestors—had once been influential at Court under Queen Mary. However they found themselves out of favour with the coming of Elizabeth I. My ancestors, you see, were secret Catholics and saw the other Mary, Queen of Scots, as a much more palatable monarch for their tastes, not to mention their ability to keep their heads.

"While they were not so foolhardy as to wear their Catholicism openly, they were quietly sympathetic to any causes which their brethren advanced, in the hope of getting a more favourable person on the throne. Rumours link them to pretty much every cause you can think of, but one that I understand the then Lord Beaumont was connected to, was the so-called *Rodolfi Plot*." She looked at them with raised eyebrows.

Spencer looked from one to the other. "All right, I'll spare everyone's blushes. What was that, then?"

Emilia gestured to Tess with a cold smile. "Would you care to answer?"

"Of course." Tess stared back at her. "It was a plot to assassinate Queen Elizabeth and replace her with Mary, Queen of Scots. 1871, I believe. It took its name from an Italian gentleman who conspired with Thomas Howard, Duke of Norfolk, who was rumoured to be a potential husband for Mary. The plot was discovered before it could come to fruition and most of the conspirators were executed." She beamed triumphantly at Emilia. "Those history lessons were not wasted on me!"

"Indeed." Emilia frowned, but then recovered herself and continued. "The then Lord Beaumont was rumoured to have some form of involvement in the plot, but nothing could be pinned on him. This is where the story starts, for the Queen of course could not allow a potential traitor to walk away scot-free, pardon the pun. So she instructed one of her more... remarkable advisors, a man by the name of John Dee, to come up with a punishment which would rid her of this potential traitor, and also provide a warning to any others who might be tempted to plot against her.

"And so the curse of Flint Hall was born. Every man who holds the title of Lord Beaumont will, when he reaches the age of sixty, come to a nasty end." She looked up at them, tears in her eyes. "My father turns sixty this coming week."

They sat and watched her as she sank her head towards the table, her shoulders shaking.

"I knew Queen Bess was said to be a pretty hard one," said Spencer. When they all looked at him, he added, "I mean, I don't have much—any—schooling, but I remember folk saying she didn't need much excuse to be lopping people's heads off."

"What is your point?" asked Tess.

"Just that, I don't get why she didn't just do what she did with everyone else. Why didn't she just chop off his head anyway? Why go to all the trouble of a curse? She was Queen, right? She could just kill anyone she wanted."

"That's what I heard she did," agreed Bart.

Emilia descended into more, louder, sobs.

"I am so sorry," said Tess. "But surely you don't believe...?"

"I do not know what to believe," Emilia said. "Except that I am beside myself with worry. In times gone by, we would have dismissed such a thing as a mere fairy tale, but these days...?"

"Your grandfather," pressed Tess. "Did he not die of natural causes? I do not remember any sort of scandal."

"Yes, but he also passed away before he reached sixty. Almost as though the weight of that impending deadline lay so heavy on him that they could not bear risking to see what happened on that fateful day."

"What sort of fate?" asked Bart.

"What do you mean?"

"You said they come to a nasty end. What sort of thing do you mean by that? How nasty?" He looked around to see the incredulous stares on the faces of the others. "What? It could be important. We need all the knowledge, right?"

Emilia shrugged. "The body of the original Lord Beaumont was found, in the March of 1572, in the grounds of the Hall, his head and limbs torn from his body. They said his face bore an expression of such painful torment…" She collapsed into tears once more.

Bart nodded at Spencer. "Sounds like a demon to me."

"Yeah, I guess," he said. "But that was then. How many folk've been killed like that since? And when was the last one?"

"I do not…" she descended into sobs once more.

"Gentlemen," admonished Tess. "Please, have some care for her feelings."

Spencer looked at the girl. "All right. We're sorry, miss. But we're just trying to understand the problem here. You know, why you need us. I mean, are you sure there's really a curse here?"

She dabbed at her eyes with a kerchief and looked up at him. "If there was a chance that your own father could be… could end up in such a way, what would you do?"

Spencer cleared his throat. "Not quite the right bloke to ask that question of. Didn't really get on with me dad, you see. A bit of beheading and disembowelling would've been good for him, truth be told."

"Didn't really know my old man," said Bart. "Although from what I hear, he'd be the one who'd be doing all the beheading and stuff."

Tess stared at them while Emilia continued sobbing.

"Anyway," said Spencer. "I get your point. And we'd want to help of course—anything for an old mate of Tess's—but why us?"

Emilia took a long swig of her tea. "I need someone I can trust, someone who my parents will trust. Tess, you are known to our family as someone of good standing. And I was hoping that, given the relationship we have, you would be able to come to our house straight away to help us."

"Come to your house?" said Spencer. "Where in London is it?"

"Not in London. In Stratford-upon-Avon."

"That's a way away?"

"It is a train journey," said Tess. "Half a day's travel." She turned back to Emilia. "I am sure…"

"Ah," said Spencer. "You see, the thing is, we're a bit busy…"

"I am sure we can help," said Tess, glaring at him.

"You can? Are you sure?" Emilia looked at her with wide eyes.

"Of course," smiled Tess. "Assuming that the fee is of course commensurate with the work required."

Emilia nodded. "I am not so good with such things. But here is a letter from my father which sets out what we are willing to pay." She handed over a folded piece of paper.

Tess opened it, her eyes widening as she read the contents. "This is… I am sure we can help you."

"You can? That is great. I leave for Flint Hall tomorrow afternoon. You can join me then."

"Erm, Tess," said Spencer.

"In a moment."

"Now, please."

"In a moment," she snapped, glaring at him before turning back to her friend. "We will meet you tomorrow. What time?"

"Three. At Euston Station."

"Perfect. We will see you then."

Once she had shown Emilia out, Tess walked back into the sitting room to find Spencer and Bart huddled in conversation. Bart tapped his friend on the shoulder when he saw her enter, and then both turned to face her.

"We're not doing it," said Spencer.

"What do you mean?"

"I mean, we're not doing it. It's not the sort of thing we should be doing."

"We're a demon hunting agency. It says so on your posters, and above our front door. Chasing after demons, saving people from harm? That sounds like *exactly* the sort of thing we should be doing!"

"No. The whole 'getting killed by a bloody powerful demon' sort of thing. *That's* not what we should be doing!"

"Oh please," she scoffed. "We have faced plenty of demons, of all shapes and sizes."

"Yeah, but something about this doesn't feel right."

Tess frowned. "What do you mean?"

"Demon that just wanders round at night. And we're supposed to believe it's biding its time until there's a big birthday party?"

"Mind you," said Bart. "Most demons don't tend to like parties. Maybe it gets cross at the thought of them?"

Spencer stared at him. "How'd you know that? How many demons have you invited to a party?"

"Never had cause to hold a party. But if I did, I'd not invite a demon."

"Because he'd get cross at all the merriment and start lopping off folks' heads?"

"Exactly!" grinned Bart. "Or maybe they're cross because they they're never invited?"

"You're my best mate," said Spencer, shaking his head. "And you know I'd never hear a bad word said about you. But sometimes…"

Tess held up her hand. "I really do not have the patience for this sort of thing right now. Please could you get to the point?" When Bart opened his mouth, she shook her head and pointed to Spencer.

"Look," said Spencer. "In our experience, demons don't tend to be the patient types, right? Don't tend to go in for planning and waiting and stuff. Right?"

"Yes…"

"That's because we mainly deal with the ones that are big blundering weapons. They're just like dumb animals: point them at something they want to smash, and they'll smash it. Get them angry and they'll go out and destroy stuff."

"All right…"

"But there are other types of demons, right? Ones which are more into planning and thinking and stuff. And just like with us humans, they're the dangerous ones. They're the ones you should always look out for, and ideally keep as far away from as possible."

"And you think Emilia's demon is one of them?"

"Certainly seems to be. Think about everything she said: biding its time, maybe waiting for some curse which strikes at a particular date. Summoned by some ancient and really powerful magician. That sort of thing can't ever end well for anyone, least of all the likes of us."

"Not even for an obscene amount of money?"

He blinked. "How obscene?"

She showed him the letter. "That obscene. Enough to solve our money problems for a good year or more."

"Keep us in pies?" asked Bart.

"Keep you in more pies than you could ever imagine," grinned Tess.

"I can imagine a lot of pies," Bart grinned back at her.

Spencer let out a strangled yell. "We've got no use for pies if our heads're no longer attached to our stomachs! No! We're out of our depths here. That's my final word."

A silence descended on the room as Tess regarded him with a cold expression. After a few long moments, she finally spoke in an even, measured voice. "Well. I did not realise that you were the one who gave the 'final word'. How interesting. I tell you what: if you can find—in the next twenty-four hours—an assignment which pays enough to cover our bills, then we will turn down the Beaumonts' opportunity. Otherwise, I will see you at Euston Station at three o'clock tomorrow." She turned and stomped out of the room.

They flinched at the sound of her door slamming upstairs.

"You think she's upset?" asked Bart.

"Yeah. Maybe, mate. But we've got that lead first thing," Spencer said. "That'll solve everything."

"Really?" grinned Bart. "That's great!" He patted his friend on the shoulder.

"Yeah," said Spencer, wincing and rubbing his shoulder. "Just great."

Chapter Five

"So tell me," said the man as he looked around nervously. "Why should I consider hiring you…" He looked them up and down before carefully adding, "Gentlemen?"

Spencer took a long swig from his mug of ale, then said, "First off, you've already told us that the authorities can't, or won't, help you."

"Prob'ly a bit of both," added Bart.

"That's right," Spencer nodded. "Not that we're a last resort or anything. Just that that's a common complaint these days: that the police and government don't want to get involved in demon stuff."

"Shush!" The man looked around while simultaneously trying to hide his face with his hands.

"I wouldn't worry," said Spencer. "No one here gives a toss about what we're talking about. It's why we choose this place for our meetings. Nice and discreet, right?"

The man had to admit that Spencer had a point. He had at first wondered why they had chosen such a shabby, decrepit tavern for their meeting. Walking through the door he had been assailed by the sour stench of stale drinks mixed with the odour of countless unwashed bodies. The floor was barely visible underneath the abandoned detritus from years—probably decades or even centuries—of rough trade, and the walls and ceiling were stained with smoke and god-knew-what-else. Hardly a place to give a new client a favourable first impression, with the most disheartening thing being how much the two men seemed at home there.

But he had to admit that it certainly did seem to be the sort of place where everyone kept themselves to themselves. He was highly unlikely to come across any of his own contacts or acquaintances there. Or indeed, anyone who was even close to being connected to anyone he knew. Polite society it decidedly was not.

He turned back to the strange pair of men keenly watching him from the other side of the splintered table. "Very well," he said. "I take your point. And I also concede your point about the authorities' singular lack of interest in intervening in matters involving our—ah—horned neighbours."

Bart stared at him in confusion, while Spencer nodded. "Absolutely. In a way, we don't blame them; it's not their field of expertise, is it? And, anyway, it keeps us in a job, eh?"

"So we may have established that the police would not really be of help to me," said the man. "What you have not done is give me a compelling reason as to why you are the ones who can help me best."

"Simple." Spencer counted points off on the fingers of his hand as he said them. "First, we're experienced: we've seen off plenty of demons. You hear about that demon that was stopped in Spitalfields yesterday? That was us." He grinned proudly.

"I heard you took half of the neighbourhood with you. Hardly what I would call a discreet assignment."

"Depends on the demon, depends on what we're employed to do. Clients there didn't insist on it being hushed up, they just wanted rid. Which we delivered."

The man inclined his head in a slow nod.

"Next," Spencer continued, counting off another finger, "We're the only agency that specialises in demons. What you get with us is real expertise. Us and our business partner."

"Ah, yes. Lady Marchant. I was hoping to meet with her..."

"Yeah, well, she's a bit indisposed right now, but she sends you her regards, and she'll gladly meet up with you, if we come to agreement over terms."

"I hear she is a rather interesting young lady."

"Oh she's interesting all right. Clever, to boot."

"She's the brains of our operation," added Bart.

"*One* of the brains," Spencer corrected him. "We're very much a partnership, and we all bring skills. She's a bit of a scientist, you see, and has loads of connections to some top Aether science types. You heard of Maxwell Potts? Well, she's really well connected to him and his sciencey stuff."

"Now that is interesting," said the man. "If there were a way to solve my particular problem without the need for brute force and wholesale destruction of property, that would certainly be my preference."

"Yeah, we can do all that." Spencer waved a hand. "We're also extremely reasonable, in terms of our costs." He produced a crumpled piece of paper from his pocket and smoothed it on the table, then produced a pencil from behind his right ear. He licked the nib then scribbled a figure on the paper, folded it and pushed the note across the table. "That is our fee for the work you described to us."

The man opened the paper, his eyes widening and an incredulous smile playing on his lips as he read it. "Really?"

Spencer leaned forward. "Maybe you compare that to what you've lost already, and would continue to lose if your problem ain't dealt with. Granted, that number might be the same as a few weeks of your takings, but you'll lose a lot more if you carry on being burdened with demon issues. Savvy? And what if word got out that you had these problems? That'd be even worse for your profits, no?"

The man frowned. "I really hope you are not threatening to blackmail me."

Spencer threw his hands in the air in protest. "Of course not! No, no, no! But you know as well as we do, there's only so long you can keep something like that under wraps before rumours start to spread."

The man stared back at the paper. "If you were willing to do something with this number…"

"Tell you what, you seem like a good bloke," said Spencer. "Tess'll kill me for this, so you need to tell her I fought really hard here, but we could knock ten bob off that. How's that sound?"

"A bit more reasonable," he said slowly. "I suppose…"

A tall shadow fell over him as a man leant over to examine the paper. "Interesting," the newcomer said. "That's the price of blackmail these days, is it?" He removed his hat and offered a hand to the man. "Inspector Jones, of Scotland Yard. No, please do not offer me your name; it is best for both of us if I do not know who you are."

Spencer groaned as the inspector took a seat at their table, smiling at them all. "Morning, boys," Jones said. "Keeping busy, are we?"

"Well actually—" began Bart, stopping when Spencer shushed him and then gestured that the two of them should leave.

Inspector Jones held up a hand. "I'd like you two to stay for a moment, please." He turned to their potential client. "On the other hand, I would recommend, sir, that you leave with all haste, and take the time to have a long, hard think about the company you have been keeping."

"I hardly know them," protested the man.

"Good. Keep it that way. But I can tell you that these two are nothing more than the lowest of crooks and conmen. I have today saved you from having your pockets emptied to no good end. Let all your contacts know as well: these men and the 'agency' they claim to represent are best steered well clear of. Now be off with you. And I'd advise you run quick until you are back in civilisation; pretty much everyone here would welcome the chance to relieve you of everything you own, without a second's thought."

The man nodded gratefully and sprinted out of the tavern, barging past a couple of workmen with a shouted "Sorry!" as he sped out of the door.

Spencer watched him go and then turned back to Inspector Jones. "Well, thanks for that," he said. "That was a solid piece of legitimate business that just ran out the door, there."

"Legitimate!" scoffed the inspector. "You two wouldn't know legitimate if it bit you on the arse!"

"Oi," protested Bart. "No one's going near my arse. You take that back!"

"He doesn't mean actually," muttered Spencer. Then, turning back to Jones, asked, "So what're you doing here? Can't get enough of our company?"

"Of sorts. A little bird told me that you two were up to no good here. Given I was in the neighbourhood, I thought I would drop in and check."

Spencer cursed as he scowled around the room, glaring at those around them. "There's a grass? In *here* of all places? What's this city coming to?"

"It's becoming a more law-abiding place to live. That's what's happening to this city. And about time too."

"But we weren't up to no good," protested Spencer. "He genuinely had a problem that he was going to pay us to fix. A legitimate problem which wouldn't have involved any sort of law breaking."

Jones shook his head. "It doesn't matter how many times you say that, it doesn't make it true. I know you two, and I know that your type never change. It's my new mission in life to make sure I put you both behind bars as soon as I catch you in the act."

Bart scratched his beard. "Might be a stupid question, but if you're so sure we're up to no good, and you want to catch us in the act, why'd you warn that bloke off? Why didn't you just wait and then arrest us when you saw us doing whatever it is you think we was going to do?" He blinked at them both, waiting to be shouted down.

Spencer grinned. "Me colleague makes a fine point, Inspector. You could've let us get on with it, then see what we're up to. And then arrest us if we did anything illegal—which we wouldn't have, as I said."

Jones frowned, his cheeks reddening slightly. "This is a not-so-friendly warning. I catch you trying anything in this town, you're in the clink. You know now that I've got more informants than you thought, and in more places than you thought. You understand?"

"But we're trying to be legit!" protested Spencer. "What do you expect us to do?"

"I don't care, as long as you do it as far away from me and my patch as possible. Starve to death, or leave town. It's all the same to me." He stood up. "But if I catch you doing anything that looks even slightly dodgy, you're for it."

They watched him walk out.

"Doesn't sound very fair to me," muttered Bart.

"It ain't. Not fair at all." Spencer downed the rest of his beer. "Oh well, I suppose that answers one question though. Let's go back and pack our bags; looks like we're going on a train trip."

*

Her bags safely stowed on board the Hackney cab, Tess was about to climb aboard when she heard a voice from behind her.

"Wait!"

She smiled to herself and then turned around to see Spencer and Bart standing there, short of breath and with bags in their hands.

"Have you changed your minds?" she asked.

"Well, we just figured that it wasn't right you heading off all the way up there without any help or company," said Spencer.

"Also, that copper turned up and drove our lead away," added Bart.

"But we could've got him," Spencer said quickly. "We just didn't think it was worth it."

She grinned and then gestured for them to board the carriage with her. She looked at the small bags they brought with them.

"Is that all you are bringing with you?"

They looked down at the items in their hands. "Yeah," said Bart. "Why?"

"We are going for at least a few days. Won't you need more changes of clothes?" She looked at them, focusing on their days-old outfits. "Never mind."

"What do you mean?" Bart asked, before turning to Spencer. "What does she mean?"

Spencer shrugged. "Don't worry about it." He turned to Tess. "We pack light. Now, how's about we get going before I change my mind?"

Tess rapped her knuckles on the roof of the carriage, and they jerked into motion. After a few minutes, Bart pulled himself forward and banged his fist on the side.

"What are you doing?" asked Tess.

"This ain't the way to Euston," he said.

"He's right," said Spencer. "Bloody cabbie thinks we don't know no better. He's trying to fleece you, charge you extra for a longer ride."

"No," said Tess. "We are not going to Euston. At least, not yet. We need to stop off somewhere first."

*

The carriage stopped in front of a large, red-brick, terraced house. The three of them stepped out onto an immaculately-swept pavement.

Bart whistled. "Nice neighbourhood," he muttered.

"Yeah," Spencer said. "You can hardly smell the dung here, you notice that?"

"Reckon they've all got them fancy indoor privvies?"

"Guaranteed. And more besides. Look in there. So much stuff, just plain on display. A King's ransom, eh?"

Tess cleared her throat. "We are not here to commit crimes. You do realise that?"

"Of course," Spencer said, an affronted tone to his voice. "We was just doing a bit of window shopping. For fun, see? Old habits die hard, you know..."

"Yes, well just try and see if you can smother those old habits. You're getting a fair bit of attention; the last thing we need is for someone to call the police on us."

They looked around, noticing the twitching curtains and the suspicious glances from the passersby.

"All right," said Spencer. "Point taken. Let's get on with whatever it is we're here to do. Which is... what, exactly?"

"Gathering supplies," said Tess, hitching up her skirts and marching up the steps to the house in front of them. She rapped on the door and looked back at them with a smile.

The door opened to reveal a swarthy man with a gaunt face topped with a mop of dark curly hair, wearing a suit which was covered in stains and grease. He peered suspiciously at them and then, when he recognised Tess, a broad grin appeared on his face. "Lady Marchant!" he said. "So pleased you could make it."

"Mister Potts, so good to see you. You received my note, then?" she said.

"I did, I did. Most intriguing. Come in. And please, call me Maxwell."

She smiled and nodded. "Then we can dispense with my surname also. Call me Tess."

Spencer tugged at her sleeve. "Maybe we should just stay out here until you're done."

Maxwell looked at the two of them, registering their presence for the first time. "While I really do not relish the idea of you two stepping foot in my house, if you stay outside I can guarantee my neighbours will have heart attacks. It would be less hassle if you were inside and out of sight." He stepped aside. "Get in. Quick, please."

They shuffled inside and, as the man shut the door, Spencer looked around in the messy gloom of the hallway. The walls were hidden behind stacks of boxes and other paraphernalia. "If you're answering the door, does that mean your maidservant ain't in?"

Maxwell grinned. "You'd prefer that, wouldn't you? No, she's around somewhere. We just have a rather informal approach to the whole master-servant relationship." He glanced around. "Actually, I'd prefer it if you forgot I said that."

"Why?" asked Bart. "Worried she'd beat you up or something?"

"No!" scoffed Maxwell, although the way he looked around told a different story.

"So you all know each other, then," said Tess.

"Not 'well'," said Maxwell. "But I do know these two crooks well enough to warn you against associating with them."

"We're not crooks," protested Spencer.

"Yeah, we've gone straight," added Bart.

"I can vouch for them," said Tess. "They are my business partners."

Maxwell peered at them and then shrugged. "I could see how some local muscle could be useful in the demon hunting game. Each to her own, I suppose." He led them through the hall towards a room at the rear of the house. "Watch out for the equipment," he said.

They navigated their way between stacks of boxes and equipment precariously balanced in uneven piles, some seemingly about to tumble messily to the floor at any moment.

"Nice place," muttered Spencer. "You just moved in?"

"This is all very important equipment," said Maxwell. "Touch, damage or steal anything, and you will regret it."

"How many times do we have to say it?!" protested Spencer. "We're not in the stealing game no more!"

They were led into a room which they suspected was a lot bigger than it appeared, its walls and floor mostly concealed by a general clutter of equipment, papers and smoking liquids. The air was thick with a chemical-tinged fug, as though they were interrupting some sort of messy experiment. The windows were hidden behind thick screens, with the only light in the room coming from a handful of strategically-placed lamps.

"Nice," muttered Bart, looking round.

"Very homely," added Spencer.

Tess had walked straight over to a collection of tubes, jars and wires at the far wall. The main part of the contraption was a large glass sphere, inside which a light flickered from one end to the other.

"Is this an Aetheric Resonator?" she asked.

Maxwell smiled and walked over to her side. "You are as discerning as your correspondence made you out to be. Yes, it is."

They discussed the equipment while Spencer and Bart looked around, taking care not to get too close to anything, to avoid them being accused of touching, breaking or stealing something. Not that either of them had the faintest clue what any of it was.

Bart made a show of peering at various items, making appreciative noises and occasionally pointing at something and giving Spencer a knowing nod. Spencer rolled his eyes at his friend's charade, hopping from one foot to the other as he glared at Tess and Maxwell, silently praying for them to finish chatting.

They were disturbed by a woman's voice from the door, which said in a strong cockney accent, "Max, what have we said about bringing any old rubbish into the house?"

They turned to see a young, dark-haired woman standing in the doorway with her hands on her hips. She was dressed in a practical skirt and top, with her hair down over her shoulders. Her face had a sharp, fierce intensity to it, her eyes flashing angrily at the visitors.

"Ah, Kate," said Maxwell. "Let me introduce Lady Tess Marchant, the person I have been corresponding with over the past few months, and who has been kindly testing out some of my equipment in the field, as it were."

Kate greeted Tess with a smile and then turned to the other two in the room. "And what are they doing here?"

Spencer cleared his throat and smoothed down his hair. "Nice to see you again, Kate."

"That's Miss Thatcher to you," she snapped.

"Right. Well, we're here with Tess—Lady Marchant—as her business associates."

Kate stared at them in disbelief. "You're having a laugh, right?" She turned to Tess. "You do know what these two are, don't you? They're common crooks."

"I know about their past," said Tess stiffly. "I also know that they saved my life, at great risk to themselves, when they could have just walked away. I do not know what your dealings have been with them." She held up a hand before Kate could speak. "And nor do I wish to. They have turned over a new leaf, and are valued companions of mine. And that is the end of it."

Kate sucked on her teeth and then shrugged. "Your funeral, love."

"Maybe we should move on to the matter at hand," Maxwell said quickly. "Your letter mentioned an assignment involving a demon of unknown origin?"

"That is correct," said Tess. "Our client has been troubled by a demon for a little while now, and they would like our assistance to capture it, or even subdue it."

"Yeah," grinned Bart. "Like permanently subdue it." He ran his finger across his neck for emphasis, nodding to Kate. "That's what we do."

"Believe it when I see it," muttered Kate.

Tess continued, ignoring them both. "We do not quite know what we are up against, or how easy it will be to locate or trap the creature, so I was wondering if you had anything that could help. The last items you lent me were very effective."

"Wait a minute," said Spencer. "Is he the bloke who made that gun and bomb thing we used the other day?"

"He is," said Tess. "They got us out of quite the sticky corner, did they not?"

"Nearly took my arm off," Spencer pointed out.

"Wasn't that more you not using them right?" asked Bart.

"It was not! I just..."

"In any case," said Tess, "would you be able to help us, Mr Potts?"

Maxwell scratched his chin and then smiled. "It just so happens that I do have a few things that might be of use. If you could provide me with a report on their effectiveness as before, then that would be satisfactory to me."

Kate tutted and beckoned to him. He went over to her, and they had a whispered conversation for a few minutes.

Maxwell turned back. "Please forgive us. My friend here is rather protective of me, and believes that I should get more recompense..."

"Look," said Kate. "I'm sure you're a lovely person and everything, but Max has a constant stream of people coming here and asking for stuff, and he's always more than happy to oblige. Problem is that all this stuff costs money. Which is the one thing Max hasn't yet managed to magic up in all his vats and tubes and stuff."

"I would never assume to take advantage," protested Tess. "I would happily pay a fair rate—"

"There is no need," said Maxwell.

"There's every need," Kate said quickly. "Thanking you kindly."

Bart grinned. "You know, I quite like her," he said to Spencer, who nodded, a look of awestricken respect on his face.

"Don't get any ideas," Kate said. "Still don't trust you two."

"I think you might find that just makes them like you even more," grinned Tess. "But now that those formalities are over, perhaps you could show us what you have?"

Maxwell nodded, a broad smile on his face which made him look like a child who had just been allowed to play with whatever toy he fancied. "Now, let me see." He rubbed his hands together. "What sort of demon are you going to be confronting?"

"We are not sure," Tess said. "Our client was not clear; to be honest, I do not think they have yet even seen it."

"Really? Are they sure it really is a demon?"

"They think so."

He nodded and led Tess over to a table. "In which case, I think these are exactly what you need."

While they talked, Spencer and Bart carried on wandering around, under Kate's watchful eye.

"So much stuff," said Bart.

"Yeah," said Spencer. He turned to look at Kate. "You don't need to follow us round, you know. We're not going to do anything."

"I should trust you, is that right?" asked Kate.

"Well, yeah."

"Trust you. You want me to forget the way you used to act? The people you used to work with? You want me to forget you're nothing more than common criminals?"

"Not any more we're not," Spencer said.

"I'll believe that when I see it," she said. "But I'm not talking about now, I'm talking about what you did back then."

"Look, I'm sorry," Spencer said. "We're both sorry. We was younger and stupider, and we didn't really have no choice."

She laughed mirthlessly. "No choice, eh?"

"You know what it's like out there, with folk like Jason. If we hadn't done as we was told, we'd have been found face-down in the Thames the next morning."

"Yeah," said Bart. "We was the lowest of the low out there."

"You always told me you were a big deal," Kate said.

"Well, you know, sometimes we exaggerate a bit… You know us… But, look, we've changed. We've seen the error of our ways."

"So now that you only do good stuff, I'm supposed to forget all the bad stuff?" she asked. "That it?"

"Yes. Well, no. Look, we're really sorry for everything we did, back then. We're trying to make up for all the bad stuff."

"Yeah," added Bart. "And if there's anything we can do for you—anything at all—you just say, and we'll do it."

"Anything?" she asked, a glint in her eye.

"Yeah," said Bart eagerly. "Anything at all."

"Steady on, mate," Spencer said quietly to his friend. "I mean, there are limits. And I don't like the way she's looking at us…"

Kate grinned. "I will take you up on that. And maybe one day I might see my way to forgiving you for what you did. But not right now. Right now, you can keep your hands off the stuff in here."

Spencer looked down at a bench which was overloaded with what looked like rubbish. "Does any of it actually do anything?"

Kate nodded slowly. "Actually, yeah." She picked up a device, which looked a bit like a funnel sitting on top of a cake box. "This here's one of my favourites; you're going to love this. Just stand there."

Spencer stared at her, his mouth twisted into a nervous grin. "Um, what do you mean?"

"Don't worry," she said, aiming the funnel at him. "This won't hurt. At least, I don't think it will."

"What? What's not going to hurt?"

"This." Kate pushed down on something, and Spencer was enveloped by a flash of white light.

Bart covered his eyes. When the light died down, he lowered his hands. "What happened? Spencer, you all right?" He looked at his friend, who was stood stock-still but otherwise looked unharmed.

"He's fine," said Kate.

"Then why's he not answering me? Why's he not moving?"

"This," she said, "is a paralysing ray." When she noticed Bart staring back at her, she explained, "It stops him being able to move."

"What? At all?"

"That's right. Quite a nice little thing, for when you don't necessarily want to hurt your opponent, but you also don't want them running away."

"Huh," said Bart. "That is quite impressive. Your man there make it?"

"He's not my man. Just a friend who I look after."

"You're not his maidservant then?"

She turned to face him. "You want me to use this on you as well?"

"No thank you," he said quickly. "So how long does it last for? How long until he can move again?"

"There are controls on this that can release him. They can also do other things. Watch this." She turned a knob and then pushed a lever and then said, "Move one pace forward."

Spencer stuck out a foot and stepped forward.

"Stand on one leg," she said.

He did as he was told.

"He does anything you say?" asked Bart.

"Yep."

"Can I try?"

She grinned and then pushed the lever again. "Be my guest."

"Put your hands on your head," he said.

Spencer again did as he was ordered.

Bart let out a short giggle. "This is amazing. And he can't speak?"

"Only if we let him," she said. "We can make him say anything." She pushed a button. "Say, 'Mary had a little lamb'."

"Mary had a little lamb," Spencer said in a strangulated voice.

She pushed another button. "You can speak normally," she said.

"This is not funny," Spencer said, the words slightly mangled by his still-paralysed face, his lips the only parts of him able to move.

"Oh, I don't know," said Kate. "I'm finding it quite funny."

"Me too," said Bart. "You'd be laughing if it was anyone else."

"Why don't we test that theory out?" Spencer said. "Let me go and give me that thing; let's see how funny it really is."

"I don't think so," said Kate. "Consider this the first bit of your payback: testing this thing for my amusement."

"All right. It works. Now can you turn it off?"

Maxwell and Tess appeared. "What are you doing?" he asked.

"Kate, I thought I told you not to play with the equipment."

"Just thought we'd test this paralysing device out," she said. "Works really well, don't it, boys?"

Bart nodded while Spencer just glared at her.

"He is truly paralysed?" asked Tess.

"And fully controllable," said Maxwell, taking the device from Kate and moving a couple of controls. "Watch this. Walk to the wall and hit your head against it."

"No, please stop," said Spencer as he matched over to the wall and then headbutted it. "Ouch!"

"Remarkable," said Tess. "And how long do the effects last?"

"Until released by the user of the device. Or around six hours, whichever is the sooner."

"That could be useful," said Tess. "I think we've seen enough now; could you release the poor man?"

"Of course." Maxwell said. He adjusted a few levers then pressed a button, and Spencer's shoulders sagged as he regained control of his body. He turned to glare at them, rubbing his forehead.

"That was not funny," he said.

"Are you all right?" Bart asked him.

"I'll live. Not that you care. Didn't see you jumping in to try and save me."

"I will buy you a beer and a pie to make up for it," said Tess. "Although I would point out that I had nothing to do with this."

"Yeah," said Kate with a wave and a beaming smile. "That was all me. You're welcome!"

Chapter Six

The journey to Stratford-upon-Avon passed uneventfully, with even Bart tiring of the novelties of the train ride after a while. As the greys of the city gave way to the unending greenness of the countryside, Spencer and Bart became more and more subdued, staring open-mouthed at the scenery passing by.

Tess watched them, intrigued. "Have you been outside of London before?" she asked.

Spencer opened his mouth and then shook his head, as though he had intended to spin some sort of bravado, but then settled for the truth. "Nah. Never seen the point; or had the coin, for that matter."

"Yeah," said Bart. "London's got everything we need; why'd we need to go anywhere else?"

"But if you spend all your life in London, just think about all of the things you are missing out on."

"Like what?" Spencer looked out of the window. "Can't see that many shops or taverns out there. Just fields and trees."

"You don't find it therapeutic, to see all this greenery?"

"We've got parks in London," he shrugged. "If it's so great out here, then why're you not living here still?"

"I had no choice but to move," she said. "My husband insisted, and wives do not tend to have much of a say in such matters."

"But he's gone now," Bart pointed out. "Why'd you stay in London? Why not come back out here? Not that I'm saying you should, you know. I'm happy you didn't. But…"

"I know what you mean," she smiled faintly. "I suppose there's not much for me to come back to. I have no family left out in Stratford-upon-Avon. Most of my friends and acquaintances live in London now. But to answer the question of what is so great out here, well, do you not think it is so much more pleasant? To smell the clean air?"

Spencer wrinkled his nose. "Don't smell too clean to me. Smells a lot like smoke and horse dung."

"But the open skies, not obstructed by fog or buildings…"

"Not sure I like it," muttered Bart. "A bit too open and empty for my liking."

"But the life…"

"What life? There's no people round out there that I can see. I miss the crowds."

"And me," Spencer agreed.

Tess puffed out her cheeks and shook her head. She turned to look out of the window, a wistful smile playing on her lips as she watched the trees and fields flow past.

She found herself slipping into a daydream, thinking about times gone by, of how she would ride horses through fields like the ones trundling past their window. She remembered lazing on grassy meadows, making necklaces out of daisies while watching the clouds float across perfect blue skies. And, when she tired of that, she would climb trees or lift stones to examine the insects which hid underneath, much to her parents' chagrin.

After a while, Spencer nudged Tess with his foot. "So tell us about this Emilia lady. You two are old friends?"

Tess blinked, forcing herself to return to the real world. "We grew up together. Our parents were friends, for a time. I believe her father and mine had some common business interests. She and I would meet up and play together, sometimes share a tutor. Although she had less interest in learning than I did."

"Not as bright as you?" asked Bart.

"No, it's not that. She was just not as bothered. She was more interested in the things she *should* be interested in: ladylike pursuits, attending parties, trying to make herself as eligible as possible for potential suitors."

Bart stared at her blankly, so Spencer explained. "She means making herself pretty for the blokes. That right?"

Tess chuckled. "In a nutshell, yes. She was always the one more likely to find herself a wealthy gentleman for a husband, while my parents despaired of me."

"That's not fair," protested Bart. "You've done well for yourself."

"In a manner of speaking," she sighed. "Although, where we grew up, the test was how well you married and how many children you produced. There wasn't much place for a girl who wanted to study subjects more properly reserved for the men."

"That's just stupid," said Bart.

"I agree," said Spencer. "All the women we knew growing up—still know—are workers. Often work harder than the men, and are a damn sight smarter, too."

Tess raised her eyebrows. "I know. It's a strange twist that in some ways the poorer you are, the freer you are."

"Mind you," continued Spencer. "When we say they work and stuff, it's back-breaking stuff, and most don't live to see out their thirties, and it's not like they have much of a choice whether to work or not; it's that or starve. So I reckon they'd happily trade places with you."

"In other words, I should stop my moaning?" Tess grinned.

"No," said Bart.

"Yes," said Spencer.

"Anyway," said Tess, "Emilia and I spent a lot of time together, growing up. We were pretty close for a time. Certainly shared our hopes and dreams. Hers was always to get married to a nobleman, live in a nice big house, that sort of thing."

"Did she manage that?"

"Not that I know. We lost touch when I became betrothed to... my late husband. I do not think she appreciated it when I achieved her dream before she did." She turned and stared out the window. "Not that it was much of a dream relationship, not by any means."

The two men shuffled awkwardly in the face of her discomfort. After a moment of frowning and working his mouth around various thoughts, Bart said, "Not your fault he tried to turn you into a demon, though, was it? And it all worked out well in the end, right?"

"It is not just that. The whole thing was a cold-hearted sham from start to finish. He only wanted to get his hands on my family's money."

"But I thought he was a Lord? Surely he was loaded already?"

"I am afraid it does not always work that way. In fact, it often does not. Just because their family once had money, does not mean they still do."

"I don't get it. They live in them big houses, do all the partying and the like, don't need to work. How come they can do that without cash?"

"That lifestyle—the big houses, the lavish parties—cost money. And it's even worse if you have a tendency to gamble or drink, or both. As most of them tend to. So they end up funding their lifestyle by borrowing or stealing from each other. It's nowhere near as glamorous a life as you might think."

"Hah!" Spencer slapped his thigh and pointed triumphantly at Bart. "It's like I've always said; for all their airs and graces, they're no better than the rest of us!"

"You've always said that," Bart agreed. "So your ex-husband was skint before he married you?"

"Not quite, but close. His father had squandered much of the family money, while my parents were much more prudent. So I was quite the catch for the likes of Lord Marchant. And my parents were too blinded by the chance to be related to a peer of the realm to see his many faults. Until it was too late."

"You never speak about your folks," said Bart. "They live up this way too, then?"

Tess turned away again, hiding her face from them.

"They're dead, aren't they?" said Spencer. "I'm really sorry."

"It is all right," she said. "It was long enough ago for it to no longer feel as raw, although I fear that coming back up to Stratford, being around old memories, might bring the emotions back to the surface. In some ways, it is for the best; mother and I never saw eye-to-eye. And father was rather distant. He wanted a son, you see, so I was always going to be a disappointment. Ironic, then, that it was when he finally had a son, of sorts, after I married, that he..."

"Marchant did it, didn't he?" asked Spencer quickly. "He killed your folks."

"I had no proof, but I always suspected. And then he confessed, just before they put that demon inside me. Maybe he thought the confession would be good for what passed as his soul, or maybe he just wanted one last chance to gloat. Probably the latter. That is why I was not too upset that I—or at least the demon-me—killed him."

Both men shuddered as they remembered her tearing her husband limb from limb with preternatural savagery. A sight that neither would forget for a long time.

"Yeah," Bart managed. "You definitely showed him. He deserved it."

Spencer cleared his throat. "Anyway, what are we walking into when we get there? Nice big happy family in a nice big house?"

"It has been some time," said Tess. "But I remember them having a typical family. Lord Beaumont—Emilia's father— always seemed a rather jovial man, if a little aloof. Lady Beamont was a nervous sort; there was some talk of scandal around her family, a wayward brother who she was always keen to distance herself from. Other than that, there was never anything that peculiar about them. Emilia has a younger brother; he always used to annoy us by hanging around, teasing us, playing pranks. You know, the sort of things boys do. I have not seen him in many years though; he would be a grown man by now.

"As for Flint Hall, well, it is a lovely manor house. Lots of rooms, lovely gardens, plenty of space for us to run around and play in when we were children. I remember lots of happy sunny days there." She smiled, a faraway look on her face.

"What about this curse?" asked Spencer.

She blinked, the question forcing her back to the present. "It is not something I recall ever coming up or being mentioned. Maybe it really is one of those family secrets that was so well-guarded, that no one outside the family ever knew about it."

"Or maybe it's not something that ever came up," said Bart. "She said it hits when the Lord turns sixty. That's mighty old, right? Maybe no one's lived long enough for the curse to work?"

"These are toffs we're talking about," Spencer reminded him. "We don't know many folk of that age, from where we come from, but the upper classes'll often live to ripe old ages. Right?"

"That is right," said Tess. "I do not know enough about her family to say if any of them did live into their sixties, or whether they met some sort of grisly end. Something for us to find out." She produced a small notebook and scribbled down a few questions.

"Still seems mighty strange," said Spencer. "Us being hired to do proper detective work."

"I suppose the proper detectives need more than just the *threat* of a curse to be engaged," said Tess.

"Yeah," said Bart. "If there's a dead body, they'll probably be crawling all over it. But that'll probably be a bit too late for Emilia and her family, eh?"

"Well," said Tess as Spencer glared at his friend. "Let us hope that we can solve this before it gets to that."

After a while, the rolling green fields and trees gave way to roads and houses as they approached Stratford-upon-Avon train station.

The train stopped and they stepped down to the platform, Spencer looking around with a confused frown on his face. "It's all so... small," he said.

"Yeah. And quiet," added Bart.

Tess chuckled. "Things are a bit different outside of London.

You will get accustomed to it, I am sure."

They were interrupted by a call from behind them.

"There you are," said Emilia, bundling over. "So pleased you made it." Trailing behind her was an older man in uniform, carrying her bags.

"You were on the train as well?" asked Tess. "We did not see you."

"Oh, I was in first class." She cast a disdainful eye at the carriage they had just disembarked from. "Shall we?" She gestured towards the exit.

Emilia led them to a stagecoach, which was driven by a surly old man with a cap pulled down over his face. He barely acknowledged their presence, treating their luggage as though its mere existence was the deepest of insults as he took it from them and strapped it to the roof of the coach.

Spencer tried engaging him in conversation, but gave up when he was rewarded with nothing more than a glare and a turned back. "Friendly sort, him," he said to Emilia as they all squeezed into the carriage. Bart tapped the wooden bench and shot a knowing look at the others, already missing the relative comfort of the train.

"That is Mr Smith," said Emilia, either ignoring or failing to notice Bart's disappointment. "He works for us at Flint Hall."

"Has he been there long?" asked Tess. "I don't recall seeing him before, but I do remember your butler: tall, thin man with a kind face."

"Henderson," Emilia replied. "He... moved on. For the time being we have Mr Smith and his wife. And the groundskeeper, of course. They have been with us for as long as I can remember, but there's no reason why you would remember them from your visits. The best servants blend into the background, you know."

"That's what I've always said," agreed Spencer. Tess hid her chuckle behind her hand as Emilia nodded and smiled.

The journey to Flint Hall was a lot less comfortable than the train journey, with them being thrown from side to side pretty much constantly. The men did their best to avoid landing on the women and risking a slap for invading their space, but it took all their strength to do so.

"Roads round here are terrible, aren't they?" asked Spencer. "I thought London was bad, but this is miles worse."

Bart had resorted to wedging his head out the window, partly to watch the scenery but also to give himself something to hold his body in place. "Not the roads," he called back. "They don't look that bad. It's your wheels, miss. They're in a right bad shape. Need replacing if you ask me."

Emilia muttered something about getting Mr Smith to look into it as soon as they got home, her cheeks reddening.

Eventually, amidst the rolling green fields, Flint Hall crept into view.

They were first confronted with a large black pair of iron gates, which Mr Smith stopped in front of, clambering down to open them. They swung open with a loud screech of protest which set all their teeth on edge.

"Don't suppose you need any guard dogs," Spencer said. "Noise like that, you'd know if anyone was coming in."

"Indeed," blushed Emilia.

"Unless they came over the sides," pointed out Bart.

"Nah. Look how high the hedges are. They've not been trimmed in ages. Not even a giant could get over, or through, them."

The coach rocked as Mr Smith clambered back into the driving seat, and then they started to crunch and bounce their way along the driveway.

It felt as though they were processing through a dark tunnel, the trees and bushes crowding in, around and over them.

In some places, the branches and vines scraped the top of their carriage and pinged off the windows. Through the foliage could be glimpsed grounds which had clearly seen better days, leading Tess to wonder to herself what it was that the groundsman did with his days; that is, if he hadn't followed the butler out of the door also.

Rounding a sweeping corner, the house itself came into view. It was a long, rectangular building with more windows than seemed reasonable, and topped with an impressive number of chimneys.

Bart whistled. "Imaging trying to clean that lot," he muttered. When they all stared at him, he added, "I used to be a chimneysweep's apprentice, back in the day. Until I got too big to fit down the chimneys. Then I got dumped on the streets."

"Is that why you ended up... doing what you did?" asked Tess.

Bart nodded. "'S'right. Not much call for a kid built like a man. No one'd take me. Not until I bumped into Spencer, that is."

"Their loss was the streets' gain," Spencer beamed. "Always handy to have a big lad as back up; never met a bit of trouble he couldn't fight his way out of."

Emilia was staring at them. "I am not sure I quite follow," she said. "Do you mean to say you were...?"

Tess cleared her throat. "My colleagues have a slightly chequered past; we will not lie about that. But I can vouch for their bona fides."

Bart frowned but, before he could say anything, Spencer said, "We're legit, and we bring skills and experience that many don't have. Especially the cops and so-called detectives. And especially when it comes to knowing about the demons. No one knows them better than us."

The driveway ended in a turning circle with a large but chipped and faded fountain at its centre, the moss growing down its side telling of the many months and years since it had last spouted water.

They stopped in front of a large black front door. Bart pushed open the carriage door and jumped down, holding it for the others as they clambered out.

"Welcome to Flint Hall," Emilia said, her voice shaking

slightly as she looked around. "I am sure my family are in, although I cannot see them at the moment."

"They were in when I left," grunted Mr Smith as he threw their bags onto the doorstep. "Lord Beaumont in his study, and Lady Beaumont in the sitting room. I'd be surprised if they'd moved."

"What about Mr Wheeler?"

"He went out riding with Master Calvin."

"Calvin is here?" Emilia shot a concerned look around them.

"Aye. He turned up just before I left. He thought you'd be happy to see him." A sly smile flitted across his face, before he turned to their bags. "I'll take these in and then see to the horses."

"It's all right," said Bart. "I can do the bags."

Mr Smith looked at him for a moment, and then nodded sharply and walked away.

Tess squinted at the front door. "What an interesting little symbol," she said, pointing at an image which appeared to have been sketched with black ink on the brickwork to the side of the door.

"Oh, that," said Emilia, lifting her hand up to play with the collar of her blouse. "Some sort of prank by my brother, no doubt. You know how he always enjoyed his art."

"Hmm," said Tess as she stared at it. It consisted of a series of three interlocking circles surrounding a pentagram, topped with what looked like a crescent moon. She looked up at the house; it felt smaller than she remembered it. But then, she was a lot smaller herself when she used to visit as a child.

The front door opened as they approached to reveal a white-haired woman with red cheeks. "Mistress Emilia," she said. "I hope you had a pleasant journey?"

"Very pleasant, thank you, Mrs Smith. These are our guests, Lady Marchant and Mr..."

"Just Spencer," said Spencer, stepping forward and offering a hand to the maidservant. "And this is Bart."

Mrs Smith beamed and blushed at the greeting, while Tess

cleared her throat. "You realise she's not the lady of the house? She is just the..." Her voice tailed off as she glanced at Mrs Smith.

"No such thing as *just* a servant, in my book," said Spencer. "House wouldn't run without the likes of Mrs Smith here, ain't that right?"

Mrs Smith stifled a giggle, as she caught the expression on Emilia's face. "I would not say..." She cleared her throat and straightened up. "Please do follow me, my lady. Sirs." She turned and led them into the house.

As she closed the door behind them, they were surprised by a loud, barking voice from the other end of the hall. "What is this? Mrs Smith, you should know better than to admit servants through the main entrance!"

Mrs Smith opened her mouth, but then looked down as Emilia said, "Father, these are not servants. Do you remember my old friend Tess, the Lady Marchant? These are her business associates: Spencer and, ah, Bart."

Tess stepped forward and offered him her hand. "Lord Beaumont. A pleasure to see you again."

He regarded her for a moment and then nodded, taking her hand and brushing it with his lips. "Lady Marchant, the pleasure is mine. Although I am rather confused as to what you are doing here."

"Well, father," said Emilia, "I have invited Tess and her colleagues here in the hope that they can help us with our problem."

He stared at her. "I am not sure I know what you mean. I think we should discuss this. In private." He looked up at the others. "In the meantime, you are of course welcome to stay here as our guests." His gaze lingered over Spencer and Bart. "Mrs Smith, I trust you will be able to find suitable sleeping quarters."

"Of course, sir," she said.

Emilia shot them an apologetic smile as she followed her father into his study, the door shutting firmly behind them.

Chapter Seven

Flint Hall was filled with dark corners and ominous portraits. Every corner, nook and cranny out of easy reach seemed to be layered with cobwebs, a thin film that on occasions reached down to tangle in the hair and tickle the noses of any who passed by.

Spencer was surprised by how cold and draughty the house was, even with fires lit in almost every room. He had thought the upper classes lived privileged lives, but the rooms he had grown up in had always been warm enough; helped of course by having lots of people crammed together in small rooms. Everywhere in the Hall felt cavernous but also tatty, as though it had been many years since the rooms had seen anything close to their best. As he walked, his footsteps echoed into the distance through rooms which felt as though they had never known laughter.

It was also surprisingly dark, in spite of the sheer number of windows. While they were large, the light they were able to let in was obstructed by either thick curtains, dirt, or plants growing over the outside. Spencer had to look away and focus on the inside of the house; looking at where the daylight should be streaming in gave him the impression of being in the darkest pit of the filthiest gaol.

He had never particularly thought of himself as an outdoors sort of person, but within a few minutes of being inside that house, Spencer wanted nothing more than lots of fresh air.

After being shown to their rooms, they all gathered downstairs for afternoon tea. The three guests were the first to arrive and milled around the large room, smiling awkwardly at each other.

"Nice place," said Spencer, examining one of the paintings.

"It is," said Tess. "Are your rooms nice? I did not see you on my landing. Presumably you are in a different part of the house?"

"Yeah. They put us near the servants."

Tess gasped. "Really? That will not do; I will speak to them."

"Don't worry," said Spencer. "We don't mind, do we mate?"

"Nah," said Bart. "We've lived in much worse places. The room I've got here's twice as big as what me whole family used to have."

"And besides," said Spencer with a sly grin. "His room's right by some maidservant we happened to spot on the way in. If we moved rooms, he might not have the opportunity to 'accidentally' bump into her..."

"Shut up!" protested Bart, his cheeks reddening as he glanced at Tess. "Don't listen to him; I wouldn't..."

"Do not worry," smiled Tess. "I think it is sweet. I have said for a while that it would be nice if you boys had a bit more of a female touch around you."

"Exactly what he was thinking," grinned Spencer. "He was thinking he'd especially like a female touch on his—"

He stopped suddenly as the door opened. Lord and Lady Beaumont entered the room, followed by a rather chastened-looking Emilia.

Lord Beaumont was a tall, dark-haired man with a long, greying moustache covering thin lips. He had a slim build, although it was showing signs of the beginnings of a paunch around his middle.

Lady Beaumont was just as Tess had described her: a timid, mouse-like creature with a skittish smile. While she was not too dissimilar in height to her husband, the way she held herself made her look almost a foot shorter.

"Tessie," smiled Lord Beaumont as he approached, his arms outstretched in greeting. "Or should I say Lady Marchant? It has been too long."

"Actually, please call me Tess," she replied. "I am still..."

"Of course, of course. Old wounds—or not-so-old wounds—and all that. Totally understand. Very inconsiderate of me. Please do accept my apologies. You remember my wife?"

"Of course," smiled Tess. "A pleasure to meet you again, Lady Beaumont." They embraced stiffly and kissed the air by each other's cheeks.

"And you, Tess," said Lady Beaumont with a tight smile. "Welcome to our home."

"Please do forgive my rather harsh demeanour when you arrived," said Lord Beaumont. "I was not expecting Emilia to come back with any house guests, let alone ones with such an... exotic pedigree."

"Nah, we're from London, mate. I mean, Lord," said Bart.

"I did not mean exotic as in where you are from. I meant what you do. I am afraid Emilia acted on her own initiative which, whilst commendable, was not necessarily how I would have preferred matters to progress."

Tess nodded, noting that Emilia was staring down at the floor, avoiding eye contact with everyone. She had heard raised voices from Lord Beaumont's study as they were being led to their rooms, so had already suspected that something was amiss.

"We do not want to cause any problems," said Tess. "If there is an issue with our presence, we can of course leave."

"No!" They were surprised by Lady Beaumont almost shouting the word. At a look from her husband, she said in a calmer voice, "We will not hear of it, given how far you have come, and especially given the fact that you are an old family friend. You and your... colleagues will be our guests. And Emilia is right; you may be able to help us. My husband is rather sensitive about our little problem, but if there is any substance to what we have been told, then any help would be appreciated."

Tess cleared her throat. "I would like to introduce you to my business associates: Spencer and Bart."

Both men stepped forward with broad grins and hands outstretched, to be met with reserved looks from the Beaumonts.

"Nice to meet you, Mister...?" said Lord Beaumont, shaking Spencer's hand as though it were made of raw meat.

"Just 'Spencer'. I don't tend to go for all them airs and graces, your Lordship. No real need for 'Misters' and the like, where we come from."

"And, truth be told, neither of us know our family names," added Bart. "Not really the sort of thing that ever came up."

"Really?" Lady Beaumont stared at him.

"Yeah. I was always just Bart, or Bill's lad."

Tess winced, making a mental note to educate them both in the dos and don'ts of introducing themselves in polite society.

"You said, where you come from," said Lord Beaumont. "And where is that, exactly?"

"London. East End to be exact. You ever been there?"

"No. I cannot say that I have."

"I'd like to say it's a nice place, but I'd be lying. Not like here. Lovely place you've got here."

"Thank you."

Lady Beaumont turned to Tess. "My dear, you do look well. My commiserations about your husband. I see you are out of mourning." She cast an eye over her clothes. "I also see that London fashion is as... unique as ever. Tell me, what is that article about your waist?"

Tess put her hand to the belt she wore, suddenly conscious of how out of place it looked against her otherwise smart dress. "It allows me to carry certain tools and items I require for my work," she said. "I do find the lack of pockets in most dresses to be rather inconvenient."

"Hmm," said Lady Beaumont with a frown. "Very cosmopolitan, I am sure."

"Now now, my dear," said her husband. "Do not forget that Lady Marchant is no longer a lady of leisure. After all, she is here on business. Is that not so?"

"Yes," said Tess, unsure whether to be grateful for his intervention, or offended by it.

"Well, shall we all go through to the dining room? I am sure the others will join us shortly." Lady Beaumont fixed her face in a smile and led them to the door.

"The others?" asked Tess.

"Yes. We have a couple of other houseguests," Lady Beaumont said over her shoulder. "You will meet them soon enough."

They were led through to an oak panelled room, which was dominated by a long dining table bedecked with a bewildering amount of cutlery and crockery. Spencer shot a panicked look at Tess, copying her as she sat down and placed a napkin on her lap.

The three servants started to bring in food, Mr Smith appearing as though he had been forced to do so, while Mrs Smith fussed around the placements and the young maidservant blushed under Bart's gaze. Perfectly-cut sandwiches, meats, fruit and cakes were placed on the table, and it took all of Spencer and Bart's willpower to resist reaching over and tucking in, watching Tess keenly for an indication of when it would be socially acceptable to do so.

Before they could start, though, the door opened and two men in riding suits burst in, laughing and joking with each other. The first was tall and tanned, with dark wavy hair, piercing blue eyes and a long handlebar moustache. The other was clearly Emilia's younger brother, his face a more angular version of hers, his mouth twisted into a sardonic grin.

"Oh, I did not realise we had visitors," said the first man, a glint in his eye. "Darling, are you going to introduce us?"

Emilia bolted to her feet and scurried to his side. "Yes, of course. This is my old friend Tess, the Lady Marchant."

"Ah yes, the demon hunters," he said with a teasing grin. "Emilia talked about nothing else before she left. We weren't sure she was going to be able to convince you to come, were we?" He looked around the room but was met only with stony faces. "I am Ralph Wheeler, and have the honour to be Emilia's fiancé."

"A pleasure to meet you," said Tess, shooting a grin at Emilia.

"And congratulations to you both."

Ralph looked at the other two men with a glint in his eye. "And who might you be?"

"I'm Spencer, and this is Bart," Spencer said, pulling himself to his feet and offering his hand. "We're colleagues of Tess's."

Ralph stared at him, making no effort to shake his hand. "Indeed. Wouldn't the kitchen table be more comfortable for the likes of you?"

"What do you mean?"

Ralph waved a hand as though to say it did not matter. "Not my place," he said, sitting down.

Spencer lowered his hand and then himself back down into his chair, his cheeks burning.

They turned to look at the other man, who was already sat down and helping himself to food, ignoring Spencer and Bart's hungry glares.

"And this is my brother, Calvin," said Emilia. "Please forgive his lack of manners."

"We have been out hunting," said Calvin through a mouthful of pie. "I have worked up quite an appetite. This is quite the spread; better than the slop you usually serve. Why have we got the good food out, all of a sudden?"

"We have guests," hissed Lady Beaumont.

"Yes," he replied, eyeing the others. "Makes a nice change. Was beginning to think you'd decided to only ever host people we're related to."

"Calvin, now is not the time," snapped Lord Beaumont.

"Sorry, I forgot. Wouldn't want us to wash our dirty linen in public, would we?"

"We had a very successful hunt, did we not?" Ralph Wheeler said, trying to change the subject with forced jollity.

"Yes, very pleasant." Calvin popped a grape in his mouth and chewed it noisily. "Don't worry, big sister, I didn't do anything to harm him."

Ralph laughed, but Emilia simply glared at her brother.

Calvin shot a sly grin at her and then turned to the guests. "So you are the demon hunters who—"

Lady Beaumont coughed and dropped her spoon in the bowl in front of her, the noise shocking them all into silence for a moment. She glared at Calvin, who beamed back at her.

Ralph cleared his throat and then asked Spencer, "What was your occupation before you joined Tess in her enterprise?"

"I do not think this is really the time..." started Tess.

"Did a bit of everything," said Spencer. "Well known in the East End, we are. You been there?"

"No," sniffed Ralph. "I cannot say that I have. Nor that I have ever had the inclination to do so."

"You're missing out," said Bart.

"I am sure," Ralph said drily. "And what exactly am I missing out on? Apart from being mugged and contracting several diseases?"

Lord Beaumont snorted with laughter, making Ralph's smile stretch even further across his face.

"It's not like that at all," said Bart, oblivious. "There's some great folk there. And pubs. Best beer and pie you'll find anywhere."

"Beer and pies. Sounds exotic." Ralph grinned over the rim of his wine glass.

"Don't know about that, but it's a treat you won't forget—" said Bart.

Spencer held up a hand to stop his friend. "He's messing with you," he said. "Just stop."

Ralph chuckled over the rim of his glass. "I am sorry. I have forgotten my manners. Tell you what, how about we make it up to you and take you out hunting tomorrow?"

"They are supposed to be here to help us with our little problem," said Lord Beaumont. "Not having a jolly at our expense."

"Oh, my dear," said Lady Beaumont, a twinkle in her eye. "It may do them some good to experience a bit of country life. And anyway, the beast doesn't come out until nighttime. There's not much else that they could be doing during the day."

"I don't know," said Spencer. "I mean, as he said we've got a lot to do here, trying to figure out where the creature hides out during the day, get some clues as to how we can stop it for you."

"Ah!" said Ralph, banging the table and sharing a glance with Lady Beaumont. "I was thinking that we would do some hunting, but maybe we could combine our hunting with yours. After all, you'll need to get a good view of the estate, get a good feel for what's where and all that. What a better way than on horseback?"

Spencer shot panicked glance at Tess for help, but she just nodded.

"They have a point, you know," she said. "This could be a good way for you to get a feel for where the demon could be hiding when it's not skulking around here. In the meantime, I could busy myself with getting to know this estate. I am particularly interested to see where the beast tends to manifest itself."

"Our groundsman can help you with that," said Lord Beaumont. "He's the best for showing you round all that sort of stuff. Don't tend to have much time for skulking around fields and gardens, myself."

"I think we should also see that," said Spencer, with one last desperate attempt to get them out of the hunt. "After all, how do we know what we're up against and what to look out for if we don't see the one place that demon hangs out?"

"Wilbur's an early riser," said Lady Beaumont. "He will quite happily show you round first thing. You can be back here in time for breakfast, and then go out with the boys on your little jaunt. That sounds like we have a plan!" She beamed round the table. "Now, enjoy this food and maybe our demonic friend will treat you to his nighttime show. So you can see for yourself what we are contending with, maybe?"

*

A few hours later, after the night had fallen, they were all settling comfortably down in their chairs, their heads foggy with booze and their stomachs full of rich food. Lord Beaumont held up his hand, silencing them all, and gestured to his ear. "Can you hear that?"

They all strained their ears.

"Is it here?" asked Tess.

Lady Beaumont nodded eagerly. "Yes, yes, I think it is. Listen!"

They all did as they were told, and, sure enough, they heard a distant howling. After a few moments, the sound came again, this time closer.

"Sounds near," said Bart. "Must be in your garden, no?"

"Probably just outside the grounds," said Emilia.

Tess scraped back a chair and darted over to the window. "Can I see it from here?" she asked.

"It seems to be coming from that direction," said Spencer, joining her and pointing. He screwed up his eyes to peer out into the darkness. "But if it's out there, it's behind them trees. We need to go higher up to see it." He turned to the others. "What room's above us?"

"I believe it is the room we have given to Lady Marchant," said Lady Beaumont. She turned to the butler, who was standing in attendance by the door. "Is that right, Smith?"

Mr Smith nodded dutifully. "That is correct, ma'am."

"Perfect!" grinned Tess, turning and running out of the room, Spencer and Bart following in her wake. After a few moments, Emily and Ralph also left the room, then Lady Beaumont walked over to the door, stopping and gesturing for Lord Beaumont to go with her.

He stared at her for a moment and then rolled his eyes. "Do I really have to?" he asked.

"Yes!" she said. "Now. Come on."

Lord Beaumont held up his wine glass. Mr Smith brought

over a bottle and poured, on Lord Beaumont's urging not stopping until the glass was almost full to the brim.

"Very well, dear," Lord Beaumont said. He raised himself from the table, somewhat unsteadily, hitting the back of Calvin's chair on his way past. "You too, Calvin," he said. "You wouldn't want to miss all this fun, would you?"

Calvin showed no signs of moving. He reached out to the table, grabbing a hunk of cheese with one hand and his wine glass with the other. "I have no desire to take part in this mummer's farce," he said, downing his drink and holding his glass out for a refill. "You go if you want, but you can't make me."

Lord Beaumont stared at him but, before he could say anything, his wife put a hand on his arm and shook her head, leading him out of the room. They made their way up to the floor above, finding the others gathered around the window in Tess's room, while Tess herself had her face pressed against the glass.

Lord Beaumont peered into the darkness of the room, holding his lamp high above his head.

"Put that light out, the glare is reflecting on the window," snapped Tess. Lord Beaumont raised an eyebrow at her impudent tone, but still complied.

They stood in silence for a moment, and then Tess pointed. "Is that it?" she asked. "Do you see that?"

Spencer screwed up his eyes to try and make out the shapes in the darkness. "Looks like something big moving around out there," he said.

"Yes," Tess said and then hissed in frustration. "It is moving behind those trees. We need to be higher." She turned round. "What rooms are above these? Can we use one of them?"

Lady Beaumont shot a panicked glance at her husband. "I am afraid not," she said. "That floor is out of bounds."

"That is correct," said Lord Beaumont. "The upper floor has been shut off for a number of years. It is too dangerous."

They all stared at him. "Are you sure?" Spencer asked. "It'd be really useful if we could go up there…"

"No," said Lord Beaumont again. "That will not be possible. That floor is out of bounds."

"We could go out there and check?" asked Bart. "Not sure why we're milling about in here, when the demon's out there."

"Bit dangerous, mate," said Spencer. "We don't know the place, don't know what the demon's like."

"It does not matter," said Tess. "It appears that the creature has gone." She turned up the lamp on her side table and then threw open her trunk, rummaging through the equipment in there.

"Can we help?" asked Spencer.

"No. Thank you. I need to get ready for the morning. I should have insisted on setting up at least some detection equipment when we arrived, rather than wasting time with dinner." She caught herself and looked up at the others. "I am sorry, I meant no offence. It was a lovely meal. But I am conscious that we are here to do a job for you. Not socialise."

"We understand perfectly," said Lady Beaumont. "We will leave you to it; it is time for us to retire, in any case."

The Beaumonts left. Spencer shut the door behind them and then turned to watch Tess, busily arranging equipment on the floor.

"So what do you think?" he asked. "Seems like there's a demon, right?"

"Maybe. Certainly sounded like one, although I cannot help wonder why it disappeared so readily. If its main motivation is to terrorise this household, then why such a fleeting visit? I saw or heard nothing which would have scared it off. Did you?"

"Not that I noticed."

"So unless it was on its way to somewhere else…" She frowned in thought. "But where?"

"Beats me," said Spencer. "So is that what you're going to figure out?"

"With this equipment? No. At least, not yet. I firstly want to check that we really are facing a demon here, and find out a bit about it. I just need to check that everything is working."

"Can we help?" Bart asked.

"No, thank you. I will need your help with installing the equipment in the morning, but for the time being I just need a bit of peace to arrange everything. Get some sleep; I suspect we will all need to be well rested for tomorrow."

*

Emilia wandered back downstairs, to find her brother still sat in the dining room. Ralph followed her into the room a moment later and stood, scowling, by the door.

"So what brings you here, little brother?" she asked. "Spent all of your monthly allowance already? Or are you hiding from some new creditors?"

"Oh, *ha ha*," said Calvin. "So amusing, as always. I am here to spend some time with my dear father. It's his birthday coming up, didn't you know?"

"Of course I knew. I'm just surprised you remembered. Which new secretary do we have to thank for prompting you?"

"Not a *new* secretary. It's still Robbins."

"Wow. That must be a record." Emilia turned to Ralph. "I hear that it is almost a badge of honour in the City to have resigned from my brother's employ. They say that if you walk into any tavern in the Square Mile, you can't move for his ex-employees."

"Oh you are so droll, my dear sister," sighed Calvin. "Is it my fault I have such high standards?"

"It is your fault that you are such an insufferable prig."

"Now come on," said Ralph. "Can we all just try and get on?"

"That's right," said Calvin. "Control your woman, Ralph."

Emilia's nostrils flared but, before she could respond, Ralph stepped in.

"You know that's not how it works, Calvin."

"No, of course not. Wouldn't want to upset my sister. Not until you've tied the knot and you're guaranteed a slice of the family inheritance, eh?"

"We're not all about the money," said Emilia.

"Of course you're not. You just stick around here out of pure love and devotion for mama and papa."

She glared at him as Calvin chuckled, standing and sauntering over to the drinks cabinet to pour himself a large glass of whiskey. "Here's to my sister: as articulate, caring and faithful as ever."

Tess, listening to this exchange from the top of the stairs, raised her eyebrows. Emilia and Calvin had always bickered as children; it seemed some things never changed.

Chapter Eight

Spencer and Bart had managed to sneak back down and steal a couple of bottles of wine from the dining room before they were cleared away by the servants, and had retired to their respective rooms with their nightcaps. It did not take long for Spencer to pass out, although a few hours later he was wide awake, staring at the ceiling and listening to a succession of noises from the floor above.

It was a loud bang which had woken him up at first. He had been shocked into wakefulness, not sure whether it had been a dream or reality which had done so.

He lay there, the room spinning slowly round him as he strained his ears to try and hear any other noises. He had almost given up and was in the process of drifting back to sleep when he was jolted awake again by a scraping sound.

He sat up and listened. There it was again: the sound of something being moved around upstairs. It was faint, as though the person involved was trying desperately to be as quiet and gentle as possible, but unmistakeably the sound of movement above.

He got out of bed, remembering what Lord and Lady Beaumont had said only a few hours earlier, that the floor above was empty and out of bounds. If that was the case, he thought, then what was he listening to?

He crept across the room to the door. The journey did not take long; his room was only a slight upgrade from where the servants slept, containing a bed and a thin, battered wardrobe with precious little floorspace between them. He pressed his ear against the rough wooden door. There seemed to be shuffling sounds coming from the landing outside now as well. He looked around for a weapon, settling on a poker from the fireplace. Holding it aloft, he grabbed the doorhandle, took a quick deep breath, and then pulled the door open.

He almost collided with Bart, who was stood right outside. They both stared at each other for a moment, wide-eyed, and then exhaled.

"I nearly brained you, mate!" Spencer hissed.

"You nearly *tried* to brain me," Bart muttered. "You hear that noise?"

"From upstairs? Yeah. You too?"

"Yeah. What you reckon it is?"

"Sounds like someone doing something up there," Spencer replied. "Up on a floor which is supposed to be empty. Fancy having a look to see what's going on?"

Before they could so do, the door to the stairway opened and Mr Smith stepped through. He jumped as he saw them. "My godfathers," he panted. "You two gave me a fright! What are you doing out here in the dark?"

"We heard something from upstairs," said Spencer. "We were wondering what it was."

"Yes, ah, that's where I was. A bat had got in through one of the windows; I was just letting it out. All sorted now, you can go back to bed."

"Do you need a hand?" asked Bart. "We can help check there aren't any others?"

"It's all right. I have dealt with it."

They stared at each other for a moment longer, and then Spencer and Bart shrugged and returned to their rooms. Spencer stood by his door for a while, listening to hear whether Smith walked away, but heard nothing; the man was clearly waiting until he was happy they would not reemerge. He shrugged, his bed suddenly looking very inviting. This all seemed like a problem for tomorrow, he decided as he collapsed onto the mattress.

*

Tess found herself tossing and turning, in that frustrating place which seemed on the verge of wakefulness and yet subject to dreams.

A face kept looming out of the darkness of her mind's eye, a face which deep down she knew but was petrified to put a name to, lest it become real.

She heard the echoes of her late husband's voice. "My dear, let me introduce my associate, Mr Emerson."

And there it was. The face congealed into solidity in front of her. She knew she was dreaming—she hoped; surely she was? Surely—but even so, she wanted nothing more than to scream and run and hide. She never wanted to sleep again, if this was what was waiting for her every time she closed her eyes.

She remembered every part of him, in more detail than anyone she had ever known. His raven black hair, his pallid skin, and those eyes: deep pools of pure black. If the eyes were the window to the soul, then this man had nothing but a void at his centre.

She saw him, first in front of her and then through the glass of the device in which he had imprisoned her, after kidnapping her from her own house. The device which he had used to inflict the demonic presence on her which had possessed her and, for a time, turned her into something terrible, gripped by a bloodlust which consumed her and everything around her.

Emerson's face swam around her, a deep evil brooding of which she knew everything and nothing.

Chapter Nine

The next morning, Spencer, Bart and Tess were down early to breakfast, before the others arrived.

"How did you sleep?" asked Tess.

"Rubbish," said Bart. "All them noises from upstairs; did you hear them?"

"I did," she said. "Quite the racket. Any idea what it was?"

"We bumped into Mr Smith, the butler," said Spencer. "He said it was a bat that'd gotten into the house."

Bart snorted.

"What?" asked Tess. "Do you not believe him?"

"Something don't add up," he said. "Thought they said it was too dangerous for anyone to go up on that floor."

"Well, if there's a bat inside the house, I suppose it is his job to get it out."

"Yeah," said Bart. "But how'd he know there was a bat up there in the first place? Who told him?"

After they had finished a hearty breakfast of fish, meat and eggs, Tess, Spencer and Bart were directed to the stables, where they were told that they could find Wilbur, the groundskeeper.

"Don't you think it's a bit weird?" asked Bart as they walked.

"What?" asked Spencer.

"If I had some great big demon messing around outside my house every night, I'd be a bit more bothered about it than they seem to be."

"I suppose. But they asked us to come here and help them. Shows they're at least a bit bothered."

"Well, Emilia did. I thought the others didn't know she went to get us?"

"Nah, you've got it wrong," said Spencer. "They knew. That future husband of hers knew all about us. Anyway, here we are."

They approached the stables, a long wooden building covered in flaking white paint. The door hung open at an angle and the floor was covered in straw and muck. They peered inside. "Anyone there?"

"What do you want?" A scrawny old man with long hair and beard to match, wearing a tweed suit that looked almost as old as he was, peered round the side of the building.

"We're looking for Wilbur," said Spencer.

"Who's 'we'?"

"I'm Spencer and this is Bart. And this here is Tess. We're staying here a few nights to help the family with a little problem."

Wilbur took off his hat to greet Tess. "Oh yeah. You'll be the ghost hunters then."

"Demon hunters," Spencer corrected him.

Wilbur shrugged, as if to say they were all the same to him.

"You were expecting us, then?" asked Spencer.

"Lady Beaumont said you might be heading round at some point. That you'd want to see the mess our little nighttime visitor's been making."

"Yes please," said Tess. "Would you be able to take us there?"

Wilbur grunted. "Follow me, please, miss."

They followed him out of the stable yard and along the path towards the gardens at the back of the house, struggling to keep pace with the older man. The sun was fighting a losing battle with the clouds, and the air had that fresh tang to it which came with the approach of winter.

"Where does that door lead?" Tess asked, pointing to a battered and faded door at the rear of the house.

"Oh, that?" asked Wilbur. "It's not been used in years. Decades probably. Pretty sure it's bricked in behind it. Certainly not something we've seen the other side of, in my knowledge."

"Maybe it leads to some old storage place," said Tess. "These old houses are always overrun with them."

"Maybe," grunted Wilbur. "I wouldn't know."

Tess stared at him, but decided against pressing any further. She looked up at the house, and a movement caught her eye on the top floor, a face at a window quickly disappearing from view. "I thought that floor was unoccupied," she said.

"What floor?" asked Wilbur.

"There," she pointed. "The top floor. We were told no one goes up there."

"That's right," Wilbur said, turning away.

"I just saw a movement in one of the windows."

"Maybe it's Mr Smith doing his rounds of the house, checking all's secure."

"Maybe," she said, squinting up but not seeing any further movement.

"Everything all right?" asked Spencer.

"Yes," she said. "Just a little peculiar. Anyway, we should keep up with Wilbur."

They made their way across a lawn which was punctuated with regular patches of weed and moss, surrounded by flower beds which were more wild than ornamental.

"They're not too bothered about nice neat flowers and stuff, then?" asked Spencer.

"I do what I can," said Wilbur. "Only so much one man can do with an estate this size."

"So it's just you doing all the work in this huge garden?" whistled Spencer. "That's a big job for just one bloke."

"Yeah, well, it wasn't always just me. Not until recently, anyways. We had one of them demons helping me. You know, one of the domesticated ones. Great help he was, doing all the heavy stuff and that. He could do in a day stuff that'd take me a week. But then the family let him go."

"Why?"

He shrugged. "Dunno. They never gave me a reason; not that they'd ever need to. But I've told Mr Smith that he can't be expecting me to just carry on with the same amount of stuff now it's just me. Not with the way my knees are these days."

"Doesn't sound very fair to me," said Tess. "When did they fire the demon?"

"Couple of weeks ago."

"How big was this demon of yours?" Bart asked.

"About seven feet tall," said Wilbur.

"And he was pretty wide?"

"Yeah. Bulky bloke, was Trevor."

"Trevor?" asked Spencer.

"Yeah. That's what I called him. He did tell me his real demon name, but there was no way I was ever going to be able to say it, so we settled on Trevor."

Bart picked around the undergrowth. "If he had a mind, you reckon Trevor could've made a mess like what you're taking us to see?"

Wilbur looked around and then said, slowly, "He could. But he wasn't like that. There's no way he'd cause trouble."

"Even if he thought he'd been hard done to, by them in that house?" asked Spencer.

Wilbur shook his head. "That just ain't his nature."

"He's a demon," said Spencer. "Breaking stuff *is* their nature."

"Not Trevor."

"All right. When he was fired, where did he go?"

"He's still hanging around the village."

"Where could we find him?"

"Down the local pub. He does some fetching and carrying there now. But I'm telling you: Trevor wouldn't do something like this."

"Even if he felt badly treated?"

Wilbur shrugged. "Not Trevor. Do you want to see this damage or not?" He reached a gate at the far end of the gardens and turned to wait for them. "You two don't do much walking where you're from?"

"We're just not used to everything being so... open," panted

Spencer.

"And grassy," said Bart. "Cobblestones and mud's what our feet are used to."

"Well, I can certainly give you plenty of mud," said Wilbur, swinging open the gate and leading them through, to the woodland beyond.

Tess stopped to look at the gate. "Interesting design," she muttered, examining an image which was fixed to it.

"Circles, stars and half-moons," said Spencer, standing next to her. "Where've I seen that before?"

"On the front door," said Tess. "Some sort of family crest perhaps?"

Wilbur grunted noncommittally as he stomped off ahead of them.

As soon as they entered the woods, it was as though the world seemed to stop breathing, a deafening silence suddenly descending on them. They looked around, feeling as though they had stepped into another world. Unkempt, overgrown trees reached down around them, blocking off the light and creating staging posts for a myriad spiders' webs which caught in their hair and stuck to their faces. The undergrowth was thick and tangled, forcing them to take huge, careful steps to make their way after the groundskeeper, who carved his way through as though it were an empty field.

"Hold up," shouted Spencer. "We're having a bit of trouble fighting our way through this lot."

"Don't worry," came Wilbur's voice from beyond the next set of trees. "It opens up here."

They stepped through, into a clearing; except on closer examination it appeared to not be a natural clearing. The foliage had been flattened, with low branches and twigs snapped off, in a trail which ran in a meandering line running off into the distance.

Wilbur stood there and looked at them. "This is what I was told to come and show you."

They looked around. "They think this was made by a demon?" asked Spencer.

"That's what they think."

"What do you think?"

"Don't matter what I think," said Wilbur, lifting his cap and scratching his head. "I weren't around to witness it, but the family were, and that's what they say happened."

"Not that impressive," said Bart. "Way they were carrying on, I thought we'd have whole trees torn down. You know, proper carnage."

They walked along the pathway, peering around.

"It's like something's just come running straight through here," said Bart, demonstrating by breaking into a lumbering jog. "It's flattened the plants and stuff, but only in this direction," he pointed at the house. "Then it looks like it stopped and kind've ran round in circles here," he gestured at a large circle of flattened ground.

"Ran round in circles. Almost like it was frustrated," said Wilbur. When he noticed them looking at him, he added, "That's what animals tend to do, when they're frustrated or scared: run round in circles."

"Could it've been an animal of some sort?" asked Spencer.

"Could be," shrugged Wilbur. "Something big like a bear or the like could do this."

"You get many bears round here?"

"Nope."

"A bloke could do this," said Bart. "Or a few of them. That'd be my guess."

"You reckon?" asked Spencer. "It'd need to be a big bloke."

"Not that big," said Bart, stretching his arms out and then up. "Someone about the size of me'd be able to do most of this, given a few hours."

"You're quite a big bloke," said Wilbur, eyeing him up.

"Yeah, most folk aren't as big as you, mate," Spencer reminded his friend.

Bart stomped up and down. "Couple of blokes then. Point is, it doesn't need to be a demon to've done all this. I'd more believe it was some blokes messing around."

"Why not a demon?" asked Wilbur.

"Demons do lots of damage, don't they?" said Bart. "Rip things up, destroy things, tear people to pieces. They don't tend to be shy. But what did this one do? Turn up, stare at the house, scream, and then do a bit of gardening? Don't make sense."

"He's got a point," said Spencer.

"What is this?" asked Tess, squatting down to examine a mark on the floor.

"Looks like someone's tried sticking a pole in the ground," said Spencer, bending down to get a closer look.

"Not deep enough for that," said Bart. "You know what that looks like; someone with a walking stick." He looked along the ground, pacing the holes. "They're about the right distance apart, for someone prodding the ground with a stick." He looked up at Wilbur. "You use a walking stick?"

"Me? No. It's probably nothing." The groundskeeper smoothed over one of the marks with his foot. "Probably just a bird or some such."

"Hmm," said Tess. "So did all this happen last night?"

Wilbur shrugged. "Maybe. There was already damage before last night. Difficult to say what was done last night and what was done before."

"And when did you first notice that there had been some activity out here?"

"About a week ago. I came out here to find all this, then the family started talking about some sort of curse."

"*Started* talking?" asked Spencer. "I thought this curse'd been in the family for generations?"

"Might've been," said Wilbur. "Although I'd not heard about it before. Not that any of them would have told me, anyway. Keep myself to myself most of the time, which suits me fine. Of course, there's always been talk of strange creatures roaming these woods at night. Even before all that stuff with the Aether happened."

"Who talked about it?"

Before Wilbur could reply, Ralph stepped out of the foliage. "There you are, Wilbur. Lord Beaumont would like to see you. Right away."

Wilbur nodded once and then stomped off.

Ralph smiled at them. "Thought I would rescue you before he started telling you stories from those old soaks down at the Red Lion."

"Red Lion?" asked Spencer.

"Oh, it's the local tavern, down in the village. But it's all stuff and nonsense. Nothing you should bother yourselves with. We are making ourselves ready for our little jaunt, if you would like to join us? Over in the stables?"

"Sure, sure," said Spencer. "Just give us a moment, yeah?"

Ralph nodded, and then turned and walked off, back to the house.

"You hear that?" asked Spencer.

"I heard him say the word 'tavern'," said Bart. "All this fresh air gives a man a powerful thirst."

"Yeah. And he seemed pretty keen to put the idea out of our heads. When a toff tries to distract me from something, that makes me want to do it even more. I think we should head over to this Red Lion this evening, see what we can find out."

"Or we could go now," suggested Bart. "You know, instead of going hunting?"

"No, you cannot," said Tess. "You have accepted an offer from our hosts; it would be rude for you to leave them in the lurch."

"But…" Bart pulled a face.

"I'd love nothing more than to miss the hunting with them two toffs," said Spencer. "But Tess is right; we should go. We'll go to the pub tonight, after dinner. Anyway, the hunting stuff might be fun."

"You don't sound like you believe that," said Bart.

"That's because I don't. But I suppose that's a part of this whole job thing we're doing now. Sometimes you need to do stuff you don't want to."

"Listen to you," chuckled Tess. "You are almost sounding like a real businessman."

"Yeah, well," he blushed. "Suppose we should go to the stables and go on this bloody hunt. You all right with us heading off?"

"Yes," Tess said, looking around with a distracted look on her face. "I will probably come out here later and set up some equipment, to see if I can pick up any readings, maybe catch our little demonic visitor in the act, tonight."

"Wait until we're back, yeah?" said Bart. "Don't like the thought of you in these woods on your own, what with that thing wandering around."

"I will be fine," she said with a smile. "I will not be here after dark."

"Even so. You don't know what could happen, and this is far enough away from the house that no one'd hear you if you did get into trouble."

She tried to wave away his concerns but, when she saw the determined look on his face, nodded. "Fine. I will see what I can find out around the house, and then we can come out here together when you get back, and set up my equipment. Happy?"

"Bloody ecstatic," grinned Bart.

Chapter Ten

"When d'you reckon we can stop?" asked Spencer.

"I dunno," said Bart. "But I can't feel my arse no more."

They were both sat awkwardly on a pair of horses, which seemed determined to throw them off at the earliest opportunity. The situation was made worse by the fact that neither of them really knew how to actually ride a horse.

So they found themselves clinging desperately hard to their respective rides, painfully aware of Ralph and Calvin's teasing.

"Not used to such a rough ride, eh?" asked Ralph, to sniggers from the other man.

Bart muttered something, but Spencer caught his eye and shook his head. "So how much further are we going to go?" he asked.

"Not far. Not getting sore, are we?" asked Calvin.

"I'm fine," he said. "We're both fine. Just wondering when we're actually going to get down to some actual hunting and the like, rather than just flouncing around the place."

The other two men laughed and then kicked their horses into a gallop, leaving Spencer and Bart trailing in their wake.

Bart glared after them. "I'm starting to wonder if they're trying to wind us up."

"You think so?" Spencer asked, shaking his head and then pushing his horse to go a bit faster.

They eventually stopped on the brow of a hill and dismounted. Each man had a large shotgun strapped to their backs. Ralph and Calvin unhitched their guns and started checking them.

Spencer and Bart did likewise, Bart struggling with the weapon's delicate mechanism.

"Not used to handling a weapon like this?" asked Ralph with a smirk.

"Not one this small and fiddly," said Bart. "What's wrong with a nice big axe?"

"We're hunting game from afar," said Calvin. "I think you will find it easier to hit them with a gun than an axe. Although I would enjoy watching you try." He turned to Ralph. "Did you pack any axes?"

"No," sneered the other man. "Nor did we pack any halberds, spears or trebuchets. You will have to make do with the shotgun."

"That's all right," muttered Bart. "I'm sure I can manage."

Spencer raised his shotgun to his shoulder and looked along the barrel, testing the weight and balance. "We've used all sorts of guns in our time."

"I am sure you have," said Ralph. "Ever killed an animal before?"

"Not on purpose, like," said Bart. "Done for some demons though. And roughed up plenty of blokes who upset us."

Ralph ignored his pointed glare. "Well, today, if we are lucky, we should snag a deer or two, or maybe a grouse or pheasant."

"What, so you just come out here and just take shots at whatever you fancy?" asked Bart.

"It depends on the season and the conditions," sniffed Ralph. "But the variety is part of the joy of the hunt."

Spencer hefted his gun. "Just wondering. We gonna be standing around here all day gossiping like a bunch of girls, or are we gonna go out there and try to kill some stuff?"

Calvin laughed. "I admire your spirit! I could grow to like these boys! Yes, let us go and kill some stuff!"

Ralph glared at him, but said nothing.

They picked their way carefully through the undergrowth, guns held across their bodies, eyes alert for any movement. It quickly became apparent that two of them were less adept at moving quietly than the other two.

"Could you be quieter?" hissed Ralph. "Every creature for a mile around knows where we are, the amount of racket you are both making!"

"We're trying our best," said Spencer. "We're not used to there being so much stuff around to push our way through."

"Yeah," said Bart. "We're more used to streets and stuff."

Ralph shook his head. "Just try and tread a bit less heavy."

"I know where I'd like to tread," Bart muttered to Spencer.

Spencer grinned in reply.

"Right on their stupid—" continued Bart.

"I know; I got it." Spencer hushed him, as the others turned to look at them.

They spread out in a line, Spencer and Bart to the right of the other two. They picked their way through the late morning drizzle, the sounds of distant birds in their ears. The season was turning, the trees showing the first signs of autumn, leaves browning and falling to the ground to form a crisp carpet which added to the soundtrack of their progress.

After a few minutes, Bart froze, holding his hand out to stop Spencer. He pointed ahead of them, at a deer which was eating from the undergrowth, its back to them.

"What are you waiting for?" Spencer hissed. "Shoot it!"

"Oh. Yeah." Bart raised his shotgun to his shoulder and aimed it at the creature. He steadied his stance, shuffling his feet further apart and squatting down slightly.

Spencer stared at him. "Are you going to do it or what?"

Bart pulled a face. "I can't." He lowered his weapon.

"What d'you mean, you can't?"

"Look at it. Standing there all nice and innocent. I can't shoot it. Not in the back, and not when it's having its dinner."

"You want to wait until it's finished eating?"

"I just can't, all right?"

"What d'you think them two toffs are going to think, if they see you refusing to shoot? They already look down on us. One thing we've got over them is we're tougher than them. If they see you won't even shoot a dumb animal, we won't even have that!"

"I ain't doing it. You do it if you want; I ain't."

Spencer glared at him for a moment and then nodded. He turned and aimed his gun, just as the deer turned to look at them. The creature's dark eyes met his as he willed his finger to squeeze the trigger, but it was as though it was stuck fast, immovable.

He gritted his teeth and then let out a strangled snarl as he lowered his gun. The deer darted away.

"See, you couldn't either," said Bart.

"I could feel you staring at me. You put me off!"

"You should've pulled the trigger. Knowing your aim, the deer was in the safest place."

"Shut up."

The bushes rustled as Ralph and Calvin pushed their way through to them. "What are you doing?" asked Calvin. "You let it go!"

Spencer coughed. "Couldn't quite get the aim right, then it bolted."

"We saw what you were doing," sneered Ralph. "Both of you had plenty of chances to kill it, and you chickened out of it."

"Hey," said Bart. "You take that back. We don't chicken out of nothing. We just didn't think it was right to kill it. Not while it was eating and everything."

"Of course," said Ralph, rolling his eyes. "What were we thinking of? Why would you want to kill an animal when it is being obliging and standing still. Much better to let them run around, make it hard for us."

"Exactly," grinned Bart. "More sporting that way."

"He's got a point..." Spencer said.

Ralph shook his head and turned to Calvin. "We are not going to have any proper sport with these two in tow. I vote we split up."

Calvin nodded. "Capital idea. We will go that way," he

pointed to their left, uphill. "You two go in the other direction, down that way. We will meet up back at the horses in an hour or so."

They turned and walked off without waiting for a response, leaving Spencer and Bart standing in the clearing.

"What do we do now?" asked Bart.

"I suppose we go for a walk. If you're not going to do any shooting, and you're not going to let me shoot anything, might as well have a wander."

"Don't mind you shooting. Just not really thinking it's fair to kill some animal that's done nothing to us or anyone else."

"Funny how you don't feel the same way back home."

"I'd not kill a deer in London either. Not if it wasn't doing me no harm."

"But you'll happily beat up or kill blokes and demons."

Bart shrugged. "Of course. They've usually done something to deserve it. My point is, that deer hadn't done anything apart from come out and try and have a bite to eat. Not sure that's worth killing over."

Spencer had to concede the point.

"And besides," Bart continued. "It was mighty sweet-looking."

Spencer snorted with laughter, and then they both started walking, holding their guns casually on their shoulders.

"Any point in us pretending to hunt?" asked Bart.

"No harm in looking the part," said Spencer. "Although feels a bit weird walking around with a gun like this. I keep expecting the Old Bill to turn up and nick us."

"Yeah. Just seems odd that the toffs do this and it's a sport for them. Yet when the likes of us do it, we end up in jail."

"Good point," said Spencer. "We don't want to wander too far away from them two, just in case someone mistakes us for poachers."

Bart nodded, looking around. "You ever done any poaching?"

"Went scrumping for apples, in some orchards down by the river a few times as a lad. Not much more than that. You?"

"When we was really hungry, a few winters when I was a kid, we managed to trap a few rabbits. They were nice meat. Caught rats a couple of times too."

"Never could get the taste for rat meat."

"Depends how hungry you get."

"True. Very true."

A sudden loud crack split the air, making them both duck instinctively and then throw themselves to the ground.

"Bloody hell!" shouted Bart. "I think I've been shot!"

Spencer crawled over to him. "Where?"

Bart held out his left arm. His sleeve had been ripped just below the shoulder, a line of blood dripping from it.

"Looks like you just grazed it," said Spencer. "You sure you were shot, though? Didn't just scratch it on something when we went down?"

"What did you think that noise was, then? And why'd you throw yourself to the ground as well?" He turned and then pointed at the tree trunk, just behind where his body had been, moments before. "And how'd you explain that?"

Spencer looked at the small round hole. "All right, that's definitely a bullet hole. Hang on, someone's shooting at us!"

"Love how you're so quick to catch on," said Bart, already scanning around them, his shotgun held ready. "I thought I was supposed to be the slow one."

"You're the man of action. I'm the thinker. Any idea where it came from?"

"That way, I think. Can't see anyone there now, though."

"Probably scarpered. Didn't want to be caught here once they saw they'd missed."

"Or they thought they'd hit me and ran off so they wouldn't be blamed. Who could've done that?"

"Let me think," said Spencer drily. "Who else do we know who've got guns round here?"

They were stood by the horses around half an hour later when Ralph and Calvin appeared. "Oh, there you are," said Calvin.

"Surprised to see us?" asked Spencer.

"Well, I suppose we wondered if you would have got lost. Then we would have had the dilemma of whether to try and find you, or just leave you to it," Ralph smirked.

"Which one of you did it?" asked Bart.

"Did what?"

"Shot at us." He pointed to his bloodied arm.

They stared at him. "We were nowhere near you," said Calvin. "I can assure you that, if you were shot at, it was not us."

"Yes," said Ralph. "Maybe another hunter who misaimed. It can happen sometimes. Maybe he mistook you for a very large deer."

"Do I look like a deer to you?"

Calvin held up a hand to placate him. "I swear, on our honour, it was not us. Hunting accidents are not uncommon. Let us go back to the house; we have had no real luck, and it looks like none of us are really in the mood for this."

They mounted the horses and started back, Spencer and Bart hanging back so they were out of earshot.

"You believe them?" Bart asked.

"Dunno. They seemed pretty convincing when they said it wasn't them. But doesn't change the fact that someone nearly hit us."

"Me. Nearly hit me."

"Yeah. All right. You were hurt. Save it for when you see that maidservant you've got your eye on. I'm sure she'll give you plenty of sympathy."

Bart scowled at him, then furrowed his brow in thought. "You reckon?"

Chapter Eleven

Spencer and Bart met Tess as they were walking back through the gardens towards the house.

"Are you sure someone shot at you?" she asked.

"Positive," said Bart. "Look." He showed her his bloodied arm.

Tess tutted over it while Spencer rolled his eyes.

"You should get it cleaned up," she said. "I am sure one of the staff in the house will be able to help."

"Yeah, I'll do that," said Bart, ignoring Spencer's smirk.

"The two lads—Ralph and Calvin—said it was probably just a hunting accident," said Spencer.

"It is possible," Tess said. "Such things are fairly common."

"Yeah, they said that. Thing is, though, we didn't see or hear anyone else out there except for them two."

"You think they tried to shoot you?"

"They denied it, but… I don't know…"

"I am not convinced they would invite us all the way here, just to deliberately shoot at you." She stared at them. "Unless you said or did something to upset them…?"

"Us?" asked Spencer, wide-eyed. "Why would we do that? We're on our best behaviour here, you know."

"Hmm," she said. "Best to make sure you definitely are on your best behaviour, going forward. We have a job to do. Speaking of which, help me with this equipment, please."

She gestured to a small pile of boxes. They picked them up and the three of them walked towards the woods, where the supposed demon had been seen the night before.

"When we're done with this, I'd like to have a nosy round that pub Wilbur mentioned," said Spencer.

"Purely for professional purposes?" Tess asked with a smile, raising an eyebrow.

"Of course. You learn all sort of things in pubs."

Tess turned to look at the house. "Is it me, or do you feel like you're always being watched here?"

"I reckon that Ralph bloke's been following us round," said Bart. "He seemed to come out of nowhere earlier, just as it looked like Wilbur was about to start telling us something interesting."

"You should try and get Wilbur alone at some point," said Tess. "See if he will open up to you."

"And the other servants," said Spencer. "Below stairs is always the best place to find the gossip."

"There's another one of those symbols," said Tess, pointing to one of the windows. "Just like the one by the front door."

"Posh folk do like their coats of arms and stuff. Never understood it myself." Spencer kicked at a stone. "So what do you think? We gonna be earning some coin out of this case?"

"I think so," said Tess. "Although something here does not quite smell right."

They reached the gate and pushed through into the woods. As they reached the clearing, Tess indicated for them to put the boxes down, and then started arranging various pieces of equipment on the ground.

They watched as she combined tubes, pipes and box-like contraptions into three equally sized devices. They consisted of a wooden box at their heart, each with brass-edged windows revealing a smoke-filled interior. Tubes snaked off at various angles and from all surfaces, which in turn were topped off with a variety of objects, from funnels to spheres to spindly insect-like antennae.

"What are these, then?" asked Spencer.

"Aetheric Detectors," she said. "Some of the items which Maxwell gave me. We will leave them at various places overnight and then check them in the morning. If there is any form of supernatural or demonic activity round here at any point—basically anything connected to the Aether—these devices will record it and, with some interrogation of the readings obtained, I will be able to determine exactly what it is we're dealing with here."

"And you'll get all that from them little boxes?" Spencer whistled. "That's clever stuff."

She directed them to hide the devices at certain points around the woods, ensuring that they were out of sight, secure, and unlikely to be disturbed. Then, after a few minutes of arranging the protuberances to ensure they were angled to her satisfaction, she nodded and they gathered the boxes and started back to the house.

"This is a lot of stuff for one demon," said Bart.

"But it looks good and makes our job look hard," said Tess.

"The harder it is, the more they pay us, right?" asked Bart.

"Maybe," said Tess. "I am a bit concerned about how resistant Lord Beaumont was to our presence when we arrived, though."

"You thinking he holds the purse strings, so he might refuse to pay?" asked Spencer.

"Exactly."

"But Emilia's your mate," said Bart. "She wouldn't do that to a mate, surely?"

"I am afraid little things like codes of honour are in short supply in so-called polite society. Especially if they feel that they have an advantage over you." She pursed her lips in thought. "I will see if I can poke the bear a bit. You both carry on seeing what you can dig up."

"Will do." Spencer tipped his cap to her, and they turned to walk back to the house. "We're going to grab some food in the kitchen, then we're going to check out that Red Lion pub. I take it the family won't mind us not joining you lot for dinner; it's just that we want to get down there before it's too late."

"Yeah," said Bart. "And with all the posh serving and chatter and stuff, it takes forever for you lot to get a meal down you. Far too much fuss."

"No offence to you and your mates," said Spencer. "But we're happier scoffing food as quick as possible. Don't need all this 'pass the salt' and saying Grace and all that messing around."

"I do not think they will mind too much," smiled Tess. "And I may get more out of them if it is just me there. They may be more relaxed. No offence."

"None taken. See you later then."

"Oh, and boys," Tess called after them.

"Yeah?"

"Don't get too drunk, please."

Chapter Twelve

Tess found Emilia in the sitting room, reading a book. "May I speak with you?" she asked her.

Emilia nodded with a smile, setting her book aside. "Of course. I have some tea here; the pot is still warm. Would you like a cup?"

"Yes please." Tess sat down opposite her. The sun streamed through the window, straight into her eyes, forcing her to adjust her position so she could still see her friend without being blinded.

"Are you and your friends being made welcome by everyone?" asked Emilia.

"For the most part, yes. Although I got the impression when we arrived that your father was not too happy to see us."

"Oh, him," she waved a hand. "You know what he is like; always so grumpy, not liking surprises."

"So he did not know that you were bringing us home with you?"

"No. None of them did, not even my fiancé." When Tess raised an eyebrow, Emilia continued, "He is a sweet and devoted man, but he is still trying to curry favour with my parents. If he had known, he would have told them and they would have stopped me. I just told everyone that I was going to London on a shopping trip."

"Why would they have been so intent on stopping you?"

"You know my family; so private, especially when it comes to rather… delicate matters. I suppose it is natural to not want everyone to know that your family is cursed. Father has always taken the view that it is best to ignore the curse, in the hope that it never comes to pass. Or maybe that he would die of other causes before the curse had a chance to take him."

"What a terrible thing to have hanging over you for all these years. Why did you never tell me?"

"We never told anyone outside of the family; it was our big secret."

"But now...?"

Emilia looked away. "I could no longer just ignore it. I had to do something, so I took matters into my own hands."

Tess took a deep breath. "I have to tell you, Emilia, that I am not sure we can help you."

"What do you mean?"

"We had a look out in the grounds earlier. The damage there looks more like it was created by humans, not demons."

"But the noises?"

"Anyone can make a noise loud and shrill enough to scare people, especially in the dead of night. Or it could have easily been some other form of animal, like a fox or cat."

"But we saw something; you saw it…"

"My colleagues are not convinced there is anything demonic at work here. And neither am I." She held up a hand as Emilia started to protest. "I am not calling you a liar; I just think that you need someone else to help you."

"We can pay. Whatever you want."

"It's not about the money."

Emilia put a hand to her mouth, her shoulders shaking as tears ran down her cheeks.

"Emilia, I..." Tess leant forward, putting a hesitant hand onto her friend's knee before then sitting back awkwardly.

"I am sorry," said Emilia. "I just cannot bear the thought of anything happening to my father. I know that he is not the best person in the world, but he is still my father. Think of how you would feel in my place." She put a hand to her mouth. "I am sorry. I am such a clumsy... I forgot..."

"Do not worry," said Tess. "It has been a fair while since my parents passed. The wound does not totally heal, but it is not so raw that I am so easily offended. But I still wonder if you would be better placed asking the police for help than us."

"But I told you; they are not interested. You really are our last hope. Please. My father's birthday is the day after tomorrow; please stay until after then. If the curse is real and is demonic, then you will hopefully be able to help us. If it is not, then you will have had a few days' break in the country with an old friend. You will also have been to the party of the year, and paid handsomely into the bargain. Either way, we will pay you for your time."

Tess stared at her and then nodded. "Very well. We will stay."

Chapter Thirteen

"So what do you think of all this talk of curses?" Spencer asked, as they sat round the table in the kitchen. Mr Smith and Wilbur looked up to glare at him, before leaning together to resume their whispered conversation.

"Don't mind them," said Mrs Smith, putting a plate on the table in front of him. "They don't like to put aside time for chitchat. Or manners, for that matter. Are you sure you don't want to eat upstairs, with the others? You are guests, after all."

"Not sure if you've noticed," said Spencer, spooning food into his mouth, "but we don't really fit in with that lot. We'll leave the hobnobbing to our friend Tess. It's more her world than ours."

"Yeah," said Bart. "Reckon they're happier with us out the way. And anyway, we want to head off into the village, go down the pub. Don't have time to do all the polite conversation and stuff they all do. Why do their meals go on for so long? All that time between courses, it's just wasted."

Mrs Smith chuckled. "I suppose you're right. It's a different world up there. And it is nice for us to have some fresh company. Isn't that right, Bev?"

The young maidservant, who was helping to prepare the food, blushed and muttered something in the affirmative. Spencer put another spoonful of food in his mouth to hide a grin at the way Bart stared at her.

"You're going to the Red Lion then?" asked Wilbur.

"Yeah. After our chat earlier, thought we'd follow up on what you'd said."

"What did you say?" Mr Smith asked, glaring at Wilbur.

"I said nothing," said Wilbur, staring down at his plate. "Nothing at all."

Mr Smith stared at him for a moment.

"It was Ralph who gave us the idea," said Spencer. "He told us it might be worth going down there."

"Did he, now?" said Mr Smith with a raised eyebrow. "Well, far be it from me to go against what my employers say, but if you take my advice, you'd be best off keeping out of all this."

"Things haven't been the same since the Lady's brother came," said Mrs Smith. "Don't know what he said to them, but they've been in an awful tizz ever since."

"In what way?" asked Spencer.

"Oh, you know. Lots of whispered conversations, tears, shouting. Young Calvin keeps threatening to leave."

"Hah!" said Mr Smith. "He couldn't stand on his own two feet even if he wanted to. Helpless, that boy is."

"He's still a Beaumont," Mrs Smith chided him.

Mr Smith responded by staring at her while ripping a hunk of bread in two.

"What're they like to work for, the Beaumonts?" asked Spencer.

"They're fine," Mrs Smith said in a high voice, turning away to the sink. "There are worse families to work for."

"Some families actually pay their staff," muttered Mr Smith.

"We've gone over this," said Mrs Smith. "Lady B explained to us there was just a bit of a delay, that's all. In the meantime, we have a roof over our heads and food in our bellies. There are plenty who can't say that."

"Good food, too," said Bart through a mouthful of meat. "You're a good cook, Mrs Smith. And Bev. You both are."

"A pleasure to feed someone with such a healthy appetite," beamed Mrs Smith. "And I thank you for your good manners."

"Don't be fooled," grinned Spencer. "He's just buttering you up so he can have seconds. Never met a cook who can fill this man."

"And he's welcome to it, as well," said Mrs Smith, taking Bart's plate and ladling more stew onto it.

"So has it happened before," asked Spencer. "You not being paid?"

"No," said Mrs Smith.

"Yes," said Mr Smith.

Mrs Smith banged her ladle down on the table, glaring at her husband. "If it's all the same to you, Mr Spencer, I'd rather we didn't talk about money matters. It's something that's between us and the Beaumonts, and I'll not hear anyone say anything ill about them."

"Of course, of course," said Spencer, holding up a hand. "Didn't mean to cause offence. Just trying to make conversation, that's all."

They watched them plate up the food for upstairs. "Who's the extra plate for?" asked Spencer. "They got guests up there?"

"Umm, yes," said Mrs Smith, ushering Mr Smith and the maidservant away to take the plates upstairs.

Chapter Fourteen

A couple of hours later, Spencer and Bart pushed open the door of the small pub in the village, walking into a cramped, smoky room with sawdust-covered wooden floors and walls which had once been covered with white plaster, but which were now a sickly, creamy-grey tint. Bart breathed in deeply and grinned with satisfaction. "No matter where I am," he said, "that smell always makes me feel at home."

"Yeah," smiled Spencer. "Almost makes me forget the mud and insects and stuff out there."

They ordered a couple of beers and perched at the corner of the bar. "Evenin'." Spencer grinned at the barman, who ignored him.

They looked round the room. "So what do you think we should do?" asked Bart. "We're here to find out information, right?"

"Yep." Spencer turned to the barman. "Here, mate. Ask you a question?"

The balding, middle-aged man put down the pot he had been wiping with a dirty cloth and walked over, casting a suspicious eye over the two strangers. "You're the ones staying over at Flint Hall," he said.

"That's right. How'd you know?"

"We don't get many strangers round here. What can I do for you?"

"The groundsman up at Flint Hall—Wilbur—said you've got a demon working for you here?"

"I do," the barman said slowly. "What of it?"

"Just like to talk to it, that's all. Find out what happened when he left Flint Hall. When the demon—"

"Trevor," clarified Bart.

"Yeah," Spencer glanced at his friend. "When Trevor left that place."

"Why'd he want to speak with you?"

"Look, mate, we know demons; been around a lot of them in our time."

"I know who you are and what you do for a living," said the barman. "Not many secrets round here. I don't want you doing any harm to my worker."

"Look," said Spencer, leaning towards him. "I'm not sure what you've heard—"

"That you're demon hunters."

"All right. I can see how that might sound. But we don't hunt *all* demons. Just the ones causing harm. Got no reason to think your demon's one of them, so there's nothing to fear, right?"

"Suppose," muttered the barman. There was a sudden loud clanging noise from behind him. "That'll be my demon, there, fetching in some deliveries. If you're quick and don't hold him up, you can talk to him now."

"Much obliged to you," grinned Spencer, doffing an imaginary cap to him.

They made their way round the bar and through a door to a storage area out back, where a large dark figure lumbered around in the half-light. Spencer and Bart glanced at each other and then cleared their throats.

"Yeah?" rumbled the figure.

"Got a few questions for you. Your boss out there said we could have a quick talk with you," said Spencer. "You able to come over here?" He eyed the large object the demon was carrying on its shoulder, something which could hurt quite a bit if it was thrown at them. "Maybe put down that big barrel, yeah?"

The demon stared at him for a moment, red eyes glinting in

the gloom, and then shrugged. He dropped the barrel, and it landed on the floor with a clang which rang in their ears.

"Here, you," yelled the barman from the other side of the door. "What have I told you about being careful with the merchandise?"

"It was empty," said the demon.

"Well even so." He poked his head round the door and then pointed at Spencer and Bart. "If you two upset him and he causes damage, you're paying for it. Right?"

"Don't worry. We just want to ask a couple of questions," said Spencer. He turned to the demon. "How long've you worked round here?"

"A few weeks," said the demon, narrowing its eyes. "Why?"

"What?"

"Why do you want to know?"

"Before you was here, you worked over at Flint Hall, right? Groundsman says you was let go, maybe a bit unfairly. Just want to ask you some questions."

"Questions about what?"

"Why you was let go. What happened."

"Whether I want to take bloody revenge on them that let me go?" asked the demon.

"Yes. No. We just want to understand what's going on here. Folk up at the Hall are getting skittish about stuff which might or might not go on. Talking of curses and the like. We just want to understand what's going on here."

"Curses? You know demons don't tend to mess with curses. At least, not our kind. It's them higher classes of demon that get involved in that sort of stuff. Us lot, we're more the fetching, carrying, following orders type."

"All right. Then you won't mind if we ask you a few questions?"

The demon thought for a moment. "All right. I'd love the chance to set the record straight. That man shouldn't be allowed to treat folk like that. I'd love to see him get what's coming to him. So I'll talk to you. But not now; I'm busy and I don't want to get in trouble with the boss. Tomorrow. Midday. Back here. And don't think about doing anything funny, or there'll be trouble."

"Don't worry," said Spencer. "We're men of our word. No trouble; just some questions."

The demon grunted and turned back to its work, while Spencer and Bart returned to the bar.

"Get what you want?" asked the barman.

"We'll see," said Spencer. "Actually, you might be able to help us. We're a bit curious about the history round here."

"You are?" the man looked them up and down with raised eyebrows.

"We are?" Bart asked his friend.

"Yes." Spencer glared at him and then turned back to the barman. "You know anything about any curses round these parts? Anything spooky or suchlike?"

The barman shrugged. "There's always talk of supernatural stuff. Just like any village; can't throw a rock without hitting someone who's a witch, or knows a witch, or seen a fairy down the bottom of their garden."

"Don't talk ill of the fairy folk," muttered an old man from the other side of the bar. He spat on the floor and then rapped his knuckles on the wooden surface.

"Why?" asked Bart. "What happens if you do?"

The old man stared at him, wide-eyed. "They're always listening, always keeping an ear out for a chance to take offence. Anyone they don't like, they spirit them away, never to be seen again."

The barman chuckled, his earlier hostility melting away. "Don't listen to him. After a few beers, he tends to get a bit fanciful."

"It's true," insisted the old man. "Remember what happened to Joe Clarkson. He was in here one night, mouthing off, and the next thing, he was gone."

"Joe Clarkson got drunk, tried walking home when he could

hardly do a straight line, and fell down a hole. He broke his neck."

"And what lured him into that hole, eh?" The old man tapped the side of his nose.

"See what I have to deal with round here?" the barman said to them. "So what sort of supernatural stuff you looking for? They say the graveyard's haunted, if that's of interest to you?"

"Was thinking more along the line of curses?" said Spencer.

"You're the second person to ask that today," said the barman. "Is there something we should know?"

"No, no. Just curious. Hang on: the *second* person? Who else has been asking?"

"Another stranger," said the barman. "Young lad. Long haired, a bit strange looking. If I'd guess, I'd say he came from London, just like you two."

"How'd you know we're from London?" asked Bart in his thick cockney accent.

"Just a wild guess," said the barman. "I'll tell you what I told the other bloke. One person it's worth you speaking to is Jack Bishop. He works the land at night, if you know what I mean."

They both stared blankly at him.

"He does a bit of poaching," explained the barman. "Anyway, he came in the other night, white as a sheet, said he'd seen something in the woods Flint Hall. He'd be a good person to talk with."

"Great," said Spencer. "Where'd we find him?"

"Hang around here; he'll be in for his evening drink soon enough. Fancy another beer while you wait?"

"Don't mind if we do," Spencer grinned, finishing his drink and handing over the mug to be refilled. The landlord stared at him until he placed some coins on the bar.

"So tell me," Spencer said to the landlord as he passed back a full mug. "What do you know about the Beaumont family?"

"Not a lot. Keep themselves to themselves, as they're entitled to do. Any big feast days, like Christmas, they'll show their face at church, occasionally put some money behind the bar for the village. Don't really know any of them personally."

"Probably just as well," belched the old man from the far side of the bar.

"What do you mean by that?" asked Spencer.

"They're up to no good up there, mark my words," he said.

"Pay no attention to Mick," the landlord said. "He gets a bit fanciful after a few jars."

"Fanciful!" bellowed Mick. "All this talk about curses out of nowhere! And then there's the missing brother."

"What missing brother?" asked Spencer.

"Hah! Lady Beaumont had a brother. When she moved into the Hall, he'd always be hanging around. Odd bloke."

"You don't know anything," said the barman. "Honestly, lads, don't listen to him."

Mick ploughed on regardless. "Bet they've not told you anything about him, have they? Ashamed of him, they are. I heard he's deformed. Got a misshapen head and a club foot."

"You don't know any of this," objected the landlord.

"I do. I know someone who saw him, years back before they hid him away. Saw him from a distance, anyway. Said he had a huge limp, had to use a stick just to get around." He took a long swig from his beer and then chortled. "Them and their curses. These well-to-do types can't ever admit that they have something wrong with them, that there's some way they're not better than us. You know what the real curse of that family is? The brother they've got hidden away in the roof."

"Wait," said Spencer. "The roof?" He turned to Bart. "Them noises upstairs in the Hall last night."

"That'd be him," said Mick. "Hidden away up there, where no one can find him."

"They said there's no one up on that floor."

"That's what they want you to believe." Mick tapped the side of his nose with a grubby finger. "Mark my words; you look up there, you'll find out what that family are trying to hide."

Then landlord tutted. "Honestly, lads. Don't listen to him. He's soft in the head. Too much beer can do that to you."

They sat in companionable silence for a little while, enjoying their drinks and the gentle quiet of the country pub.

"So who'd you think the other man is? The one the landlord said was also asking about curses?" Bart asked Spencer.

"Dunno," said Spencer. "But if there's other people sniffing around, maybe there's more to all this than we thought."

They looked up as a scrawny man with long dark hair came in through the door. The barman poured a drink and put it in front of him without being asked, and then nodded to Spencer and Bart, muttering something to the man. The man stared at them, took a long swig from his beer, and then walked over.

"Seth tells me you wanted to speak to me," he said.

"You're Jack Bishop? The poacher?" asked Spencer.

"I'm a man who makes his living off the land," he said. "Not a poacher. Poaching's illegal."

"Of course," said Spencer. "Sorry for the misunderstanding, mate. Your man there said you know something about a curse up at Flint Hall?"

Bishop looked around and then gestured with his hand. "Let's talk outside." He led them out the door and then, when he was happy they were out of earshot from those inside the pub, continued as they stood in the greying light, pulling up their coats against the cold. "Hope you don't mind," said Jack. "But I've had enough of them lot in there making fun of me for talking about this sort of stuff. They all think I'm seeing things, going mad."

"Seeing what sort of things? Something to do with the curse?"

"Don't know about any curse," he said, "but I do know that there's some strange stuff going on in the grounds round Flint Hall."

"What sort of stuff?"

"Strange noises. Howling and stuff. There's been something wandering round that house the past week or so. Something big."

"You seen it?"

"From afar. Been keen to keep my distance, truth be told." He looked around. "Folk round here think I'm mad, even for mentioning it."

"We don't think that," said Spencer. "We've seen plenty of strange stuff in our time."

"I'm sure you have. Where you from?"

"London."

"I heard it's crazy down there; demons everywhere, ever since the Aether opened."

"That's about right, although they tend to keep to their own places most of the time. Bit of a truce, if you know what I mean."

Bishop nodded. "Out here, in the sticks, most of that stuff's passed us by. There's been mainly rumours and the like, but most folk don't tend to stray too far from where they live, so there's not really much opportunity for us to see what's happening elsewhere. It's just what we're told by outsiders like yourselves."

Spencer looked around. "So it's almost like the old days here."

"Kind of, yeah. We get the odd weird thing. Anyone stupid enough to be walking the roads after dark runs the risk of running into a wraith or something like that. But most of the time, we just get on with life. That's why them lot in there think I'm mad to be talking about this sort of thing."

"Do you think you're mad?"

"I don't think so. Do you?"

"I think you look like the sort of bloke who knows what he sees. I think you're a good hunter and tracker. Bloke like you's going to know the difference between a fox or whatever you'd normally find roaming these parts and... something else."

"Thank you," Jack said.

Spencer patted his pocket. "Let us buy you a drink and—"

"Jack Bishop!" A young woman marched over to them.

Bishop turned with a wince and then switched on a smile. "Darling, there you are," he said. "I was just having a quick relax before coming home. These lads are—"

"I don't give a toss who they are," she said. "You turn up drunk to supper again, I will take your balls and turn them into a stew. And then feed it to you."

He put his hands on her shoulders. "I'm not going to get drunk. Just need to deal with a bit of business, and then I'll be back home with your tea before you know it."

"What have you caught?"

"Nothing yet. But I'll get you the juiciest—"

"You're not going out again. Not tonight. Not after what you saw..."

"Don't worry; I'll be fine."

She stared at him with wide eyes, anger melting away into pure fear. "Please. Don't go out there again." Tears filled her eyes.

"All right," he said, placing a kiss on her forehead. "I won't."

"Promise?"

"Promise. I just need to finish chatting with these two, then I'll be home."

She peered into his eyes and then nodded. "Thank you," she said, then turned and walked away.

Jack watched her go and then smiled at Spencer and Bart. "Now," he said. "How's about that drink?"

They went inside and gathered fresh beers, settling in a corner as far away from the rest of the patrons as they could. "Your wife; she seemed pretty scared," said Spencer.

"Yeah, well, it was the other night. I came back having had a close brush with the creature near Beaumont Hall. She saw how worked up I was."

"Tell us what happened."

"It was late; probably not far off midnight, a couple of nights ago. I'd gone out to check my traps; I've got a few not far from the Beaumonts' estate. I'd been held up that evening, so it was later than I normally would go out.

"Anyway, I was checking the last one, just getting a nice big rabbit out, when I heard something. At first I thought it were a gamekeeper come to catch me. Then I thought it was a couple of gamekeepers, or a couple of kids messing about. But then I realised it was a lot bigger than that. Making an awful racket, it was. Blundering into trees, trampling around the bushes. Almost as though it were trying to get as much attention as it could. Which was strange in itself, as there's no one around the woods that time of night to be attracting their attention."

He wiped a hand across his brow, took a long swig, and then continued. "Anyways, I stayed as still and quiet as I could, thinking I could hide it out, whatever it was. But then I saw it. It was huge. Biggest thing I've ever seen; it was like it blocked out the whole sky."

"Can you describe it?" asked Spencer.

He shook his head. "Didn't see too much of it to be able to make out any stuff. It was really big, though. And it had these big, glowing eyes..." He shuddered. "I froze up, totally stiff. Could've sworn I was going to die, right there and then. But then it moved away and I realised it hadn't seen me yet, so I just ran off, fast as I could. Didn't stop running until I was home. Took me an age to calm down." He downed the rest of his drink.

Spencer looked at Bart.

"Sounds like a demon to me," Bart said.

"Yeah. Me too."

"Then you believe me?" asked Bishop.

"Yeah. Tell me, where was this?"

"In the woods round the back of Flint Hall. I can take you there if you want."

"You'd go back there?"

"Not now. Not after dark. But tomorrow, yeah. Meet you at dawn, at the gate at the back of the Hall. You know it?"

"Yeah, we know it. See you then."

Jack nodded, holding up his beer. "Nice meeting you, gents."

"You too." They watched him wander over to the bar to talk to the barman.

"So you believe him?" asked Bart,

"I believe that he believes it."

The door opened to reveal Ralph, followed by Calvin and a couple of other men. They had clearly already been drinking, and were laughing and shouting as they made their way to the bar, totally oblivious to everyone else in the room.

"Ah," bellowed Ralph as he spotted Spencer and Bart. "Our esteemed guests. We missed you at dinner."

"We had things to do," Spencer said.

"So I see. Barkeep, drinks for my friends. And for these two as well." He waved at Spencer and Bart. "I am glad to see you finally decided to socialise at your correct level."

They glared at him, but still accepted the drinks.

Calvin wandered over. "Word to the wise," he said. "If I were you, I would get as far away from here as you can, and I would take Tess with you."

"Is that a threat?" asked Spencer.

"Not at all. More a warning." He looked up at the sound of his voice being called from the other side of the pub.

"Leave the riff-raff, Calvin," called Ralph. "Come, join us!"

"I don't like him," said Bart, after Calvin had walked away.

"Who? Calvin?"

"Nah, not him. He seems all right. For a toff. No, I mean that Ralph bloke."

"Me neither. And I don't think we're the only ones." Spencer gestured to the corner, where Ralph was now talking rather insistently at Jack Bishop. The poacher was trying his best to ignore him, but Ralph was doing everything he could to pester the other man.

"Reckon we should help him?" asked Bart.

"Not our fight," said Spencer. "Let's just watch."

"All right," Bart grumbled into his beer, his body tensing as he watched the altercation on the other side of the room.

Ralph had turned away and said, loudly, to one of his friends, "Maybe he should try making a proper living, rather than just profiting off other people's work."

"That's rich coming from you," snapped Bishop. "I'd be surprised if you've ever done a day's work in your life!"

"At least I don't steal."

"You and your kind do nothing *but* steal!"

"I'm intrigued," Ralph sneered. "Pray elucidate. That means *'explain'*, by the way."

"I know what it means," snapped Jack. "You and your lot just live off the labour of others. Folk like me. You don't make anything yourselves."

Ralph laughed, his friends joining him in a raucous cacophony of braying.

"That noise there," said Bart. "Surely that's enough excuse for me to just go over there and knock a few heads together, to make it stop?"

Spencer grinned and shook his head.

Bishop and Ralph were now standing close together, practically nose-to-nose. They were saying something, but whatever it was that was being said could not be heard over the sound of Ralph's friends. After a moment, something Ralph said clearly proved to be the final straw, as Bishop punched him square in the face.

Ralph collapsed to the floor, before being helped up by a couple of his friends. Others restrained Bishop, stopping him from surging in to do yet more damage.

Bishop shook himself free. "I'll do what I want!" he yelled, before charging out. "You can't stop me!"

Ralph waved in an exaggerated manner at the door before turning back to his friends. "Always nice when the rubbish takes itself out, eh?" he said, holding a kerchief to his nose to try and stop the bleeding.

Chapter Fifteen

"I really don't like that bloke," said Bart as they left the pub. "Would you mind if I taught him a bit of a lesson? You know, with my fists?"

"I wouldn't mind," grinned Spencer. "But our hosts at the Hall might not look too kindly on it. Best to wait it out. These things come around, you know?"

"Wait until after we've left the Hall. Got it."

They walked on in silence as they left the meagre pool of light cast by the tavern, and on into the darkness. It was blackly quiet, making the two city dwellers feel as though they had fallen into a featureless, blank hole. The crunching of their footsteps on the ground was their only companion, the sole sign that there was anything around them, aside from the cloying night.

Even the moon and stars seemed to have deserted them, retreating behind a covering of clouds. Their eyes slowly adjusted to the darkness, but even so they found themselves stumbling off the side of the road and almost turning their ankles in potholes.

Mrs Smith had given them a lamp to light their way home, and Spencer stopped to strike a match and hold it to the wick, grunting with satisfaction as it caught and the light flared up. He closed the hatch and held it up, frowning when all it did was lighten up empty space.

"Well that worked a treat," he muttered.

They both jumped at a shrieking sound from the distance.

"Probably just a fox," said Spencer, sounding like he was not even convincing himself.

"Here, where'd you reckon that Bishop bloke went to?" asked

Bart.

"Dunno. Home probably. Hopefully not wherever that sound came from."

"Thought you said it was a fox?"

"Yeah. Of course it was. Just prefer not to be around it, that's all."

"You're not scared of a little fox, are you?"

They both jumped as another piercing sound cut through the night, a bellowing shriek which echoed around them. They looked at each other,

"That didn't sound much like a fox," muttered Bart.

"No. Let's get back to the Hall. Quick."

They ran as fast as they dared, stumbling in the lantern's shaky light, which threatened at any moment to be blown out by the way it swayed in Spencer's hands. They came to a fork in the road and skidded to a halt.

"Which way?" asked Spencer.

"I dunno. I don't remember a fork on the way out."

"Nor me. Bugger. You reckon we took a wrong turn?"

"I..." They both jumped at another skin-crawling screech. "No, wait," said Bart. "I remember that tree there. We go that way." He pointed to the right.

"You sure? I really don't fancy wandering around all night."

"Nor me. Yeah, I'm pretty sure. I remember looking at that tree and thinking it reminded me of a girl I once knew."

Spencer peered at the tree and at then his friend. "I don't want to know," he said, shaking his head. "Sometimes, you come out with some really strange things, mate." He led the way down the right-hand path, Bart following him with a shrug.

*

As they approached the Hall they heard the roar again—this time a lot closer—followed by a distinctly human yell. Without thinking, both men broke into a run.

"Where did it come from?" asked Spencer.

"This way," Bart said, charging into the woods in front of the wall around the property, pausing only to pick up a large plank of wood. They ran through the trees, yelling as they stumbled over low roots and bushes until they came out into a clearing.

At the far end, a large form was bent over, its back to them. At the sound of their approach, it turned to face them, sharp eyes glinting red in the moonlight. It towered over them, even at that distance appearing to blot out the scarce moonlight, its head brushing the branches of the nearest trees, even though it was stooped forward. It was a brutal shadowy form, a huge blackness which oozed violence and menace. The head was angular and horned, with the outline of its shoulders and arms hinting at spikes and scales.

It swung its head round at the sound of more feet coming from another direction, from the direction of the Hall. Raised voices came to them, shouting out: "Hey!" "Who's there?" "Spencer, Bart, is that you?"

The creature looked in the direction of the Hall and then, with a snarl, spun and disappeared. They turned to see another figure turning and running away. It looked like a man, and he moved in a strange, stumbling sort of run, away from the sound of the approaching people from the Hall.

"Hey!" shouted Spencer. "Come back!" He tried running after the man, but after a few paces gave up; the darkness and the foliage had swallowed the figure up, making any attempt to chase him pointless.

A moment later, Tess sprinted into the clearing, followed by Wilbur. "Are you all right?" she asked them.

"Yeah," said Spencer. "Bit of a run-in with... not quite sure what it was. You get any clear views, Bart?"

"Not really. Was more focused on hoping it wouldn't rip our heads off."

"All went really fast," said Spencer. "And it's so dark here. Hang on; who's that?"

They ran over to a groaning form at the far end of the clearing; a man who was clearly the source of the yell they had heard. Tess turned him over; he had been attacked quite violently—presumably by the creature which had just run away—blood covering his face and one leg lying in an unnatural direction.

"He's still alive," Tess said. "We need to get him inside."

"I recognise him," said Spencer. "We were talking to him just a couple of hours ago, down the pub. Name's Jack Bishop; he's a poacher."

"So it is," said Wilbur. "Can't say I'm upset to see him in this state. Causes me nothing but trouble, that man."

"This is a human being, and he needs our help," Tess snapped at him. "Now, come on all of you and help me get him into the house."

Bart carried Bishop's limp form in his arms to the Hall, where he was laid on the kitchen table. "We need a doctor," Bart said.

"There's one in the village," said Mr Smith. "Come with me; we'll go get him."

"Me?" asked Bart.

"Yes, you," said Mr Smith. "There's something big and dangerous out there, so if I'm running around out there at night, I want someone big and dangerous with me on my side."

"Fair enough," nodded Bart, running out of the house with him.

"He can't stay here," said Mrs Smith.

"Are there any spare beds?" asked Tess. "Maybe on the upper floor?"

"No, that will not do. The Beaumonts will not stand for that. What did you bring him in here for, anyway? Nothing but trouble that man, and what's happened to him is clearly just his comeuppance."

"That's what I said," Wilbur muttered.

Tess stared at them. "This is a person. It doesn't matter what he's done, we can't just leave him out there; he would die!"

"Pretty sure the Beaumonts would have a thing or two to say

about all this," said Mrs Smith. "Dirtying up my table; probably delay breakfast in the morning while I tidy all this up. Or are you saying I should work longer, me already working all hours God sends? Your kind don't think about that, or care."

Tess glared at her. "My kind?"

Mrs Smith looked down. "Anyway, I just... I don't like Mr Smith going out at night. Not with someone or something out there which is clearly out for blood."

"Bart's with him; he'll keep him safe," pointed out Spencer.

"Did you get any a look at the villain before it ran off?" asked Tess.

Spencer shook his head. "It was too dark. Was bloody big though, whatever it was."

"Demon?"

"Maybe. But it was distracted by someone other than you and us. I saw some bloke standing in the distance, opposite direction to where you came from. Tried to run after him, but lost him pretty smartish."

"A man? You are sure?"

"Definite. Looked like some sort of toff, from what I could make out. First thought I had was it could've been Ralph Wheeler."

"Why him?"

"We saw him down the pub. Had a bit of a set-to with Mr Bishop. He could have followed us back here."

"Followed you?" asked Mrs Smith. "But he is Mistress Beaumont's betrothed! He has more right to be here than you do! "

"I just meant he had a bit of an argument with our man here." Spencer gestured at the bloody figure lying on the table.

"What are you suggesting?"

"I'm not suggesting anything. Apart from Ralph has a fight in a pub with a bloke, who a few hours later gets a good kicking. Pretty obvious connection, ain't it?"

"I'm not sure I like your tone," Mrs Smith muttered.

The door opened and Mr Smith charged in, followed by Doctor Wilson and Bart. The Doctor ushered them out of his way and examined the patient.

"What happened to him?" he asked.

"Got beaten up, we think," said Bart.

"By what? A train?"

"Couldn't quite see. But, yeah, it was big."

"I need to get him back to my surgery, right away. Help me get him to my carriage."

"Will he live?" Tess asked.

"Too early to tell. But the fact that he's still breathing is a good sign."

Chapter Sixteen

A memory. Something she had tried to bury, long ago. Something she did not want to remember, was desperate to never remember. And yet here it was. Again.

She tried to push it down, to drive it away, out through the top of her head, but it stubbornly stuck fast, her struggles to thrust it away just giving it more strength to cling to her mind.

She was back in her old home in London. He was there. Her beloved husband. Her toes curled as she remembered his slimy grin and liquid eyes. How had she ever managed to convince herself there might be some sort of future with this creature?

She had put on a show of being busy when she heard him enter the room, peering at her book in the hope he might realise she was occupied and leave her alone. But she knew that was a forlorn hope; things like social niceties and empathy meant as much to him as clouds in the sky did to a fish.

"Put down your book," he said. "I have someone for you to meet."

He was followed into the room by a figure which seemed to suck all the light out of the room. He was a tall, dark man, dark in almost every aspect—his clothes, his hair, his eyes—except for his skin, which was a pallid grey. This, she thought, was the very essence of a creature of the night, a man who was created to dwell in the shadows.

He walked towards her, tapping the floor with a cane which seemed to serve no purpose save to provide a tattoo to his progress, and possibly so he could have a weapon to hand at all times.

"This is my wife, Lady Tessie Marchant," her husband said to the man, then to her, "My dear, this is Mr Emerson, an associate of mine."

She held out her hand and suppressed a shudder as he pressed his lips to it. It was like being kissed by a dead fish, and it took all her energy to resist the urge to snatch her hand away and run, screaming, from the room.

Instead, she composed her face into as natural a smile as she could. "A pleasure to meet you, Mr Emerson." She tried to pull her hand back but realised with alarm that his grip was unyielding. She looked up at him, and found her eyes locked with his, stuck as firmly as her hand.

Those eyes... They were unending pools of sheer black, two unyielding obsidian pits that seemed to have a gravity all of their own. And she was trapped in their pull, helpless, unable to escape.

"The pleasure is all mine," he said in an oozing voice. "Surrender your will to mine. Focus on my voice, my eyes..."

Everything swam around her as the world collapsed into the singularity of those piercing black holes. The room and the world melted away, with his voice the only thing remaining which she could focus on. Words came thick and fast, a soothing jumble which bypassed her conscious mind, arrowing straight into somewhere deep inside her.

She remembered the sensations, but not the words. As hard as she tried, they remained elusive, slipping away from her as soon as she got close to them. All of the words, that is, apart from at the end.

"Your conscious mind will not remember any of this," Emerson said. "You will forget everything, forget you ever met me, but your subconscious mind will remain affected by what I have just done. When you wake up, you will pick up your book and continue reading, and forget that we were ever here.

"Now, wake up!"

She blinked, sat down, picked up her book and continued

reading. Something itched at the edge of her mind, but she could not put her finger on what it was. She did not register the two men leave, nor Emerson's words as they left the room.

"She will do just fine. She has all that we need. I will need some more sessions with her, but she is ripe."

"And she will not remember any of this?"

"Not a thing."

Tess woke in a cold sweat, the memory, suppressed for so long, raw in her mind. She remembered it all—well, everything except for whatever he had said or did while she was in that enforced fugue state. She concentrated, trying to pull those hidden commands or whatever they were from the depths of her mind, but they remained as elusive as ever. Worse, the more she tried the more she could feel the other—new—memories threatening to slip away.

She lit the lamp by her bedside and grabbed a pen and a sheet of paper, quickly scrawling down everything she could remember, before collapsing once more into a deep sleep.

Chapter Seventeen

The next morning, Spencer and Bart accompanied Tess down to the woods to check on the devices. All seemed calm and bright in the morning sun, making the events of the previous night seem even less believable; surely nothing so bad could have taken place in such a serene part of the English countryside?

They helped Tess retrieve the boxes, placing them on the ground in a line, and then stood back to watch as she examined the devices. Both men kept a wary eye out for anything approaching them.

"You reckon it's still here?" asked Bart.

"Nah. It wasn't even here when we came out last night. Can't see it hanging round now. Especially not in daylight."

"I hope you're right. I don't like being out here without a weapon. You should've let me bring something."

"Stop worrying. It's fine." Spencer looked down at Tess. "Anything?"

"That's funny," she muttered.

"Funny in what way?" Before she could respond, a movement caught his eye. A figure over at the edge of the clearing, moving slowly around as he examined the ground with his back to them.

"Oi, you!" shouted Spencer, starting towards what appeared to be a tall, well-dressed man.

Thaddeus glanced round, and then turned back to the patch of ground he was studying.

"You stay right there," Spencer continued. "We want to talk to you."

"Not sure you needed to say that," pointed out Bart. "He

doesn't look in a hurry to go anywhere."

Spencer glared at him. "I know that..." They stopped as they reached the magician, staring at his back.

"What?" asked Thaddeus, making no effort to turn to face them.

"What are you doing here?"

"I could ask you the same question."

"We're working here. We were invited. What's your excuse?"

"You are working?" Thaddeus straightened up and turned to look at them. "Ah yes. Your little agency thing. How is Lady Marchant? Is she here?" He peered past them.

"Never mind her," Bart said, moving to block his view. "You don't say her name."

Thaddeus grinned. "You don't have to be jealous of me."

"Answer the question," said Spencer. "What are you doing here?"

"I heard there was some form of demonic activity here. I have decided to lend my skills and knowledge to the investigation."

"You have *decided*? Well, that's mighty kind of you," sneered Spencer. "What makes you think anyone needs your help?"

"I am assuming you actually want to make some form of progress towards actually solving the mystery and stopping any further injuries, or even deaths. Or are you just planning to do your usual trick of causing chaos and then running away?"

"Hey! That's unfair! We very rarely run away, unless we really have to!"

"That's right," agreed Bart. "Most of the time there's nothing left for us to run away from, anyway; so you're wrong there."

"And anyway, how'd you know there was any demonic activity here?"

"I am attuned to such things."

"And of all the demonic stuff going on, all over the place, this is the one you decided to check in on? Something special about this here?"

Thaddeus glanced past them.

"That's it, ain't it? It's Tess. You're stalking Tess!"

"I am not stalking. It is just that, wherever your lady friend goes, strong demonic activity tends to follow. Call it a professional curiosity. And unfinished business."

"There you are!" They turned to see Tess walking towards them. "I was looking for you." She stopped short when she noticed Thaddeus. "You! What are you doing here?"

"I thought my skills could be of use. And I am curious to see what manner of demonic activity you have attracted here."

"Me? Attract? I have not… We are here to investigate some unusual activity on behalf of a client."

"Of course." Thaddeus waved his hand dismissively. "My mistake," he said in a way that implied he did not believe he ever made a mistake. "I am here to lend a hand to your investigations."

"How did you…?"

"Know that there was some form of arcane activity here?" He gestured to himself. "I am a magician, remember?"

"He's an *evil* magician," said Spencer. "And given he's suddenly appeared here, just after some poor bloke's been near torn to pieces, I think it's safe to say we now have our main suspect."

Thaddeus laughed at him. "Oh, very good. But do you really think I would be so stupid as to present myself here in this manner, if I was actually the one who had committed the crime?"

Spencer shrugged. "Might be some sort of double bluff sort of thing."

"I am flattered that you rate my intellect so highly."

"I know what you're capable of," Spencer said. "We both do. Don't we?"

"Yeah," said Bart. "Still have nightmares remembering how poor Nicky ended up, you cursing him with that kind of living death." He shuddered.

"How is it that you have suddenly appeared here, of all places?" asked Tess.

"I am highly attuned to arcane activities."

"Well," said Spencer. "Given everything that happens every day all over the country, with demons and wraiths and whatnot, that must mean we've got something really strong and powerful here. Is that what you're saying?"

"It is unclear at present... I need to..."

"You've been stalking Tess," said Spencer. "That's it, ain't it? You were hanging around our offices like a bad smell, and then you followed us up here."

"No, that is not it at all," said Thaddeus, as he straightened his back.

Spencer grinned. "I know folk. And I 'specially know perverts, having been around my fair share of them. And I know an undergarment sniffer when I see one. She gets your cold little heart a-flutter, don't she?"

"I will not take that from the likes of you. I will—"

"You'll what?" Spencer leaned in. "Make sure you say it nice and loud so she can hear, yeah? Will you do to me what you did to that poor bloke last night?"

Thaddeus glared at him and then took a deep breath. "That was a nice attempt at baiting me. But I am not as dense as the people you would usually deal with. Present company excepted, of course."

"Thank you," Tess said coldly.

"I had nothing to do with the events of last night," continued Thaddeus. "Aside from right now, where I am attempting to be of assistance in unravelling the mystery of what has happened."

"That still does not explain how it was that you came to be here," said Tess. "It almost feels like you are evading the question. Are you following me?"

Thaddeus shrugged. "I am particularly attuned to what you term, ah, 'Aetheric energy'. I sensed a large amount emanating from here, and so thought I would investigate."

"A large amount of energy?" asked Tess. "When?"

"Over the past week or so, with a particular surge last night."

She stared at him. "Interesting. And were you able to pinpoint exactly where this energy was coming from?"

"Not exactly. But certainly down to the general area of this house and its grounds."

She beckoned. "Come with me."

"You're asking him to help?" asked Spencer, running to keep up with her.

"There is something I would like to get his opinion on. He may be of use, yes."

"Just don't expect to get paid," Spencer said to Thaddeus, then turned to Tess. "We're not splitting the fee with him. No way we're doing that."

They reached the devices, and Tess squatted down to examine one. Thaddeus stared down at her. "What are these?"

"Aetheric Sensors," she said. "They detect any supernatural energy and tell me what created it."

"I could do a spell which would tell you that," said Thaddeus.

"I would wager that your spells draw on Aetheric energy," she said.

"Yes. And?"

"And that would contaminate the readings from my sensors. So please do not do that."

He shrugged. "Suit yourself."

"Something is not right, though," she said.

"In what way?"

"We heard and saw a demon out here last night. And the poacher seemed to have been attacked by a demon. But the readings I am getting from these devices do not appear to match that."

"How's that?" asked Spencer.

"Well, if there was a demon of any reasonable level of power within a few feet of any of these devices, I would have expected the readings here to show a much higher level." She pointed to a dial on the front of one of the machines, the face of which showed two needles, one red and one black. "This black needle shows the current level of Aetheric energy—you will see it is close to zero—while the red one shows the peak since I last set it, which was last night."

"Red one's higher than the black one," said Bart, leaning over her shoulder. "That's good, right?"

"It should be a lot higher than it is," she said. "If a demon were here right now, I would expect it to be closer to a reading of seven or eight, not three, which is what we are seeing here."

"Were they close enough to the demon?" asked Spencer.

"Yes. You saw where we put them; they were spaced all around this clearing. And we found Mr Bishop in this clearing, so the demon must have gone past at least one of the devices, close enough to trigger a reading at least in excess of five."

"Could someone have messed with them?" asked Spencer. "You know, done something to change them. Open the front and move the needle back down?"

"No. That is not possible. I would be able to see very easily if there was any tampering. They have been set up in a very particular way, by Maxwell, who is a very meticulous man. I can see nothing that would suggest foul play from that regard."

"Maybe your devices are faulty, or not set up correctly?" asked Thaddeus, leaning over her to have a look.

"Maybe, although... Huh, that is funny," she said as the black needles all started to quiver and move upwards. Thaddeus stepped back and they returned to their previous resting levels.

They all looked at Thaddeus. "I do a lot of work with the supernatural," he said. "Surely it is to be expected that there would be some form of residue which affixes itself to me."

"Maybe," she said, watching him thoughtfully.

"Before you go," Tess said to Thaddeus, "I would like you to walk with me."

"Shall we come too?" asked Spencer.

"No. I wish to speak to him in private."

"Maybe we hang around," said Bart. "Just in case, you know?"

She smiled. "Do not worry; I will be fine. I just have a couple of things to discuss with Thaddeus." She led the magician away.

"What's that all about?" asked Bart as they watched them go.

"Don't know. But I don't like it."

"So we'll just leave her with him on her own?"

Spencer looked up at him. "What do you think? You want to try telling Tess what to do?"

"I suppose," Bart said, kicking at a root. "Huh, that's funny."

"What?"

Bart squatted down to examine the ground. "These marks. Same as the ones we saw the other day. Little holes."

"Oh yeah. Like a walking stick or something. Here, wasn't this where Thaddeus was looking when we found him?"

"It was. He didn't have a walking stick with him, though, did he?"

Spencer looked after the disappearing forms of Thaddeus and Tess. "No, he didn't. Let's tell Tess about this later. Might be nothing, or might be some sort of clue."

Tess walked in silence for a few moments, until she was happy that they were out of earshot of the others. Then, she said, "I had a dream last night. A very vivid dream, about Emerson. But it was more than a dream; it was a memory. A memory I had suppressed." She told him about the dream, of meeting Emerson before she remembered meeting him, how he had somehow mesmerised her, and then made her forget.

"And you do not recall what it was he said to you while you were in this trance?" asked Thaddeus when she was finished.

"No. I have tried hard to force the memories back, but to no avail."

"I think I know what it was. It was all a part of the process which culminated in you being possessed by the demon. He was testing what you were capable of. Preparing you. Do you recall any other similar sessions."

"No."

"I would wager that there were in fact other occasions, which you still do not recall. Maybe over time you will remember more. I would be very interested in hearing the details when you do." He looked at her. "I could accelerate the process, you know. I have means of extracting memories."

"So in order to find out whether Emerson messed with my mind, you want to mess with my mind?" She shook her head. "No thank you. I do not trust you enough to allow that."

He shrugged. "As you will. Then do it the longer way. Just try remembering on your own."

"I will keep notes should I do so." She paused and then, looking down, asked, "Do you think he did anything permanent?"

"What do you mean?"

"Did he... change anything in me that cannot be reversed?"

"It is difficult to say. I would need to know more about what he said to you when you were in the trance, and any other trances you may have been subjected to. That is why it is important that you note down, and tell me, everything you remember."

"I understand." She shivered. "One thing is bothering me, though. Why now?"

"What do you mean?"

"Why am I remembering it now? It has been so many months... Months in which I had ample opportunities to remember. And yet it is only here that the memories start to come back. Why?"

"Maybe it is linked to us talking through what happened," he said. "That may have prompted your mind to begin exploring the memories connected to those experiences." He looked around. "And I understand that you spent time here as a child? That could certainly have an impact; encouraging your mind to look inward and backward."

She nodded slowly. "Maybe."

*

Back at the house, having brought the equipment back to Tess's room for her to examine, they joined the Beaumont family for breakfast. Tess had invited Thaddeus to join them, but he had quickly declined and left without offering an excuse or explanation. Walking into the dining room, they found the Beaumonts in a rather subdued mood, the news having spread to those who had been in bed at the time the events had occurred the previous night.

"So terrible," said Lady Beaumont. "I cannot believe I slept through it all."

Spencer let out a loud yawn. "Know how you feel," he said.

"You do look exhausted," Tess said to Spencer. "You usually sleep like a log after a few beers."

"Yeah, well I would've done if it weren't for all the racket. Are you sure there's no one above my room?"

"There certainly is not," said Lady Beaumont quickly. "I did ask Mr Smith to check that the whole house was secure; that could be what you heard."

"Well he wasn't quiet about it. I had half a mind to go up there and tell him to lay it off. Don't worry," he added quickly. "Wouldn't dare to wander places you don't want me to in your gaff."

Lady Beaumont shot him an appreciative smile. "So have we heard anything more about how the poor man is? The poacher fellow?"

"Not yet," said Tess. "I plan to go and visit the doctor after breakfast, to check on him."

"We'll come with you," said Spencer. "Bit of fresh air'll do us good."

"I do not know why you bother," said Ralph. "Surely it would be better all round if the fool has finally learnt his lesson. A few months laid up and incapacitated could be the best thing for him. Certainly the best thing for the rest of us."

"You want to be careful, mate," Spencer said. "Talk like that could get people thinking you had something to do with this."

"How dare you!" spluttered Ralph. "Lady Beaumont, are you going to allow him to talk to me like that?"

Lady Beaumont stared at him. "I am sure you do not need

me to stand up for you. You are a grown man, after all. And my daughter's betrothed. Surely a man of honour such as yourself would have no problems in proving to be false, any allegations that these people may throw at you?"

Ralph stared at her and then swallowed and took a deep breath, regaining his composure. "I can assure you I had nothing to do with it," he said through gritted teeth. "You can ask my friends. I was with them until long after you say you found the man."

"Anyway," said Emilia. "Did you not say it was a demon that mauled the poacher so?"

"Bishop," said Bart. "He has a name, the poacher. And yeah, we heard a demon. Didn't get much of a look at it though."

"And there was the mysterious figure you saw running away," said Tess. "You thought it was a man?"

Spencer nodded. "I reckon so."

"Probably another poacher," sniffed Lady Beaumont. "Lacking the moral fibre to help his friend, he instead ran away at the first sign of trouble."

"That would certainly fit the profile," said Ralph. "There's enough of them hereabouts; I recall Wilbur once telling me that, at certain times of night, you could not throw a stone in the woods without hitting a poacher!"

Spencer stared at him. "How's your nose?"

"Fine. Why?"

"It's just it looked like Jack Bishop whacked you quite hard last night. If a bloke did that to me, I'd be pretty cross."

Ralph shrugged but, before he could answer, Calvin appeared at the door, his eyes red-rimmed. He wordlessly accepted a cup from the maidservant and Bart noticed the way he stared after her as she retreated.

"Could you tell your man to make less noise at night?" he asked his mother. "Took me forever to doze off, what with all the banging upstairs."

"Mr Smith, you mean?" asked Lady Beaumont. "Checking

on the security of the house?"

Calvin looked at her and then noticed the others in the room watching him. He shrugged with a half-smile. "Yes, well, I know it's a valuable job and everything, but a bit less banging and crashing would be appreciated." He looked over at Mr Smith, who had appeared in the doorway with a plate of meats. "Could you manage that, Smithy, old chap? Maybe wear softer shoes at night? Or no shoes at all? Fellow's got to sleep after all."

Mr Smith looked from one to the other and then nodded. "Of course, sir."

"We finally have something we can agree on," Spencer said, raising his cup in a salute to Calvin.

*

After breakfast, Spencer and Bart went to Tess's room, finding her surrounded by the Aetheric sensor devices, which were in various states of dismantlement.

"This a bad time?" asked Spencer. "You said you only needed a few minutes to get ready…"

"I know," she said. "But I just wanted to check up on a few things." She screwed a tube into one of the devices, opening a valve on the box it was connected to, then held it to her ear for a moment before nodding in satisfaction. "I will leave these to do their thing for a few hours, and check on them when we are back. I want to make sure they are operating correctly, or whether Thaddeus was right."

"Pah! That idiot don't know nothing," said Spencer. "At least, not about your stuff." He looked around, as though he was checking that the magician was not skulking behind him.

Tess chuckled. "Maybe. But it does not hurt to check. One thing I have learnt, is that you should always make sure that you have discounted all other alternatives before you come to a conclusion." She did one last check and then ushered them out of the room, closing and locking the door behind her.

"Now," she said. "Let us go and see how Mr Bishop is."

Chapter Eighteen

Jack Bishop's house was a run-down cottage at the end of a row of run-down cottages. The walls were a muddy brick which showed signs of at one time having been treated to a lick of white paint, which was now all but faded or flaked away, except in a few scarce places. The windows and door all sat at odd angles to the ground and the rest of the building, as though they were trying to dissociate themselves from the house, while the roof showed every sign of being ready to cave in at any moment.

Tess knocked on the rickety door, wincing as it rattled alarmingly, and a few moments later it haltingly opened to reveal a timid-looking dark haired woman, her eyes red from a night of tearful worry.

"Mrs Bishop?" asked Tess.

"I might be. Who's asking?"

"My name is Tess. These two are my colleagues, Spencer and Bart. We are staying up at Flint Hall with the Beaumonts."

"Ah yes. You'll be them demon hunters, then."

"That is correct," Tess blinked. "News spreads fast around here."

"Don't get many strangers round here. And when trouble follows them, we all tend to take notice."

Spencer opened his mouth to speak, but Tess held up a hand to stop him. "We were the ones who found your husband last night. We wanted to check up on him."

She looked at them for a moment and then nodded. "Kind of you." She stepped aside. "You'll be coming in, then."

"Thank you. But only if it is all right. We do not want to

intrude."

"It's all right," Mrs Bishop said. "Don't get much company. And he'll probably be happy to see anyone, given his injuries mean he ain't likely to be leaving his bed much for a while now."

They stepped into a dark, dingy space, a single room which served as kitchen, sitting room and bedroom. The windows let a minimal amount of light into the room, given the amounts of dirt stuck to the panes. The majority of the light in the house came from a fire at the far end, and the sunlight streaming in through the cracks in the walls and ceiling.

Bart whistled. "Nice place," he said, with genuine admiration.

Tess looked at him to check that he was not being sarcastic, as did Mrs Bishop, but his face was set in innocent appreciation.

"He means it," said Spencer. "You should see some of the hovels we lived in, growing up back in London."

"They must've been bad," said Mrs Bishop, slumping into a small chair in front of the fire. "You can't know what to do with yourselves in that big fancy manor house, up at Flint Hall."

"A lot more posh than we're used to, that's for sure," agreed Spencer.

"Not to mention weird and creepy," added Bart. "What do they need all them rooms for? Just more chances for stuff to hide and sneak up on you."

"Is that why the Beaumonts invited you to stay?" asked Mrs Bishop. "Demons and ghosties in the spare rooms?"

"Not quite," smiled Tess. "But we are wondering if what attacked your husband could have some supernatural connection. How is he?"

"He's over there." She nodded to the bed in the corner of the room.

"Is he recovering?" asked Tess.

"Why don't you ask him yourself?" She picked up a ball of wool and started knitting.

They walked over to where she had indicated, squinting down at the blanketed lump on the bed. The figure stirred and rolled over, to reveal a face with two black eyes and a cut lip.

He blinked at them. "I remember you two. From the pub last night, right?" His voice was raspy, coming between gasped breaths.

"That's right," said Spencer. "Talked to you about the thing you'd seen up at Flint Hall. Looks like you had a close run-in with it afterwards."

He laughed, a short bark which turned very quickly into choking gasps. When he had regained his breath he said, "Should have listened to my own advice and steered well clear of that place."

"Can you tell us what you remember?" asked Tess.

"I'll tell you what I can. I remember going out to the woods."

"You'd had a fight with Ralph, hadn't you?" Spencer asked.

He frowned. "Yes. Can't remember what about. Something about nothing though. He's a nuisance, that man, nothing more."

"So you went to the woods," said Tess. "Why?"

"Can't remember."

"You shouted something at Ralph as you left the pub," said Spencer. "Something about him not telling you what to do. That anything to do with it?"

Mrs Bishop tutted from the other side of the room.

"No." Bishop shook his head and then winced. "I can't remember, but it's nothing to do with him. Anyway, I'm in the woods and I hear something. Something big coming towards me."

"Did you see it?"

"No. I don't think so. But I felt... something. Something really bad. Something which made me want to run away as quick as I can."

"Did you?" asked Bart. "Run, I mean."

"I couldn't." The man's face grew more and more pale as his eyes focused on the memory. "It was like my body wouldn't listen to me. I wanted to move, run away, anything, but I couldn't.

And then... Well, I'm not sure. Something hit me from behind, and next thing I know I wake up and the doctor's peering all over me." He collapsed into another coughing fit, which then lapsed into moaning.

"That's enough for now," said Mrs Bishop, putting down her knitting and standing to open the door. "He needs his rest. You can come back later if you want to ask him anything else, but I don't think he has anything else to tell you."

"No," said Tess, staring at the man, who was already lapsing into a doze. "I am not sure he does." She followed the others out of the door. "Thank you for allowing us to speak with him. If there's anything we can do for you, please do let us know."

Mrs Bishop grunted. "There's one thing you can do. Tell your fancy friends from Flint House to leave us alone."

"What do you mean?" asked Tess. "Has someone else been here this morning?"

"He has. Big posh man, a few hours ago. No idea what he said to him, but he damn near scared my husband to death. I don't want them lot bothering us again. Tell them we'll keep away from their damned woods, if they keep away from us." With that, she slammed the door shut.

They looked at each other.

"Sounds like Ralph's been here to do mischief, don't you think?" said Spencer. "Probably worried he'd be the one blamed for what happened, so wanted to make sure Bishop wouldn't say nothing. That'd explain why he wouldn't say anything against him just now, right?"

"Maybe," said Tess. "Although when did he manage to do that? He was with us at breakfast..."

Spencer shrugged. "Them horses can ride pretty fast."

Tess nodded slowly, a thoughtful look on her face.

They started back along the lane, meeting a flustered man coming the other way, towards the cottage.

"Hey," said Spencer. "You're the doctor. Come to check up on Mr Bishop?"

"I have." He blinked at them. "You're from Flint Hall. The demon hunters."

Tess nodded. "That is right."

"You've just been to see him?" The doctor nodded to Bishop's cottage.

"We have," said Spencer. "Thought we'd check up on him. Check he's all right."

The doctor grunted. "That's kind of you. Can't say the Beaumonts would do that."

"Yeah, well, we're not them."

"I can see that."

Tess cleared her throat. "Mr Bishop seems to be recovering."

"Is that right?" The doctor looked at her, as though challenging her to prove some form of medical qualifications.

"He was talking to us, he seemed lucid. I would have thought that is a good sign?"

The doctor gave a curt nod. "That would be the case. I of course need to examine him to be sure."

"Of course." They stepped to the side to let him pass. "I was wondering, though," Tess continued. "What was the extent of his injuries?"

"Well, you saw him last night. He was pretty badly beaten up."

"What do you think could have caused the injuries?"

"Was it a demon, do you mean?" He scratched his head. "Certainly could have been. The injuries were very extensive and could have been fatal. Although…"

"Although what?" asked Spencer.

The doctor looked around. "I haven't had too much experience in dealing with injuries from demon attacks. I suppose you've had more experience in that regard than me. I always assumed that they would be more in the way of… I don't know… tooth and claw. Ripping the victim into small pieces, eating him, or stomping him into the ground. That sort of thing."

"Tends to be how it ends up," agreed Bart.

"So why did this one not do any of that, if it was a demon?" asked the doctor. "There were no signs of any cuts or tears. He simply looked as though he had been hit hard from behind with a blunt object, and then left for dead."

"Maybe it was running and he was in the way?" said Spencer.

"Maybe. Although running from where, to where? Anyway, I suppose that's what you three get paid to figure out; I'm just here to patch up the wounded. Speaking of which, I should go and check on the patient. Good day to you."

They watched him go and then Spencer turned to Tess, noting the thoughtful look on her face. "Interesting?" he asked.

"Yes," she said. "Very interesting."

Chapter Nineteen

At midday on the dot, Spencer and Bart left Tess and went to the tavern, circling round to the rear entrance to make their appointment with Trevor the demon.

The sun was forcing its way through the clouds, the hint of rain giving the air a musty, close smell. The world around them seemed to be holding its breath, the birds quieter than usual, the cows hiding out of sight under the shelter of trees and walls.

As they rounded the corner, they saw the demon standing against the far wall, staring at them impassively as they approached.

"I thought it was just going to be you two. Who's this?" asked the demon.

"She's a friend of ours," said Spencer. "She's all right."

The demon grunted. "What is it you want to talk to me about?"

"We're just trying to piece together what's been going on up at Flint Hall. We heard from Wilbur, the groundsman, that you'd been let go, not that long ago. Just want to understand what happened, whether there's anything you might've seen that could help us."

"Help you to find out who hurt the poacher?"

"Well, yeah. But also understand about this curse that the Beaumonts keep banging on about. Not sure if there's a connection or not, but we need to check all this stuff out."

"We're detectives, you see," chipped in Bart.

"Really?" the demon rumbled sceptically.

"Kind of," said Spencer. "But we're not Peelers or anything

like that. You can trust us."

"Even though you call yourselves 'demon hunters'?"

"We're just trying to understand stuff. Don't mean you no harm."

"What if I was the one that beat up the poacher and plan to do off with Lord Beaumont?"

"Did you? Are you?"

"Nope."

"Then we'll be all right. We don't know what to think, right now. So anything you can tell us, that'd be great."

"Why should I help you?"

"Because they're already starting to blame all their problems on a demon," said Spencer. "And sooner or later they're going to stick all that blaming on the only demon round here."

"That's you," added Bart, helpfully.

The demon looked from one to the other. "I wouldn't do that sort of thing though."

"So why don't you help us to nip any unfortunate assumptions in the bud by helping us find the real reason behind what's going on up at Flint Hall?" asked Spencer.

"And that'd stop me getting in trouble?"

"Can't promise anything," shrugged Spencer. "But we can promise that if you don't help us, and we don't find out what's really going on... Well, you ever seen a whole village lynch a demon?"

The demon scratched his head with a huge hand, the claws making a noise like rocks clattering down a cliff. "All right. Guess you've got a point. I've got nothing to hide."

"Good. So how's about we start with when you started working for them up at the Hall?"

"It was a few years ago. Not long after I came through from the Aether and then it closed. You see, when that happened, we didn't know what to do. We'd all been told we were here to invade, that the humans'd be all ready to be conquered."

"Then it turned out we was up for a fight," said Bart.

"Well, yes. You see, some of us were made for one thing, and one thing only--fighting and killing. But most of us weren't like that. Yeah, we're stronger than you lot, but we'd rather do stuff less... well... bad. You know?"

"Yeah," said Bart. "I know exactly."

Spencer looked up at his friend and then turned back to Trevor the demon. "So you made your way here and found work up at the Hall?"

"Yeah. I was just wandering round the fields, then saw Wilbur struggling with some rocks. Thought I'd give him a hand. Of course, he ran off at first, but then when he saw I was trying to help, he came back. Then he got me helping with other stuff, then offered me food and lodgings and a job if I carried on helping. We can be good workers, you know."

"Yeah, I get that," said Spencer. "We've got some doing similar around London. Them that aren't causing chaos in the demon areas of the city."

"You ever been in them demon areas?"

"Yeah, a few times."

"Then you'll know better that it's more than just demons running around causing chaos."

"I dunno. A few have tried to rip us to pieces and serve us up as lunch," commented Spencer.

"All right, I accept some might be bad 'uns. But that's no different to you humans, right?"

Spencer frowned as he tried to get his head round this concept. "I dunno. Maybe." He shook his head. "So you worked for the Beaumonts for a few years. Anything unusual you noticed there? I'm thinking 'specially in the past few weeks or so?"

"Tended to keep myself out of the way of them as much as possible," said Trevor. "You know, the Lord and his family. Staff that worked for them were always good to me."

"You ever hear about any curse?"

"Only when the brother appeared. That's when they started talking about it. And that was when I was let go."

"The brother?" asked Bart. "That's that Calvin lad, right? Always thought he was up to no good."

"Didn't catch his name. Didn't like the look of him though; creepy looking. Well, more creepy than most humans, anyway."

"What you mean about that?" protested Spencer.

"Come on, you must see it. You're just wet sacks of meat. The only bits of your bodies that make sense is your nails, and you cut them too short to be any use. Any species that has to make its own armour to protect itself rather than growing its own... well, it ain't natural."

Spencer chuckled. "All right. So the brother appears, folk start talking about some curse, and then you lose your job. That about the size of it?"

"Pretty much."

"Who fired you?"

"Wilbur. He wasn't happy about it, he said as much. But said orders was orders. I couldn't carry on working there."

"Did he say why?"

"No. But I know it had something to do with that brother. He came to watch me when I was working one day. Then just after that, I was told to go."

"You been back since?"

"No. I've had no cause to."

"So where've you been staying?"

"Round and about. I get some supplies, and just hide out on my own, out in the hills. I got friends, you know?" He looked up, his eyes widening as he stared past them, into the distance.

"What is it?" asked Spencer, turning to look. He caught a glimpse of a tall, dark figure; a well-dressed man who seemed familiar but, before he could figure anything further out, he found himself flying through the air.

He landed awkwardly on a hard patch of ground, inches from a brick wall, Bart on top of him. "Hey," Spencer shouted. "What're you doing?"

"Saving your life," grunted his friend, picking him up and

forcing him into a run as the wall exploded in a shower of stone.

"What...?" Spencer looked back to see Trevor charging at them, murder in his eyes. He swung a huge fist, which missed them by a fraction, thanks to Bart's quickness of feet and hands, barging them both into a ditch.

Spencer groaned. "I think I've broken something. Do me a favour; next time you try and save me, maybe do it without trying to kill me?"

"Stop moaning; you're fine. We need to keep moving. Come on."

They scrambled along the ditch, trying to ignore the rank smells kicked up by their progress. A shadow fell over them, and they looked up to see Trevor bearing down on them, fists raised and ready to pummel them into the ground.

They spun away, one to the left and one to the right, as Trevor's claws gouged the dirt where they had been just moments before.

"Oi!" shouted Spencer. "What's going on?" He ducked under another fist and ran back. "Why're you doing this? What did we say?"

"I don't think he's in the mood to chat anymore," panted Bart. "This way." He ran and dived over a low wall, Spencer following close on his heels.

They scrambled away as that wall exploded in a cascade of stones.

"Thought that might slow him down a bit," Bart mumbled.

They backed away, finding themselves with their backs against the wall of a house. Spencer looked left and right, trying in vain to find a door or window that they could flee through. Whichever way he looked, the stonework was stubbornly opening-free. He cursed, then picked a direction at random but, before they could move, the demon was looming over them.

"Help!" shouted Spencer. "Anyone? Help!"

Then Trevor's eyes widened. He blinked, staring at them as though he had just woken from a dream before turning and running away.

They both stood there, breathing heavily, not daring to move until they were happy that the demon had definitely gone.

"That was weird," said Bart.

"Yeah. Wonder what he saw that made him do that? Looked like some bloke, a toff by looks of him, but didn't have enough time to work out who he was."

"Calvin?"

"Maybe. Would make sense if Trevor's holding a grudge against him. Wouldn't be first person to flip into a rage in that sort of circumstance, right?"

"Hey," said Bart. "That was a long time ago. I'm a changed man now. And anyway, he deserved it."

Chapter Twenty

Bruised, battered and no further forward, they met back up with Tess and, after updating her on their encounter with Trevor the demon, together made their way back to Flint Hall, enjoying the unseasonable warmth of the sun on their faces as they walked. They walked in silence, Tess and Spencer lost in their own thoughts while Bart busied himself with seeing how far he could kick the stones on the path.

"Could've been that demon," said Spencer. "If he went into a rage like he did with us, nothing could've stopped him, he could've run right through Bishop."

"Yes," said Tess. "That is certainly possible. But you were there last night; did you see anything that a demon could have been running to or from? Anything chasing it?"

"Well, no. But it was dark, right?"

"How many creatures did you hear?"

He frowned. "Just the one, I guess. Yeah. Just one demon. So maybe he wasn't being chased. He could've run off, like he did when he saw that toff just now."

"Hmm. You did say you saw someone else there though, running away?"

"Yeah. Could have been the same bloke as Trevor saw just now."

"But what could it be about the mere sight of a man that could cause a demon to react like that?"

They rounded a bend and Flint Hall came into view, the house peeking through the wrought iron gates.

"So what now?" asked Spencer. "Must be getting close to

dinner time."

"I would like to place one of the sensor devices back in the woods. Just in case we have another visitor tonight. And then I would like to do a bit more exploring," said Tess. "Have a wander round the grounds for a few minutes."

"We'll come with you."

Bart was holding the gate open for them and as they passed he asked, "What about dinner? You said it was close to dinner time."

"Don't worry; we'll not be long. Right?"

"That is right," said Tess. "But you can leave me to it if you want to go and eat."

"No," said Spencer. "We're not letting you wander round on your own out here."

"That's right," said Bart. "And while you're getting your stuff from your room, I'll make sure Mrs Smith knows to keep some food aside for us. Just in case, like."

They met back at Tess's room a little while later, and found her standing in the middle of a chaotic mess, her devices in varying states of disrepair scattered all over the place.

"What did you do?" asked Spencer.

"This was not me," she said, her face flushed with exasperation. "Someone broke into my room and did this; they destroyed all of the sensors. All of the readings, all of the gases needed to power the devices: destroyed."

"You locked the door," said Spencer. "We saw you."

"Yes. And when I came back, it was unlocked."

"Who'd do that?" asked Bart.

"I'll find out," said Spencer. He examined the door for a moment and then ran along the corridor, through an unremarkable door and down a set of narrow stairs to the servants' quarters, where he found Mr Smith. "Oi, Smithy, a word."

"How dare you talk to me like that..." the butler started.

"No time for pleasantries. You been in the house all day?"

"Yes."

"You know who's been in and around the bedrooms?"

"Well, the maidservant will have cleaned the rooms…"

"Did she do Lady Marchant's room?"

"I don't know. We can ask her. What's this all about?"

"Lady Marchant's room's been broken into, and a load of her stuff smashed. I want to know who did it."

They found the maidservant in the kitchen. "Bev, a word please," said Mr Smith.

She turned and cast a quick glance at them both, before looking down at the floor. Spencer noticed that she had wide blue eyes, brightening up an otherwise plain face. Every inch of her bearing screamed that she did not want to be there, did not want to be talking to them. He knew straight away what Bart saw in her; his friend had always been a sucker for a damsel in distress.

"Yes, Mr Smith," she muttered.

"Did you clean the bedrooms this morning?"

"I did, sir."

"Including the guest ones?"

"Yes, sir. Well, apart from Lady Marchant's. The door was locked, and I did not have a key with me, so I was going to go back later but I am so sorry I forgot and I will go and do it right now. I'm so sorry sir…"

"It's all right," said Spencer. "You're not in trouble for that. So you didn't touch that room?"

"No, sir." She shot a quick glance up at his face, checking that there was no sign of mockery or deception there.

"What time was it you were up there?"

"It was before midday. Probably around eleven. Yes, just after eleven; I remember hearing the clock chime as I was moving to the next room."

"And it was definitely locked?"

"Definitely. I remember being annoyed that I'd not got the keys with me."

"Did you go back there afterwards? Walk past the room or anything like that?"

"No," she said.

"Where's the keys kept?" asked Spencer.

"Over here," said Mr Smith, pointing to a row of hooks on the wall.

"They all here?" asked Spencer.

"You mean: is the key to Lady Marchant's room here? Yes. It's this one."

"That the only one to her room?"

"No. There are two others. She has one, and the other is on the set which I keep on my person at all times." He patted the thick ring of keys clipped to his belt, causing them to jangle dully.

"You been near her room today?" Spencer asked him.

Mr Smith pulled a face as he thought. "I could not rightly say. I will typically do rounds of the house, to check all is in order, when I am not needed for other duties. I did so today a couple of times. But I did not stray into any bedrooms, if that is what you are implying."

"Not implying anything. Just asking. So them keys never left your side today? You never lent them to anyone?"

"No."

"And these keys here. They stay on here all day?"

"Mrs Smith!" the butler called out. A moment later his wife appeared at the pantry door. "Anyone come in and take any room keys today?"

"Not that I remember."

"You been in here all day?" asked Spencer.

"Near enough. Why?"

"Someone broke into Lady Marchant's room today," said Mr Smith.

"Oh no! What did they steal? Nothing valuable, I hope."

"Not sure if they stole anything," said Spencer. "But they smashed up a load of her equipment."

She put a hand to her mouth. "Who would do such a thing?" she asked.

"Someone who didn't want us finding out what the sensor thingies picked up from last night," said Spencer. "And someone who doesn't want us using them sensors again."

*

Dinner that night was a more subdued affair, all of them warily watching each other while they picked at their meal.

"I was sorry to hear about your room," Lady Beaumont said to Tess. "Was anything stolen?"

"Not that I can tell. But some of my equipment was damaged."

"Oh dear. How terrible. I hope it was not too expensive."

"I do not know," Tess said. "It was not mine."

"Do you know who did it?" asked Lord Beaumont.

"No. At least, not yet."

"Well, I am sure that Mr Smith is doing everything he can to find the culprit."

"Indeed," said Tess, noting the way that Lord and Lady Beaumont looked at each other.

Emilia cleared her throat. "I understand you had a trip into the village earlier."

"Yes. We went to see Mr Bishop."

"Oh, how is he?"

"He's alive," said Spencer. "Just about."

"Well, that is good news."

"He was grateful that someone came to check on him," said Tess.

"Yes, of course," said Lady Beaumont. "Very Christian of you to do that. We should arrange for something to be sent to him, by way of compensation."

"But it was not our fault he was injured," said Ralph. "He should not have been wandering around near the Hall."

"That is not the point," Lady Beaumont said in a cold voice.

"A man was badly hurt."

Calvin chuckled. "Really, mother. Sounds almost like you are developing a conscience."

She stared at him for a moment and then returned to her food.

"What about you lot?" asked Spencer. "Anyone make a trip into town?"

Ralph glared at him, still red-faced from the rebuke by Lady Beaumont. "It is none of your damned business what any of us did today."

There was precious little conversation after that, and they all retired to their rooms before the clocks struck ten.

Tess lay in her bed, willing herself to go to sleep. The dark wrapped around her like a cloying blanket. Shapes loomed at her out of the shadows, bringing to her mind all sorts of images, half-drawn devils and the outlines of ghostly figures.

Her rational mind tried to take control. She closed her eyes and forced herself to relax.

Finally, she drifted off to sleep.

And she dreamed.

She was in a dark, formless room, looking around at walls which were little more than mist. In front of her a chair congealed into being, and on it a figure.

A feeling of deep dread overcame her. It was him.

"Lady Marchant," Emerson said. "So good to see you again."

She looked around, desperately seeking a door, any way out of that place. As she did so, she became aware that her hands were bound by rough leather straps. She realised with panic that she was back there, in that device, the one which had enabled her demonic possession.

She struggled against the bonds, sheer terror coursing through her veins. But they held firm.

"It has been so long," Emerson continued. "And we never really had a chance to get properly acquainted. Of course, I know more of you than you do of me. At least, I remember more; although I see you are starting to recall our little hypnosis sessions."

"You monster," she said. "What did you do to me?"

"I? Do? Why, nothing. Nothing, aside from prepare you for your destiny, your purpose. Or at least, what should have been your purpose, if those idiots had not intervened. But now it is time to end it all."

"What do you mean?"

He leaned forward. "You thought you were all so clever, thought you could thwart my will. Such things cannot happen. Will not happen. Say goodbye to your friends, and say goodbye to your pathetic little life."

She struggled with even more force, and managed to work a hand free. She thrust her hand out at the glass dome in front of her and it shattered, sending her cascading away into the blackness.

She woke up, her heart beating heavily and her skin slick with sweat. She realised with a shock that she was no longer in bed, but was instead stood by the window to her room, which was wide open. She had clearly sleepwalked while she was dreaming and, if she had not awoken when she did, could have found herself falling through the window and down on to the flagstones below.

She shuddered and went to shut the window, wondering how it had been opened in the first place; she certainly did not remember doing so. Could she have worked the latch in her sleep? She supposed it was not beyond the realms of possibility. But why?

Before she could put any more thought to the problem, her attention was caught by a movement in the garden below.

A bulky figure was stumbling across the lawn, making its way towards the woods.

"Bart!" she shouted through the window. Her friend carried on regardless, not heeding or caring the way that his nightclothes were getting soaked by the wet grass under his bare feet.

She ran out of her room and ran down the corridor, stopping to rap on Spencer's door. After a few moments the door opened and he blinked out at her.

"What is it?" he asked.

"Bart. He's outside, walking out to the woods. I think he's sleepwalking."

"Can't be. He wouldn't do that."

"Trust me, he is. Come on; if that demon's out in the woods, he could be walking straight to his death!"

They ran down the stairs and out the house, shouting to Bart as they approached him. As they drew level with him, he stopped and looked at them.

"What's going on?" he asked. Then, looking around, "Where am I?"

"You're outside," said Spencer. "You were sleepwalking."

"What? No. No, I was dreaming about..." he frowned.

"About what?"

"Can't remember now. But it was something strange." He scratched his head. "Nope. It's gone."

They heard a crashing sound from the woods, over the other side of the gate. Bart turned to the others. "While we're out here, shall we bag us a demon?"

"Mate," said Spencer. "Look at us all; we're unarmed and in our nightclothes. I don't think we're really kitted out to fight a demon."

"He is right," said Tess. "Not without any weapons."

"Give me a few minutes," said Bart. "I'll run in and get my axe." He looked around. "Actually, isn't there a shed around here? They must have something I can use as a weapon in there."

Spencer held up his hand and they listened as the sounds of the demon receded. "Sounds like we're too late."

"Can I go chase it?" said Bart hopefully.

"In the dead of night, in our bare feet? And by the time we've gone in and got some clothes on, it'll be long gone. Anyway, we'd be chasing round in circles out there. Sure recipe for us winding up lost, or dead, or both."

"But…"

"Mate, just for once, use your brain. It's not worth the risk. We'll get another chance, and that time we'll be ready."

"And there's something else that bothers me," said Tess. "You were sleepwalking towards the demon. I also sleepwalked tonight; I woke up at my window, which was wide open."

"Is that how you knew I was out here?"

"Yes. But two of us doing that on the same night? When neither of us have sleepwalked before?"

Bart conceded the point with a shrug. "Sounds strange. But I'm cold and hungry. If we're not going to chase the demon, can we go back inside?"

They walked back to the house, relieved to find that the back door was still open. None of them fancied a night outside while they waited for the staff to wake up.

"What do you reckon's going on?" asked Spencer.

"I have a theory," said Tess. "At least, I have an idea. You see, my dream tonight, just before I woke up, was about someone who has been haunting my dreams ever since we arrived here."

"Who?"

"Emerson." She looked at him, a meaningful look on her face.

Spencer raised his eyebrows. "So?"

"So, I believe that he is behind all this. Think about it; it matches his pattern of behaviour. Demonic goings-on. A house with women in it. And me."

"So, what?" asked Spencer. "He came all the way out here to create a demon to torment Flint Hall? Bit of a coincidence, isn't it? Him coming all the way out here, to the same place we've come to, only a few months after we handed his arse to him, back in London?"

"You could look at it that way. But we are the only ones really offering the type of service we do. So of course we would be asked to come here."

"I don't know. What've you got to make us think it's him behind this?"

"The dreams?"

Spencer laughed. "Sorry Tess, but you do know dreams aren't real, right?"

"They seemed real enough."

"Dreams can do that. I once dreamt I was a pigeon. Didn't mean I suddenly sprouted wings and started doing my business all over Nelson's Column."

She scowled at him. "I know that. This is not some flight of fancy, you know. And I am not some sort of silly little girl who needs everything explaining to her." She turned and stomped off.

"I know that... I didn't mean..." Spencer started after her, then stopped and turned to look at Bart for support.

His friend was gnawing on a chunk of meat he had found in the larder. "Could've handled that better, don't you think?" Bart said, before offering him the meat. "Want some?"

Spencer shook his head and then also stomped off.

"Suit yourself," said Bart, taking another bite and chewing contentedly.

Chapter Twenty-One

The next morning, they told their hosts about the adventures of the previous night.

"How scary that must have been for you," said Lady Beaumont in a distant voice. "I had an aunt once who sleepwalked. Terrible nuisance, it was. We ended up having to tie her to the bed every night."

"I know folk who'd pay good money for that," quipped Spencer, to disapproving stares from everyone, apart from Calvin, who spluttered into his drink, his shoulders shaking in silent laughter.

"Did any of you hear anything?" asked Tess.

"Not particularly," said Lord Beaumont as the others shook their heads. "I of course heard the carrying-on from the demon, but that is becoming as common as the hooting of owls now."

"Father, please do not be so blasé," said Emilia.

He waved a hand. "It is all fine. And I am sure our guests here will get rid of it soon enough, and everything can go back to normal."

After breakfast, Tess decided to have a wander around the house. As she passed the drawing room, she saw Emilia and Lady Beaumont huddled together. When they noticed her, they stepped apart.

"How are you faring?" asked Tess.

"Oh, it is just so dreadful, is it not?" said Lady Beaumont. "I am beside myself with... with concern for that poor man and his family. Is that not right, Emilia?"

"Yes," Emilia managed, looking up with red-rimmed eyes. "It

is so dreadful."

"It is," Tess agreed. "I just cannot believe that such a thing could happen, in such a place as this. You know, I have nothing but pleasant memories of your home."

"Thank you," smiled Lady Beaumont. She shook her head. "It just... was not meant to be this way."

"What way?" asked Tess.

"Oh." Lady Beaumont glanced at her daughter and then back at Tess. "I just meant... that we were supposed to have a nice, pleasant time this weekend, and then there was all of this... terrible stuff around the curse."

"Yes," said Emilia. "It is supposed to be a celebration. My father's birthday. And then... this..."

Tess frowned. "But I thought you specifically brought me here because of the curse?"

"Well, yes." Emilia glanced at her mother. "But we did not expect it to unfold so soon, and in this way."

"And as for you and your strange companions," Lady Beaumont said to Tess, "we are paying you good money, and I am not entirely sure we are seeing any form of return for it." She stomped out of the room.

Emilia shot an embarrassed smile at her friend. "I am sorry," she said. "I think the stress is just getting to us."

Tess frowned as she stared after Lady Beaumont.

*

"Smells delicious as always, Mrs S," said Spencer as he walked into the kitchen.

Mrs Smith turned and smiled at him. "Thank you, Mr Spencer. Is this your way of getting a chance to get a taste?"

"It's just Spencer. No 'mister'," he reminded her. "And if you're offering, I'll not say no."

She ladled him a helping of stew, which he tucked into enthusiastically. "So," he said through mouthfuls of food, "is it always this lively round here?"

"What do you mean?" she asked.

"Folks popping up beaten up all over the place. That Ralph lad mouthing off at everyone."

She chuckled. "Mister Wheeler is a character. But he's harmless."

"Harmless?" asked Spencer. "As in: wouldn't kill a random poacher?"

"Oh, he wouldn't hurt anyone," she laughed. "Nor would Master Calvin. He's a little kid at heart, that's all."

Spencer raised an eyebrow. "If I'd talked to my folks the way he does, I'd've been given a thick ear in no time."

"No doubt you would. But they just have their own way of raising their family. And I'll have no bad talk about them, do you hear?"

Spencer raised a hand in surrender. "All right. Tell me about this place then. You've worked here for a while?"

"More years than I care to remember. Seen Mistress Emily and Master Calvin from cradle to… well, where they are now."

"Just you and Mister Smith?"

"There were more of us, at one time. Used to be the case we'd be rushed off our feet with one dinner party or another, day after day. Very sociable family, the Beaumonts. You know how they are, the aristocracy?"

"Oh, yeah," lied Spencer. "But that's not the case no more?"

"Things have quietened down over the years. Don't get so many guests these days, to be honest."

"That's why there's less of you staff here these days, then? What happened: they run out of money?"

She stared at him and then resumed her washing up without responding.

*

Bev hummed to herself as she folded the washing, then screamed as she caught sight of a huge figure in the doorway.

"Sorry," said Bart. "I didn't mean to scare you."

"No, it's all right, sir," she said. "You just surprised me, that's all." She put a hand to her chest as she calmed her breathing. "I'm sorry sir, how can I help you?"

"I'm just... Nothing. I just was enjoying hearing you sing. You've got a nice voice."

"Thank you." She looked down, a faint reddening in her cheeks.

"Can I help you with that?" Bart asked, gesturing to the pile of clothes.

"Help? No, that wouldn't do. It couldn't... You're a guest, sir."

"Don't know if you've noticed, but me and Spencer ain't your usual house guests."

She giggled and then stopped herself with a hand over her mouth.

"You've got a nice laugh," Bart said.

"Thank you."

They stood in awkward silence for a moment, then the girl said, "If it is all right with you, sir, I'll get back to my work."

"Of course. I just wondered though if I could talk to you. You know, about the stuff that went on the other night?"

"Yes sir," she said.

"Please," he said. "Call me Bart. Ain't never been a 'sir' in me life. Anyway, did you hear anything the other night? You know, anything weird that might be part of what happened to Mister Bishop?"

She shuddered. "I heard that horrible howling, if that's what you mean."

"Happen a lot, does it?"

"Sometimes. Not that often. Mister Wilbur, he says he thinks it's just some sort of wild animal, trapped or in pain or something. Maybe caught in some nasty poacher's trap."

"Are poachers a problem round here?"

"So I hear. Not really something I get involved in though."

"'Course. So the howling noise. How often you heard it, before last night?"

"Once or twice."

"When did it start?"

"First time I heard it? Probably about a week ago. It was just after the demon who Wilbur had working for him left."

"Could it be the demon making that noise?"

"What, Trevor? Doubt it. Never one for making noises, was Trevor. And after the way he'd been treated by that man, wasn't much chance of him wanting to come back here."

"What do you mean?"

"Oh. Nothing. I meant nothing, sir."

"But what man was it? Wilbur? I thought he didn't want to see him go."

"No, he didn't—"

"Then one of the toffs? Lord B?"

"No, I... I should not be talking to you about this. Please, leave me alone."

Bart stood there, staring at her for a moment and then bowed his head. "Sorry, miss. Didn't mean to upset you. And don't want to get you in trouble. I'll be off."

He lumbered out of the door, leaving the maid breathing shakily behind him as she checked around to make sure they had not been overheard.

Chapter Twenty-Two

Tess found herself at a loose end, wandering aimlessly through the corridors in the great hall. Many of the rooms and spaces held old memories for her, the echoes of feet running up and down stairs, of giggles and games, of happy days charging through a house that always felt full of life.

She was used to adulthood taking the shine from childhood memories, but there was something much more abrupt and melancholy about how different Flint Hall was from the playground of her memories. And the people... It was almost impossible to reconcile the family she had known, not that long ago, with the bitter, paranoid shells which now inhabited the Hall.

Lord Beaumont had always been aloof and remote—that was the way of the patriarchs of such families, after all—and Calvin had always been an insufferable boor. But Emilia and her mother had been a key part of her happiest childhood memories.

On a whim, she found herself wandering upstairs, to where the guest quarters had always been. Funny that she had not been offered one of those rooms this time, even though they had been clear that there were no other guests in the house.

She made her way onto the landing, expecting to find it mothballed or damaged. But it seemed to be as well kept as the rest of the house; that was to say, not pristine, but not showing signs that it had been left empty for ages. In fact, the lack of dust showed that it was still being cleaned regularly. But why, if there was no one staying there? It was not as though the Hall was overrun with servants; if they were being run as efficiently as she knew Lady Beaumont liked to run her household, then such vacant spaces would be left alone, rather than waste time cleaning it.

She remembered on the first morning, when they were going out to the woods, seeing what she thought was a face at one of the upper floor rooms, one of the rooms on this very floor. In fact, she remembered the house well enough to know which room it must have been; the way the trees grew at the rear of the house meant that there was only one room on that floor with a clear line of sight all the way down the garden to the point where she would have seen it.

She counted the doors and ended on the one she knew would have been the location of the mysterious observer, if one existed. There was, of course, every chance it had just been a trick of the light or a product of her imagination. But she had precious little else to do with her time right now. And she was pretty sure that, in the world of being a detective, it was important to investigate every occurrence, no matter how strange and unrelated it might seem.

She tried the handle; the door was unlocked. The room beyond was thick with half-light; the curtains pulled only partly back, as though the inhabitant was still forcing themselves awake through a particularly tricky hangover.

She looked round the room; it was thankfully unoccupied. The bed, though, showed signs of having been slept in, the bedclothes rumpled and pulled partway back. While this could have simply been a failure to tidy up after some historic occupant, that was at odds with the way the rest of the floor seemed to have been regularly cleaned and tidied. So whoever had slept in that bed had done so very recently.

She walked over to the window. If she had really seen someone watching from there, the curtains must have been pulled further back from their current position; yet more evidence pointing to someone having been in that room in the past twenty-four hours.

There were some papers on the desk, although from close inspection they were a blank pile of plain white writing paper. She picked up the top sheet, held it up to the light, and then rolled it up and pushed it up her sleeve.

She wandered over to the wardrobe, but before she could open it, she saw something which made her stop and gasp. She stared at it for a long moment, her mouth working soundlessly while her heart pumped loudly in her ears.

A sound from the landing outside broke her out of her tortured reverie, and she darted to the door, breaking into a sprint towards the stairs which then turned into as close an approximation of a saunter as she approached them.

Mr Smith almost collided with her, coming the other way.

"Lady Marchant," he said. "What are you doing up here?"

"I am sorry," she said. "I appear to have got myself quite turned around. This place can be such a maze, can it not?"

He peered past her. "This floor is out of use, ma'am. None of us are allowed up here. The servants rarely venture here."

"Really? I am sorry. May I ask why?"

He cleared his throat. "That's one for the Lord and Lady to answer, begging your pardon. I would not presume to reply. But we don't come up here. Not to clean or nothing. I was only coming up here because I heard a sound, which I presume was you."

"That is probably the case," she said. "Although I thought I heard something up here. Are you sure no one is staying here?"

"Not for many months, if not years, ma'am." He shifted his stance, hiding something behind his back. "Now please, can I escort you downstairs?"

"Escort?" smiled Tess. "So formal. Is there danger up here? My, how exciting."

"Nothing exciting, ma'am. I just... worry. This floor is not visited much." He leant forwards. "There is a risk of pests, such as wasps' nests, or spiders, or bats. I would not want you to be surprised."

"If you had not heard," she said with a smile, "I and my colleagues are demon hunters. It has been some time since I have been frit of insects, arachnids or flying things."

The smile he gave in response showed exactly what he thought of her bravado. "Of course, ma'am. But even so, if you would come this way..."

She dodged his hand. "It is quite all right, Mr Smith. I know the way down. I will not deter you from whatever duties you have up there." She marched down the stairs before he had a chance to respond.

She reached the bottom and looked back to see him ducking out of sight, having clearly been watching her to make sure she was actually heading away. She shook her head and then made her way along the corridor.

Before she reached the sitting room, she could hear the shouting. Lady Beaumont's voice was the first one she heard, although she could not quite make out the content of what she said. But there was no doubting the intent of her words; an indignant shriek.

"And so I am supposed to just put up with that?" Calvin's voice rang out in response.

"You will do what we tell you," Lady Beaumont said in a raised voice.

"Hah! Or what? You will do for me like—"

"That is enough" bellowed Lord Beaumont. "I will not have you talking to your mother—"

"Like you do?" Calvin laughed in an exaggerated manner. "I am so sorry, father. I would hate to outdo you."

"That is enough!"

A scrape of chair legs and a few forceful footsteps gave the impression of Lord Beaumont standing to physically confront his son.

"None of your business!" The man's voice rang out, slightly muffled through the thick door.

There followed more heated words, although the content was

not clear from where Tess stood. She edged closer in the hope of making more out, while keeping half an eye on where she had come from, in case Mr Smith was following her.

"Ungrateful... Own good... For best..."

She ducked out of sight just as the door was flung open and Calvin charged out, thankfully choosing to storm off in the opposite direction to where Tess was hiding. As he marched away, something dropped from his pocket. Tess crept forward and picked it up; it was a piece of jewellery, like a broach, and the design on it was very familiar.

Chapter Twenty-Three

As he was walking towards the kitchen, Bart heard the sound of crying. He stopped and listened, then opened the door nearest to him. Bev quickly turned her back as soon as the light hit her.

"Hey, what's going on?" he asked.

"Nothing. Please leave me alone." She sniffed.

"Sorry love. Hate to call a lady a liar, but I heard you crying from out there. What's the matter."

"I'm... Not a lady, sir. I'm just a..."

Bart shuffled into the room, raised a hand as if to stroke her face, but stopped when she recoiled violently away from him.

"It's all right," he said. "I'm not going to hurt you. I just want to help. And don't ever say you're 'just' anything. You're... a really nice person."

She smiled. "I'm sorry. I just." She took a handful of gulping breaths. "I would really like some water."

"I'll get you some. Wait here." He ran off, returning a few minutes later with a glass which was overflowing with water.

She eyed it. "I can't drink out of that. That's one of the family's glasses."

"I won't tell," he said. "Drink."

She did so, and then perched on a stool in the corner while she regained her breath. "I am sorry. I did not mean to back away from you. I know you are not someone who would do me harm. I just... I have fears."

"Fears of what?"

"It's nothing."

"By the look of you, I know you're lying. Begging your pardon and all that. But I don't believe you."

She cleared her throat and looked down. "I cannot. It would not be proper. You do not understand."

Bart stared at her for a moment. "I'm not the brightest of fellers, but I know a thing or two about people. I've been around enough ladies who've been badly treated by a man to know one when I see one. And the way you've been acting and hiding away, I'd say it's not Mr Smith or Wilbur or any of the other staff. I'd say it's one of the blokes in the family."

She flinched, but still kept her eyes rooted to the floor.

"So I'm right," he said. "Which one?"

She shook her head. "I cannot."

"Look," Bart said. "I can help. I can stick around you, make sure nothing happens."

She looked up, tears in her eyes. "You cannot. You cannot be with me all the time. And what of when you leave? I will be alone here again."

"I could take you with us."

"And do what? I'm no use to anyone. Not like this." She turned and pulled down the back of her top to reveal angry red welts criss-crossing her skin.

"Who did this?" Bart asked, a cold venom in his voice.

"I cannot tell. The brother, he would—"

"So it's him." Bart turned and marched out, ignoring her muffled cries from behind him.

He passed Spencer a little way down the hall. "All right, mate. What's going on?"

"Where's Calvin?" Bart asked. When Spencer stared at him he said louder, "Where's that snivelling coward Calvin?"

"I don't know. I think he went out. What's going on, Bart? What are you doing?"

"Going to sort something out," he said, starting in the direction of the kitchen.

Spencer darted in front of him. "Hey, mate. I don't know

what's going on, but I know that face, and I know it never ends with anything good. You should think before you do anything too..."

"Get out of my way, or I'll put you down. This is important."

"Let's talk about it, all right? Let's calm down and—"

"Don't want to be calm. Something I need to do before it's too late." The sound of sobbing caught their attention. "If you want to be useful, look after her, back there."

Spencer looked in the direction of the sobbing. "But..." He looked back; Bart was already halfway down the corridor. "Bloody hell," he muttered, heading in the direction of the sobbing.

*

"Calvin!" Bart bellowed as he ran out of the kitchen door into the deepening twilight, leaving Mrs Smith and the rest of the staff staring after him.

He peered around the gardens, his eyes slowly adjusting to the darkness. He saw a figure disappearing through the entrance to the woods at the far side of the garden, and he started in that direction. His foot skidded on the damp grass and he slid sideways, landing with a wet thud on the muddy ground. He swore under his breath and then scrabbled to his feet, wiping the dirt from his hands onto his trousers.

He dimly heard his name being shouted from the house behind him, but he was solely focused on catching up with Calvin. Rage consumed him as the image of the sobbing girl played through his mind over and over again.

He reached the gate and stormed through, the hinges squealing as he shouted Calvin's name again. But his voice was drowned out by another noise: a deep, vicious snarling roar, followed by a strangled yell which was cut short almost as soon as it had begun.

That snapped Bart out of the red mist. He blinked, suddenly

regaining control of himself and realising where he was. He was on the edge of the woods, alone and unarmed, and the demon was somewhere nearby. He could imagine what Spencer would say to him, berating him for his stupidity and hot-headedness. He should do the sensible thing, turn around and go back to safety, if only to get a weapon.

But the demon was out there, and so was Calvin. Was that his cry he had heard? He looked around for something he could use to defend himself, picking up a thick branch and testing it against a nearby tree. It splintered, but did leave a jagged edge which could at least cause a bit of damage.

"Bart!" he turned to see Tess running across the lawn. "Bart, where are you?"

"I'm here," he said, stepping back through the gate. "Stay back. I heard the demon, and I think Calvin might be with it."

"Wait," she said. She put something into his pocket.

"What's that?" he asked.

"Just something that might help," she said.

"What? A weapon?" He pulled it out, turning it in his hand. "A badge?"

"Just something Calvin dropped."

"You want me to give it back to him?"

"Take it with you," she said. "Keep it with you. It is very important that you do so. Understand?"

"All right. I need to go. You wait here, yeah?"

He plunged into the trees before he could change his mind, or she could try changing it for him.

His breath was loud in his ears as he pushed through the branches, each contact making him tense in anticipation of the attack which was surely coming at any moment.

Bart burst into the clearing where they had found Bishop just a few nights earlier, holding his improvised wooden weapon above his head, ready to strike.

At first, it appeared to be empty, and he blinked as he looked around in confusion.

And then he noticed the bloodied and broken form on the ground.

"Oh, bugger," he said.

Chapter Twenty-Four

"Looks like he's not been dead for long," said the police constable, standing over the body.

"How can you tell?" asked Tess.

"Look at his arms and legs," said Spencer. "Not rigid enough." He looked up at them. "Not my first dead body," he explained.

"Indeed," said the constable. He turned to Tess. "Madam, once more I really must insist… this is no place for a lady."

"In case I come over all faint and peculiar?" she snapped. "Because of my delicate disposition? Because of my being a member of the inferior sex?"

"Not inferior," the constable stammered. "Just…"

"I'd give up if I were you," grinned Spencer. "She's not going to budge. And to be honest, she'll be a lot more use to you here than most others. We're a demon hunting agency, you see."

The constable stared at him. "I thought you were joking."

"We never joke. Not about stuff like this."

He looked from one to the other and then shrugged. "And you were the ones who found him?"

"Yeah. I was," said Bart. "I heard something, came to see what was what, found him like this. And that there, and there." He pointed at where the rest of the corpse's remains had been scattered.

"Well," said Tess, "at least this answers the question of what we are dealing with here. The way he was ripped to pieces certainly looks like it was done by a demon."

"Oh, before I forget, this is yours," said Bart, handing Tess the amulet.

"Thank you," she said.

"What's that?" asked the policeman.

"Oh, nothing," Tess said quickly before Bart could answer. "Just an heirloom of mine, which Bart was looking after for me."

"Very well." He turned back to Bart. "Was anyone with you when you found the body?"

"I was," said Tess.

"Well, not really," Bart said. "I told you to stay back, didn't I? In the garden. Didn't want you to be in danger in case the demon was still here."

"So you were alone when you came into the clearing with," he checked his notes, "a bloody big stick. No one else could verify that the victim was dead by the time you got here."

Bart blinked at him. "You think I did this?"

"I don't think anything," said the policeman. "I've sent for an inspector from Scotland Yard, and until he gets here, you're all suspects and I'll ask you all to remain in the Hall."

"But—" started Bart.

"And given that you were the last to see the victim alive, and was the one who found the body, it's especially important that the inspector speaks to you." He pointed at Bart. "So no attempts to do a runner, or I'll be forced to arrest you."

"Nice," said Spencer. "You give that speech to everyone, or have you saved it just for us, given who we are?"

The policeman leant in. "And what exactly do you mean? Is there something about your background that is of relevance here? Anything you'd like to admit to now, before the inspector arrives?"

"No, no," said Tess quickly, shepherding her two colleagues away. "Nothing at all. It's just the shock, you understand. No one wants to find a dead body. I will take them back to the house now, and we'll wait on your inspector. It is late, so we should get some sleep, anyway. Thank you so much, constable."

"He was accusing us of stuff, just because we're—" started Spencer.

"Shut up!" she hissed. "Do you enjoy being arrested? Does playing the bad guy, being the centre of attention, give you some sort of twisted pleasure? We're here to investigate, not to be the prime suspects!"

*

The next morning they all gathered in the sitting room of the Hall, waiting on the imminent arrival of the inspector from Scotland Yard.

Lord and Lady Beaumont sat in high-backed chairs at opposite ends of the room. The Lady was in floods of tears, being comforted by a similarly distraught Emilia, with Mrs Smith hovering just behind them with a seemingly endless supply of handkerchiefs.

Lord Beaumont was studiously ignoring everyone as he hid behind a large newspaper, trying to keep up the pretence that this was simply a day just like any other.

Ralph paced the floor in front of the window. "I do not know why we all need to wait here, and with them," he nodded at Tess, Spencer and Bart. "It clearly had nothing to do with us, and it is clear who did commit the murder."

"What you trying to say?" asked Bart.

"I am not *trying* to say anything," Ralph sneered. "I am stating that you murdered Calvin. It is as plain as the nose on your face."

Bart put a hand to his nose and then shook his head. "You've got it wrong. I was the one that found him. He was all dead and torn to pieces by the time I got there."

Lady Beaumont let out a shriek at these words.

"Have some care," snapped Emilia. "This is my brother, her son, you are talking about."

"Sorry," said Bart. "But it weren't me, it was the demon."

Ralph snorted.

"Hang on, though," said Spencer. "You lot've been so keen to tell us there's a demon stalking your family, ever since we got here. We all heard it last night, just like the night when Jack Butler was attacked. Which you were so keen to believe was a demon. But as soon as it's one of your own who's attacked, suddenly it's our fault?"

Tess put a hand on his arm and shushed him.

"But…" said Spencer.

Tess shook her head. "Not now," she said. "Now's not the time."

Spencer looked around the room, at the grieving family, and nodded. "Point taken."

They lapsed back into an uneasy silence.

The doorbell rang and the atmosphere in the room grew even tenser, Lord Beaumont jumping out of his seat before lowering himself back down. "Mr Smith will answer it," he muttered.

They listened to the sound of the servant's feet echoing on the hall floor, making their measured way from the servants' landing up to the hall and then across. It felt as though ice ages came and went as he made his slow progress, finally ending at the front door. The door creaked open and there was a muffled conversation, followed by the slamming shut of the door.

They all held their breaths as they watched the door to the hallway, counting the steps as they approached. Finally it swung open to reveal Mr Smith, who stepped aside to announce the arrival of the police inspector.

"Well, well, well," said Inspector Jones as he fixed his eyes on Spencer and Bart. "What a surprise to see you two here."

"Uh?" said Bart.

"Bugger," said Spencer.

Chapter Twenty-Five

Inspector Jones requisitioned the dining room to question the suspects, and the first one invited in was, naturally, Bart.

"Take a seat," Jones said, gesturing to the other side of the table.

Bart did as he was told, glancing over his shoulder at the constable stood behind him. "Do I need to be worried?" he asked.

"I don't know," said Jones. "Do you think you need to be worried?"

Bart shrugged. "It's just you asked me here first, there's a plod breathing down my neck and another one outside the door. That sort of thing makes me a bit twitchy."

"I am sure it does. Why don't we start by you telling me what happened last night?"

"I found a dead body."

"Yes, all right. Let's go back a bit further. Why were you out there in the first place?"

"I was going after Calvin."

"Why?"

"I found the maidservant really upset. She said Calvin'd done something to her."

"And that upset you?"

"I was bloody furious! I don't like blokes hurting women. It's not right. Especially when they can't fight back."

"Which she couldn't?"

"Well, no. What's she going to do? Get herself fired?"

"So what were you planning to do, when you went after

Calvin?"

"Don't really know. Didn't think that far ahead; truth is, I don't tend to think ahead much normally. Not that kind of bloke."

"So you were going to have a word with him."

Bart spread his hands on the table. "Look at me. I'm not the kind of bloke to have words. I was ready to kick his head in."

Jones stared at him and then shook his head in wonder. "So you admit you wanted to do harm to him."

"Yeah, of course. But then I was running out there, just got through the gate, and I heard it."

"What?"

"The demon."

"Demon," said Jones, deadpan.

"Yeah. The one that killed Calvin. I heard it, this huge roar and then someone shouted out, like he'd been attacked. Reckon that was Calvin."

"And then what did you do?"

"Well, that shocked me, you know. Suddenly realised what I was doing. 'Being an idiot' is what Spencer'd say. Out there without a weapon or nothing, and a demon somewhere in front of me. So I grabbed a bit of wood and went in, and then I found Calvin's body."

"And no demon?"

"Nope. Must've run away before I got there."

"Demons often do that? Run away, rather than wait around and try killing you, too?"

"Well, no. But if it was afraid of being hurt it might."

"You think it was afraid?"

"Dunno. I didn't see it, remember?"

Jones sighed. "All right. So there were no other witnesses?"

"Well, no. Not when I first found him. Not that I knew, anyway. But Tess saw me before I went in."

"Tess? You mean Lady Marchant?"

"Yeah, that's her. She told me I could call her Tess." He

beamed proudly. "She ran out after me. I told her to stay in the garden when I went in, and then I found the body."

"So she saw you beforehand? And she will be able to confirm exactly when you ran into the woods, and how long you were in there?"

"Yeah. I came out and got her as soon as I found the body; she ran and raised the alarm. And then everyone started blaming me."

"Why do you think that is?"

He shrugged. "They don't like me. I'm an outsider."

"And you were the one who not only found the body, but also ran out after him, before he was killed, wanting to do him harm."

"I didn't say I wanted to hurt him. I just... All right, maybe I wanted to hurt him a bit. But I got over it. As soon as I realised the demon was out there."

"Yes. So you said." Jones read through his notes and then looked him straight in the eyes. "I need you to tell me the truth here. Did you kill Calvin?"

"No! Haven't you been listening to what I've been saying? It was the demon!"

"Which you didn't see."

"No, but what else do you think would make those noises and do that sort of damage to a bloke? You see all the claw marks on him?" He held up his hands. "These look like claws to you? And the way he was all ripped up; I'm strong, but I ain't that strong!"

*

"All them people in there," said Spencer, "and you decided to interview us first."

"I wonder why," said Inspector Jones, leaning back in his chair.

"It's victimisation, that's what this is."

"I prefer to call it common sense. There's a murder in a quiet, sleepy village. I arrive at a sedate country house, full of upstanding citizens, and who do I find there but two ragamuffins who cause nothing but trouble wherever they go. And one of them was the one who found the body. Doesn't take a genius to piece this one together."

"Yeah, well, if you know anything about us, you'll know we've never been in the murdering game. And definitely not the type of murder that happened to that poor bloke."

Jones tipped his head slightly. "Let's start at the beginning. What are you two doing here?"

"Working."

"What kind of working?"

"The legitimate type. We've gone straight, just like I told you."

Jones wrote slowly and deliberately on a notepad. "Let's just say for the moment that I believe you. What sort of work are you doing here?"

"Demon hunting. You've seen our business cards."

"Ah yes. The 'Great Big Demon Hunting Agency'. Snappy name."

"Thanks," beamed Spencer, oblivious to the sarcasm in Jones's voice.

Jones stared at him for a moment. "So you are here to hunt demons?"

"Kind of." Spencer leaned back in his chair and crossed his legs. "We was hired by this family—well, by Miss Emilia, to be exact—to help them with a problem that they thought was to do with demons. You see, they've got a little curse thing going on here."

"A curse," Jones deadpanned again.

"Yeah. Apparently, they're worried that, when her dad turns sixty in a couple of days' time, some demon's going to turn up and kill him."

"Would that be the same 'demon' that killed his son, Calvin

Beaumont, last night?"

Spencer nodded. "Looks that way."

Jones scribbled on his notepad. "Where were you last night?"

"You mean around the time Bart found the body? I was with that maidservant."

Jones made a note. "Why were you with her? And what were you doing?"

"I was trying to calm her down. She was in a state."

"Why was that?"

"Don't know. She wouldn't tell me. Although I think it had something to do with Calvin. At least, that's what Bart thought."

"So Bart was there as well?"

"No. Bart had gone running off after Calvin. He told me to look after the girl as he went running off."

"So you went to the maidservant rather than with your friend."

"Yeah. Well, he asked me to. And he can look after himself."

"What would you say Bart's state of mind was, when he went running off?"

"He just wanted to talk to Calvin."

"Really?"

"Yeah. He was really calm and stuff."

"So he wasn't agitated, cross, angry? None of that?"

"No. 'Course not."

"Because he told me he was—" Jones flicked back a couple of pages in his notebook "—'bloody furious'."

Spencer stared at him for a moment. "He said that?"

"He did."

Spencer swore. "This is why I'm the one who does the talking! So he doesn't incriminate himself like that!"

"You do realise that lying to me doesn't help your case?"

"Never hurt us in the past," Spencer smirked.

Jones cleared his throat and stared at him. "You tell me that you are trying to turn over a new leaf, to be fine upstanding citizens."

"We are."

"So why don't you start by answering my questions properly, rather than treating this like a game? If you've got nothing to hide, like you claim, then there's no harm in telling the truth, is there?"

Spencer frowned and then bobbed his head in vague agreement. "I suppose you're right. Sorry. Force of habit, you know. But you can't blame me for wanting to protect him."

"Let's try again. What exactly happened when and after you saw Bart."

"All right. So I was walking along the hall, going to get ready for dinner, and then Bart came barging along towards me, face like thunder. I asked him what was going on, and he just told me to look after the girl."

"And by 'the girl', he meant the maidservant?"

"Yeah. That was who he was talking about. She was in a right state. Wouldn't talk to me though. Just kept saying about how it wasn't him, but wouldn't really tell me anything else about what she meant. She was in a right state, though, so I could see why Bart wasn't happy."

"Keen on her, is he?"

"Yeah, but it's not just that. He's got a thing about not liking blokes beating up on girls. Never has done."

"That's understandable. So he thought Calvin was mistreating the maidservant?"

"That's what he said. But look, even though he was angry, he'd never kill for that. Rough him up, yeah, but not kill him."

"He's a strong lad though, isn't he?"

"Yeah…"

"Wouldn't take much for him to do serious damage, if he was out of control."

"Not the sort of damage done to Calvin though. That was definitely a demon. You just have to look at the body to know that."

*

"You are really working with those two individuals?" Jones asked Tess as she sat down opposite him.

"I am. We are business partners."

"How do you...? I mean, you seem to be an intelligent woman, someone of good standing."

"Thank you."

"I just do not know how you can put up with them on a daily basis."

"Let us just say they have hidden depths," she said. "Was everything acceptable, what they told you?"

"Spencer was remarkably cooperative, something I've not been used to from him. I have no reason to think that he was hiding anything from me. At least, not so far. Bart was..." He shook his head. "I am not quite sure what to think. But I am hoping that, speaking with you, I may get closer to the nub of the matter."

"I will be happy to help in any manner I can."

"Good. Well, you can start by telling me why you are here, and what has transpired thus far."

"We are here because we were invited, by the family."

"Invited?" asked Jones. "How so?"

"We have been engaged by them in a professional capacity, to assist them with a rather delicate matter."

"Namely?"

She stared at him. "That is a private matter."

He shut his notebook and lent forward. "Lady Marchant, you need to understand that we are essentially on the same side here. In spite of what your... ah... colleagues may say, I am not the devil. I am trying to do my job, and it would be a lot easier for all of us if you did not put barriers in the way of me doing so. So, unless you are the person who committed the murder—and I very much doubt that you are—then surely it is in as much your interests as it is mine for me to get to the bottom of what happened last night, find the person responsible, and bring them to justice before they have a chance to hurt anyone else. Do we understand each other?"

Tess cleared her throat. "Perfectly," she said, her cheeks reddening. "And for the record I am not trying to be in any way obstructive. I am simply thinking of the interests of my clients."

"Given that the murder happened on their estate, the victim was a member of their family, and all this has led to them being held here until I understand what has occurred, surely it is not in their interests for you to withhold information from me."

Tess pursed her lips and then nodded. "Very well. I was approached by Emilia a few days ago. She came to our offices in London and asked us to help the family with an issue relating to a family curse." She paused, searching his face for any sign of ridicule or disbelief. "They believe that there is a curse which results in the death of the Lord of the Manor on his sixtieth birthday."

"And Lord Beaumont's sixtieth birthday is…?"

"The day after tomorrow."

"Why you?"

"Pardon?"

"Why did they approach you for help?"

"You would have to ask Emilia, but I am known to the family—I grew up near here and my family was friendly with the Beaumonts. I believe they have sought assistance from others, including the police, but with little effect. You and your colleagues are of course not really interested in the *idea* of a crime; but by the time the deed has been done and you are in a position to investigate, it would be too late. For Lord Beaumont, anyway. When they heard that I had established a business in the demon hunting arena, they thought I might be able to help."

"So you believe that this is a demon curse, then."

"Possibly. They do not really seem to know; aside from some tales of seeing large figures and hearing loud and terrifying howling at night."

"Howling? Like a wolf or some other kind of wild animal?"

"Maybe. We only arrived the other day, so opportunities for us to dig into the matter have been rather limited."

"What were your movements last night?"

"I was going down to dinner. I heard some commotion, saw Calvin storm out of the sitting room, then Bart run from the servants' area. I went after them to see what was going on, and I then encountered Spencer, who told me Bart was upset with Calvin. I went after them and caught up with Bart at the edge of the gardens."

"Before he confronted Calvin?"

"That is correct."

"Are you sure?"

"Positive. I had him in view at all times. Before he could go into the woods, after Calvin, we heard the demon."

"The demon."

"Yes, the demon we have come here to stop. And which killed Calvin."

"Did you see it?"

"No."

"Then how did you know it was a demon?"

She rested her elbows on the table, steepling her fingers and resting her chin on them as she stared at him. "Inspector Jones, my line of work requires me to recognise a demonic roar when I hear one. And, trust me, I have heard more than my fair share over the past few months. I do not think that anyone can be in any doubt that what we heard was a demon, the same one that the Beaumont family have been hearing on a regular basis recently. It does not require a huge leap of imagination to come to the conclusion that not only was what we heard a demon, but also that it had something to do with the terrible demise of poor Calvin Beaumont. Especially given the state of his body."

Jones cleared his throat. "So you heard a noise which you believed to be a demon. What then?"

"Bart had paused and picked up a thick branch, presumably

to defend himself. I spoke to him, and he told me to stay where I was. He went into the woods, and then a few minutes later he reemerged, telling me that he had found a dead body."

"And how long was he out of your sight?"

"No more than a couple of minutes. Long enough for him to reach the clearing, see the body and then come back. Not long enough to stage a demonic-style killing, if that is what you are asking."

Jones ignored the edge in her voice. "And did you hear anything while he was gone?"

"The sound of him ripping a man to pieces, you mean? No. And he was unbloodied as well, which everyone else will attest to."

Jones made another note in his book. "So the family were all very mindful of the risk of a demonic encounter if they ventured out at night. Do you have any idea why Calvin stormed out the way he did?"

Tess shrugged and looked down. Jones let the silence stretch between them until she finally spoke. "I overheard an argument between Calvin and his parents. I did not gather exactly what they were fighting about, but that was why Calvin stormed out."

"Had you noticed any tensions between Calvin and his family before then?"

Tess pulled a face. "Is this conversation confidential?"

"You are worried about offending your hosts?"

"They are also old family friends."

"Lady Marchant, I am here to do a job: to discover what happened to Calvin Beaumont and, if there was a murder, to apprehend the guilty party. If it were to transpire that you withheld some information from me, no matter how trivial it may seem, and by so doing it led to another member of the family being murdered… Well, would you be able to live with yourself?"

"I suppose not."

He leaned forward. "I assure you that I am a professional.

I will treat anything I am told with the utmost discretion, and will seek to preserve confidences wherever I can. But rest assured that, if you deliberately withhold something which could have assisted with my investigation, then I will not hesitate to bring the full force of the law on you. Do you understand?"

She glared at him. "You do not need to threaten me, Inspector. I want the same as you; to find the guilty party and ensure that there are no other attacks."

He nodded and waited for her to continue.

"I had noticed some tension between Calvin and his sister, Emilia," she said. "Although that had always been the case, even when they were children. You know how siblings can be. And he was rather cold towards his parents, even before the argument I overheard."

"Was there any particular tension or words which struck you as unusual, since you arrived here?"

"Calvin did seem rather detached from everything. He was drunk for most of the time we saw him, making snide comments to anyone and everything."

"So he was unhappy, maybe?"

"Maybe. Or he had developed an unhealthy relationship with drink. Some people can be nasty drunks, as you know. I had not seen him since he was a little boy, so I could not say whether that is his usual behaviour. I do know that Emilia did not take too kindly to the way he acted. She upbraided him on a number of occasions. In particular she felt he did not seem to be taking this demonic curse seriously."

"He didn't believe there was a curse?"

"He seemed rather dismissive." She frowned. "There was a short altercation between them about their inheritance; it seemed to me that Calvin was implying that Emilia and her husband-to-be were almost willing there to be a curse, so that they would inherit on Lord Beaumont's death."

"Presumably Calvin would have benefited as well," said Jones.

"Probably. I do not know what arrangements Lord Beaumont

195

has made. But now that Emilia is the sole child, presumably she inherits the lot."

"And she is not yet married?"

"Not yet; but soon to be married."

"Do you know when?"

"No."

"You have not had an invite?"

Tess shook her head, her cheeks reddening. "We were childhood friends, Emilia and I, but we have lost contact in recent years. It was somewhat of a surprise when she arrived at our offices to ask us to help her."

"And the argument you overheard; you have no idea what it was about?"

"No. I turned up just as they were finishing. I recall something said about... Yes, that was it. Calvin's parting words as he left the room were something along the lines of him refusing to take part in their games. Something like that."

"Their 'games'? Any idea what that could be?"

"I assume it is to do with society matters. There are so many hoops to jump through, parties and dinners to attend. Calvin did not strike me as the type to relish attending such things."

"One sympathises," said Jones.

She looked at him. "I can assure you that, while it may sound far from drudgery, being forced to attend one event after another, making conversation with the arrogant bores who frequent high society... Let us just say I am much happier in the company of Spencer and Bart, fighting demons."

Jones chuckled. "I am sure you are. Finally, what is your perception of Bart's character?"

"You mean, could he have killed Calvin? No. He may be a huge hunk of a man, and can be slow-witted, but he is soft at heart. He would only kill if there was no alternative; and as I said, not even he would surely be capable of the wounds inflicted on Calvin's body."

Jones checked his notes. "There was another incident, though, was there not? A couple of nights ago; a poacher badly beaten up in pretty much the same spot? And wasn't Bart the first on the spot again that time?"

"Yes..."

"And the first person to the scene of that crime was again your friend Bart."

"It was, but…"

"And the injuries to that poor man, from what I can tell, were consistent with something a man of Bart's size could inflict."

"He did not, though. And anyway, what motivation would he have to do such a thing?"

"I do not know, Lady Marchant. But that is one of the things I am seeking to understand."

*

The maidservant sat down opposite Inspector Jones, perched on the edge of her seat and playing with the edge of her apron. She stared down at the table, her cheeks red and her eyes brimming with tears.

"Miss Turner," Jones said in as gentle a voice as he could muster. "I appreciate this is all very overwhelming for you."

"I am sorry, sir," she said quietly. "I'm not used to speaking much with folk, you see. 'Specially not policemen."

"Do not worry. You are not in trouble. But I do need to understand what happened last night, from your perspective."

"I did not see the… thing that happened," she said quickly.

"I know. But you did see other things. You were with Bart, just before he left the house."

She shot a darting look around the room, as though she was looking for a way out.

"I have been told as much by the others," said Jones. "You are not betraying any confidences by telling me."

"I… was."

"Good. So tell me, in your own words, what happened."

Again, she looked around.

Jones sighed. "I am a reasonable man," he said, "but I am also a professional with a job to do. And as a result my patience is not limitless. Answer my questions and we'll get along just fine. But if you don't, or if you lie to me, or delay, and I will have no choice but to arrest you." He leaned forward. "You ever been to prison?"

She shook her head.

"No," he said. "I can see you're a good girl. So do yourself a favour; tell me exactly what happened, and you won't have to worry about going there."

She took a deep, shaking breath. "I was doing some housework. Bart came to see me. I… I was crying and he wanted to know what was the matter."

"And what was the matter?"

She shrugged. "Nothing."

"You were upset. Upset enough to make someone like Bart wonder what was wrong with you. And you say it was over nothing?"

"It was nothing, really. I just sometimes get upset by stuff."

"What in particular upset you this time?"

"I can't remember." She looked down at the table.

"I need you to tell me the truth. This could be important."

"It's not. It's nothing. Please can I go, sir?"

"No. Not yet."

"After Bart left you, I understand that Spencer came to be with you?"

"That's right. For a few minutes."

"A few minutes?"

"Yes, sir. He sat with me and then ran off as well. I'd pulled myself together by then."

"Where did he go?"

"Don't know, sir."

"All right. After speaking to you, Bart left the house and that led directly to him finding Calvin Beaumont's body. It is therefore important to know exactly what you told him."

"I didn't tell him anything, sir."

"Then why did he run out after Calvin?"

"I don't know. Honestly, I don't."

"So you didn't tell him Calvin was the one who had upset you?"

"No! Mr Calvin has never been anything but kind and a gentleman to me. He would never do anything to hurt me."

Jones stared at her. "And you are certain about that?"

"Completely! Sir, I would never suggest that Mr Calvin would do anything bad. To me, or anyone."

"So why did Bart seem to think that it was Calvin who had upset you?"

She blinked at him. "He said that?"

"Yes." Jones looked down at his notes and read, "He told me that you said Calvin had 'done something' to you, had 'done stuff' to you."

Her cheeks flushed even deeper. "No, that's not true."

"So you didn't say that?"

"No. Not about Calvin."

"About someone else?"

She looked around.

Jones closed his notebook and pushed it to the side. "Is there someone bothering you?"

She shook her head rapidly and stood up. "I would like to go now, please, sir." She ran out of the room before he had a chance to respond.

Chapter Twenty-Six

The silence stretched between the two sides of the room as they waited for Inspector Jones to finish interviewing the rest of the servants. The family had been in and out, one at a time, none of them adding much more to the picture.

Jones had asked Lord and Lady Beaumont about the row which Tess had overheard, but they had not been overly helpful. Lord Beaumont had straight out barked at the man that it was none of his business, while his wife had simply dissolved into inconsolable tears.

"Why can't we go?" Spencer asked. "He's already spoken to us. What's the point in us staying here."

"He told us to stay," said Tess.

"Yeah, but why?"

"Take a wild guess," said Ralph.

"What's that supposed to mean?"

They were interrupted by the door opening and they all turned to look, as Jones walked into the room, flanked by the two constables.

The constables were, between them, carrying a large axe, the blade of which was stained dark red. They laid it down on the ground with a loud and resounding *thunk*.

"Do you recognise this?" Jones asked Spencer and Bart.

They both shook their heads.

"Do you know where it was found?"

Spencer shrugged. "The garden shed?"

"Your room."

"Mine?" Spencer asked. "Not possible. I've not seen it before."

"Constable, please tell us where you found it," said Jones.

The first constable cleared his throat. "It was found in the room allocated to Spencer," he said.

"You planted it there. You're trying to frame me!"

"I was accompanied by my colleague, PC Anderton, and also the butler," said the constable. "They will bear witness to the fact that it was already in the room when we entered, together."

Mr Smith nodded. "It's true," he said, looking at the floor.

"And that looks suspiciously like blood on the blade," said Jones. "I would wager that it is human blood, from last night."

Lady Beaumont let out a low moan.

"My apologies, Lady Beaumont," Jones said. "But I believe we have found our murder weapon."

"Look at the size of it, compared to the size of me," protested Spencer. "I'd barely be able to lift it, let alone swing it and do any sort of damage!"

"Indeed," said Jones. "But *he* would. Wouldn't you, Bart."

Bart shrugged. "Looks like a good axe, that. But it ain't mine. Never seen it before."

Ralph bounced in his chair excitedly. "You talked about wanting to use an axe, when we went hunting! I remember now. It all makes perfect sense!"

"You are both under arrest," Jones said to Spencer and Bart.

Ralph let out a barking laugh. "I knew it!" He shared a grin with Lord Beaumont, who nodded approvingly.

"But… This ain't right," said Spencer. "We had nothing to do with it."

"We have witnesses who place you both at the scene. Not only of that crime but also the assault of Jack Bishop," said Jones.

"I was with the maid the whole time!" said Spencer.

"That's not what she said," said Jones. "You were only with her for a few minutes, and then you left her. You therefore had plenty of time for you to meet your accomplice and retrieve the axe to be taken into hiding. Meanwhile, Bart could reemerge into the garden, in full view of Lady Marchant and the rest of the house, and play the innocent who had found the body, rather than who you really were: the murderer."

Both men started to protest but were stopped by Jones holding up a hand. "Constables, take them away."

Spencer turned to Tess, his eyes wide. "Help us?"

Tess watched as they were led away. "Inspector…" she said.

"One moment please, Lady Marchant." He looked around the room and nodded. "I thank you all for your patience and assistance. There is not much else I can do today, so you are free to leave this room and go about your business; although I would ask that none of you leave the house or the village for the next few days, until I have finished my investigations."

"I have an appointment in London the day after tomorrow," said Lord Beaumont. "I will need to leave for that."

"I am afraid you will probably need to cancel that engagement," said Jones.

Lord Beaumont started to bluster at the impertinence of the man, but was cut short by the inspector raising his hand in the air. "I have to insist, sir," said Jones. "It is vitally important that I have access to all of you until I tell you otherwise. I appreciate that this is a troubling time, but I am willing to use the force of the law to compel you to do as I say. In any case, surely you want to be with your family, to comfort them at this time?"

Lord Beaumont looked around, his cheeks reddening, then pursed his lips and sat back in his chair, his arms folded tightly across his chest.

Lady Beaumont turned her tear-stained face to Tess. "I want you out of my house," she said.

"I am afraid I cannot allow that," said Jones. "She needs to stay here until I have finished my investigations. I want to know exactly where to find her, should I need to ask her any more questions."

"But this is preposterous!" said Lady Beaumont. "This is my house. You can't—"

"Mother," said Emilia. "Tess is our guest. Why are you…?"

"Guest!" she spat. "She brought those two thugs, who were responsible for what happened to poor Calvin! And she betrayed confidences. Listening in on private conversations..."

"Lady Beaumont, please forgive me," said Tess. "I was simply helping Inspector Jones with his inquiries. He said that anything that had happened could help. Surely you want to find out who... did what they did last night?"

"We already know!" she wailed.

Lord Beaumont walked over and bent down to whisper something in his wife's ear. After a moment, she gulped and then nodded, burying her face in her handkerchief once more.

"Please forgive my wife," he said. "You will appreciate that this is a traumatic day. Especially for the mother of..." He turned to Tess. "You are of course more than welcome to continue as our guest."

"Good," said Jones. "So that's settled then. I'll remind you all again to not stray too far. I may need to speak to you, and I do not want to be forced to traipse around the country to find you." He nodded and then left the room.

Tess sat, staring at the doorway, feeling the eyes of the others on her. Then she stood and walked out, heading down the hallway after the policemen and her friends.

"Inspector Jones," she said. "May I have a moment of your time before you go?"

He turned and looked at her, then nodded. "Of course." He gestured to the constables to continue on with Spencer and Bart. "I'll catch you up," he said to them. Then, to Tess, "How can I help?"

"Maybe we could walk and talk?" she asked, leading him away from the house. She glanced behind them, checking that they were out of earshot from the windows before starting to speak. "I am concerned that you are following the wrong lead here."

"Let me see," he said. "We are called to a house where there was an assault and then a murder, both of which happened shortly after two well-known criminals had been invited to stay. I don't think it's unreasonable for me to draw a conclusion here, don't you?"

"Ordinarily, maybe. But you're wrong."

"Please, do enlighten me."

"They really have turned over a new leaf. I know they did not do it."

He smiled thinly. "Your loyalty to them is touching, but totally misplaced. I do not think that you know them as well as you think you do."

"I would say the same to you."

He chuckled. "I admire your spirit. Really, I do. But how can you be so sure that they did not commit the two crimes? On both occasions, Bart was near or at the scene when the crime was committed."

"I told you: when Calvin was murdered, he was with me."

"Are you completely sure of that? You said yourself that he was out of your sight for at least a few minutes. Plenty of time for a hardened criminal—and a well-known bruiser—like Bart to commit murder."

"No. It was not them."

"And you would testify to that?"

She looked him in the eye. "Yes, I would."

They stood for a moment, staring at each other. Then Jones shook his head. "And that is why I am the professional and you are..."

"What?"

He opened and closed his mouth and then clearly thought better of responding. "I have to go."

"Why are you here, Inspector?" Tess asked.

He blinked at her. "There has been a murder. That is my job. To investigate murders."

"Yes, granted. But what I mean is, why are *you* here? Your usual area of work is London, is that not correct?"

"Well, yes. But it is not out of the ordinary for officers to be asked to assist other forces. Especially if there is a particularly complex case or something which falls within the officer's field of expertise."

"Like this case?"

"Exactly."

"Tell me, Inspector—and do forgive me for being blunt—but what is it about this case which falls under your field of expertise? Aside from the presence of my two friends, of course."

He snorted with laughter. "I can assure you that I am not here because of them. It is a mere coincidence."

"Then what is it about this case that meant that you should come so many miles to investigate it?"

"I..." He frowned. "I was told to come here."

"By your commanding officer?"

"Well, no. I told him I wished to be on this case. That I had to be the one assigned to it."

"Because you have dealt with demonic murders in the past?"

His cheeks flushed. "I am aware of them. Like any other London officer. There are a lot of demons in London, as you know."

"Indeed. So why you? Why not a different officer?"

"I..." He stopped and then shook his head. "I do not answer to you. And I have better things to do than continuing this conversation. Good day." He stomped off.

Tess watched him go, a thoughtful expression on her face.

Chapter Twenty-Seven

Tess watched the police and their captives disappear from view, clenching and unclenching her hands at her sides. She turned back to the house, pausing when she saw the faces at the window which immediately ducked away from view, no doubt red-faced at being caught in the act of watching her.

She took a deep breath. She could not bring herself to face the Beaumonts. Not yet. Maybe not ever again.

She turned and walked away from the house, idly picking her way along the gravel path. Everything around her—the trees, the midmorning sun, the birds in the sky and the ground beneath her feet—felt like it was a million miles away, happening to someone else.

She had not realised how much she relied on the presence of Spencer and Bart. But as soon as they had been taken away by the policemen, she had felt a deep sense of loss. It was amazing how, in a short space of time, she had found herself in a place where they were such an important part of her life.

She felt a rising sense of panic as she wondered what to do. Inspector Jones had clearly decided on their guilt, and all the evidence seemed to point to that. She knew that they were innocent, they had to be. But she had no way of proving it.

And anyway, who was she to try and prove anything? They were the police, the professionals here, while she was just... What? An heiress playing at being a demon hunter. Chasing after her own idea of respectability on her own terms, wanting people to look up to her as some sort of maverick scientific avenger. And what was her reason for doing this? To rail against the status quo, against the role she should have quietly assumed all those years ago. The role in life her parents always ordered her to adopt.

And what did she have to show for this hubris? An expensive office and a client list which was sparse at best, propped up by an inheritance which was being depleted by the day.

And now she had doomed her friends to the gallows for a crime they had not committed. All because she had wanted to prove to her old friend and her family that she was more than just a pathetic wastrel of a widow, that she was making something of her life, in spite of what they were all no doubt saying behind her back.

Her cheeks burned with the shame of it, of being found out for what she really was: a failure. Why could she not have done what any respectable lady would do in her position? Find an eligible bachelor or widower, get married, and settle into her proper place in life.

The thought brought an image to mind: her late husband's face, leering at her. Then it shifted to another, that of Emerson. The faces brought a different set of emotions to the fore: a shame of a different type, that of allowing herself to be beaten down, made to feel less than she was, mixed of course with a healthy dose of disgust.

She could almost hear their voices in her ears. *"Just a woman." "Know your place." "Do as you're told."* She felt the heat rising from the pit of her stomach, a rising tide filling her with the urge to run and hide. Or fight.

That was it. In a sudden moment of clarity, she realised what she had been doing wrong. Her parents, and then her husband, had died knowing nothing of what she was capable, mainly because they could not countenance the idea of her being more than the dutiful daughter and housewife. She had never been able to show them what she could do, so had for the past few months been trying to make up for lost time, to prove to anyone and everyone exactly who she was and why they were wrong to underestimate her.

She had been fighting so hard to prove her worth, that she had lost sight of the real fight. It was pointless trying to prove herself to other people. More than that; it was a complete waste of her time and energy. Better to direct her efforts where they were needed: helping her friends.

She looked back at the house. She knew exactly what she needed to do.

Chapter Twenty-Eight

Tess squatted down on her haunches as she stared at the house, thinking through what had happened over the past few days, and in particular the night before. She felt as though every window had a member of the household in it, staring back at her, but yet when she focused on each one, it was empty. Yet she could not shake the feeling she was being watched, and not for the first time, either.

She shook her head. *Think, Tess. Walk through exactly what happened the night Calvin was murdered.*

She had overheard the row between Calvin and his parents, after which he had stormed out, clearly upset. He had dropped the amulet as he left. Or had he thrown it away? She pulled it out from a pouch on her belt and turned it over in her hands. The patterns on it matched the styling on the house and gates. Presumably some sort of family insignia. Was his discarding it some form of protest? A way of him showing that he was making a break with the family?

Calvin had clearly been upset, no doubt not thinking straight, which would explain why he went straight out to the woods, where the demon was known to haunt. Unless he was going out there to meet someone. Or confront them. Someone connected to the row with his parents, perhaps.

Bart had been with the maid, who was upset. Something she said had made him believe that Calvin was the one who had upset her, and he had marched off after him.

Tess frowned. The way Bart had explained it, the maid was acting as though whatever incident had upset her had only just happened. And yet Tess had seen Calvin in a completely separate room with his parents. The impression she had gained was that Calvin had been there for some time. So either the maid had been extremely upset, to the extent that the passage of quite a few minutes had not been enough for her to calm down, or it had been someone else who had upset her.

She clicked her fingers, allowing herself a smile at the realisation. Someone else. Not Calvin. That is also what the girl had told Inspector Jones, which he had used as a basis for suspecting Bart was not telling him the truth. But what if they were *both* telling the truth?

Move on, she told herself. *Keep that thought for later and move on.*

Spencer had seen Bart and, when he had tried to stop him, had been told to look after the maidservant, which he had done. He had wandered away, presumably to check through the window for Bart. But Jones was clearly accusing him of using that time to help Bart, by hiding the axe which he claimed was used to murder Calvin.

A key question was whether Spencer had had enough time to do all of that. He was in the house when Tess had gone back in to raise the alarm, which was not long after Bart had emerged from the woods. So there could not have been more than five minutes when he was unaccounted for. Was that long enough? Spencer was a fast runner, so it was possible, although she did not recall him looking out of breath when she went back in the house.

The bigger puzzle, though, was how he could have got in and out of the house. The servants were all in the kitchen, which was directly off the rear door, so he would have been seen if he had gone that way. And the front door was unlikely, as Mr Smith locked it religiously, with multiple locks, which would slow down even someone with Spencer's lockpicking skills. So surely there would not have been enough time for him to go in and out through that door, including unlocking and relocking it after him.

So where else? The windows? Possible. He said he had gone to look out of one of the windows. If it was in an empty room on the ground floor, he could have opened it and climbed out.

But then there was the size and weight of the axe itself. It had taken two police constables to carry it into the sitting room earlier. Could someone as slight as Spencer have run unseen across the garden with it, let alone lift it through a window and up some stairs, in a short enough time to not be overly missed, and without anyone seeing or hearing him? At best the idea was unlikely.

She knew the inspector's theory was wrong, and it surely would not stand up to sober scrutiny. It was her job, then, to make sure that the police saw sense, before this charade continued for too long.

The axe had clearly been planted in Spencer's room, and probably by the same person who had broken into her own room and destroyed her instruments. Find that person, and she would clear Spencer's name.

But if the axe was the murder weapon, and had been brought into the house and placed in Spencer's room by someone else, then that begged two questions: who and how?

Her mind flitted over all the people in the house. Who would have had a motive to murder Calvin and frame Spencer and Bart?

Ralph had always seemed to have it in for Spencer and Bart, and arguably had an incentive to murder Calvin, as now his wife-to-be was due to inherit the entire family wealth. He was definitely a suspect.

Emilia? Tess could not believe that her old friend was capable of murder, but she had seen enough of the bad that people could do—by accident or otherwise—to not completely discount it.

Lord and Lady Beaumont did seem genuinely upset about Calvin's death, and the argument, while it had prompted Calvin to storm out the house and to his doom, hadn't seemed orchestrated.

211

Assuming the axe was the murder weapon, how did the person who planted it in Spencer's room get it across the garden and into the house without anyone noticing? The most obvious answer was Mr Smith: he had the keys to the front door, so could have got in and out of the house easily. And he had access to all of their rooms, and no one would question why he was in their rooms if he was caught in the act; he would say he was simply doing his job.

The same could be said for the maidservant, and there was the fact that the girl had cast suspicion on Bart's version of events, by denying that Calvin had upset her, even though that was clearly the impression she had given Bart. She seemed to have been at the centre of the events that pointed the finger at both Spencer and Bart, but what reason would she have for getting them in trouble? Was she trying to protect someone, or being forced to lie and implicate them?

That was the core of all of this; the plain fact that, whenever something had gone wrong, Spencer and Bart had been there. The only logical conclusion, given she knew they were innocent, was that they were being framed.

The sudden realisation hit her, and she laughed aloud at her own stupidity.

She looked at the house, at the window where she had believed she had seen someone watching her on the first day, the top floor room which everyone had told her was empty. But what if it was not as unused as people were telling her?

Her eyes drifted down from the room and settled on the mysterious door, which she now noticed was directly below the window she had just been looking at. She remembered Wilbur telling her that the door had not been used for years, and that it probably led to just a storeroom. But the more she thought about that, the stranger it seemed. Not that there would be an unknown or useless door in a house, but that the groundsman would be unaware and seemingly incurious about its use. In her experience, groundsmen not only knew every inch of the outside of a building, but they also were hungry for space to store things. She remembered the groundsman at the house where she grew up; he took pride in all the nooks and crannies he used to keep his equipment, not to mention the places where he could hide away for a rest or a snack. Wilbur seemed a canny enough fellow; there was no way that he had not explored the space beyond that door and, if it really was storage, he would be using it.

So what was he hiding? She decided she had to find out.

She approached the house, walking casually and making a show of inspecting the flowers, just in case anyone was watching her. She reached the door and looked around, pleased to note that she was out of sight of all the windows. She reached into one of the pouches in her belt and pulled out a small lockpicking set. Spencer had been teaching her how to pick locks, something which she found to be an entertaining diversion, certainly more fun than needlepoint. She was still a bit raw, but she fancied her chances of testing her new skills on this lock.

With one last look around to make sure she wasn't being watched, she first tested the door to check it actually was locked— the first lesson Spencer had drummed into her, and one, he said, he had learnt the hard way on more than one occasion when he was growing up. It did not budge, so she selected her tools and bent down to insert them into the lock. As she did so, she noticed that the ground in front of the door had been scraped back; the door had been opened very recently. She smiled; she was clearly on the right track.

It took a few minutes of scraping, wiggling and teasing with the pick before she felt the lock start to ease open. A few more jiggles and it opened with a satisfying click. She smiled to herself; her boys would be proud of her.

The door swung open soundlessly; it was clearly well oiled, lending yet more evidence to the case that Wilbur had not told the truth about the door not being used. Beyond was a narrow, dark servants' staircase, leading up.

She looked around and picked up a reasonable-sized rock,

then stepped inside and placed the rock in the doorway to wedge it open. She did not fancy being inadvertently locked inside, especially if she needed to make a quick exit. She took a deep breath and started up the stairs.

They went up four short flights, each flight she estimated to be half a storey, turning sharply back on themselves each time, and ended at a solid-looking door. She tested the door; it was unlocked and again the hinges were well-oiled, the door swinging silently open.

Beyond was a bedroom, and stood in the middle of the room was her worst nightmare.

*

Tess found herself back in her room, sat on the edge of her bed, staring at the door.

What was she doing there? She remembered going through the mysterious door, up the stairs and then... Had she hit her head? She put her fingers up to her scalp. There was no tenderness, no bumps or scratches as far as she could tell.

She looked at the clock and then frowned. Two hours had passed since she had gone through the door and up the stairs. What had happened to her?

She wracked her brain, but it was almost as though there was an impermeable membrane blocking the way to the memories of... whatever it was that had happened to her. Whenever she tried to push her thoughts past that, she bounced off and away to something else entirely.

Maybe she should retrace her steps? No. As soon as the thought entered her head, her heart started racing and her body shaking.

Interesting, a distant part of her noted. An extreme physical and psychological reaction to even the thought of going back to that place. Now where had she come across such a thing before?

She stood. She knew exactly what she needed to do. She

needed to go and find a magician.

Chapter Twenty-Nine

Spencer paced the dingy cell, pausing only to kick the door each time he passed it. Bart sat on the hard bed, watching him while picking dirt from under his nails.

"You know that's not going to get us out any faster," said Bart.

"No. But it makes me feel better. And it reminds them we're still here, in case they're thinking of leaving us here to rot."

"You'd be better off saving your energy. Have a nap or something."

"A nap! I don't mind being banged up when I've done something wrong—"

"That's not true."

"All right. I *do* mind being banged up when I've done something wrong. But it's even worse when I've not done anything!" He stopped and glared at his friend. "How can you sit there like that? Aren't you even a bit cross?"

Bart shrugged. "We're innocent. They'll figure that out soon enough and then we'll be on our way."

Spencer stopped and stared at him. "After all the years you've spent in and around Peelers and prisons, haven't you learnt anything? When they have the likes of us banged up, they don't tend to work that hard to find a way to let us out."

"Tess is on the case. She'll sort it."

"Don't know if you've noticed, mate, but Tess has hardly been on top form lately. She's probably run straight to Thaddeus so he can poison her mind with more useless stuff. She'll not be any help to us."

"Nah." Bart shook his head. "You're wrong."

Keys rattled in the door and they both turned to see Inspector Jones standing there, a distant expression on his face.

"About time," said Spencer. "You actually going to question us, or charge us, or something? We have got rights, you know."

Jones ignored him. "Got a visitor for you boys." He stepped aside.

Spencer and Bart backed away as a huge shadow fell over them, and a massive demon folded itself into the cell, its eyes glowing with murderous intent.

"Hey, now come on," shouted Spencer. "What's this? What...?"

The cell door slammed shut, the keys turning in the lock as the demon advanced on them.

*

Thaddeus watched Tess from his chair on the other side of the dark room, his fingers steepled in front of his nose as he listened to her recount the events of the past day to him.

"And you have no recollection of what happened to you before regaining consciousness in your bedroom?" he asked.

"Not a jot," she said. "It is frustrating. I know there is something there, but my mind slips off it any time I get close enough. Almost like..."

"Like the times Mr Emerson mesmerised you, all those months ago. But I would argue it is not *almost* like that; it is *exactly* like that." He stood up. "I think I need to do some mesmerisation of my own."

Tess took a step backwards. "You... You want to do the same thing to me? No. I do not think so."

He shrugged. "It is up to you. But if you want to fully understand exactly what has been happening to you, and why, then you will need to trust me."

She stared at him. "Spencer and Bart have told me everything about you. I know exactly what you are capable of, and how devoid of morals you are."

"And yet time and again you come to see me."

"Because I want to make sense of what happened to me. To understand how I can ensure it never happens to anyone else, ever again. And to do that through conversation, that is all. But this suggestion of yours... That goes too far."

"There is only so much that I can achieve through just talking. But it is of no consequence to me, so if that is your final answer then I suppose there is little else for us to do."

He picked up his book and started reading, while Tess pulled a face of frustrated concentration.

"Wait," she said. "How do I know that I can trust you? If you are right, and there has already been at least one person playing around with my brain, why should I let you loose in there as well? I would argue it is crowded enough in there, without also letting you have a play. How do I not know that you will not just do something to suit your own ends, rather than help me?"

"I will give you my word?" he said.

She raised an eyebrow and folded her arms.

"Very well," he sighed. "I should be able to unpick what has happened to your brain without having to mesmerise you. To be honest, I find it a blunt tool at best. I have a certain method which will enable us to view what has occurred, both of us as observers. You will be conscious and aware throughout, and you will be a willing participant in anything I do; free to refuse should you not agree with what I say at any point."

"I am still relying on your word," she noted.

"It is the best I can do. Others with my training could vouch for what I am saying, but you may have noticed that we are a little short on the ground in terms of high-level magicians here. So what say you?"

She stared at him, thinking. Then she was struck by something. "You put on a pretence of not being bothered either way, but you really do want to do this, do you not? Why?"

He opened his mouth as though to deny everything, and

then changed his mind. He looked away as he spoke. "Your case is intriguing because, right from the start, it involved people meddling in things which they have no right to get involved in, things which are way beyond their abilities to control."

"Mr Emerson."

"Indeed. Whilst I enjoy a bit of chaos as much as anyone—probably more than most people—there are limits. I have to live in this world, and I do not have any interest in it being destroyed on the whim of an incompetent."

"Better it be destroyed by competent people."

"Well, yes."

"Like yourself."

He held up his hands. "Lady Marchant, my interests in this particular matter are benign. Indeed, our interests align fully here. I, too, wish to know who has been doing whatever it is they are doing, and to what end."

"And to stop them?"

"Maybe."

She laughed. "You are not helping your case here! If your intention is to reassure and convince me..."

"I am being truthful. I thought that was what you wanted. I cannot state with certainty that I will stop them, because I do not know what they are doing or why."

"So if we discover that what they are doing is something that you agree with?"

"I will reconsider my actions, if and when that occurs. But for the time being, you can trust me to undertake the task we discussed. Is that sufficient for you?"

She ran her fingers through her hair, thinking through her options. From where she was standing, it did not feel like she had any. And with her friends languishing in jail, if there was a connection between whatever had been done to her and the wider case, she had a duty to help them.

"Very well," she said. "But you saw what I did to my husband; if you even think about crossing me, that will be nothing compared to what I will do to you!"

*

Spencer and Bart backed away from the demon as it approached them.

Spencer shot a sideways glance at his friend. "What do we do?"

"Don't ask me," said Bart. "Got nothing in here I could use as a weapon." He looked around, testing the only item of furniture in there, the bed, to see if it could be picked up, but it was only the mattress that came away. He looked at it for a moment, noticing how flimsy it was, and then shook his head.

"Yeah, I don't think that will do it."

Spencer backed away, grabbing his friend's arm, pulling him with him. In no time they were pressed back against the wall.

"Hey!" shouted Spencer. "Inspector Jones! Officers? Anyone? What's going on here?"

Bart shook his head. "No one's coming. Looks like they plan to bump us off."

"Brilliant!" said Spencer. "The one time we do nothing wrong, the one time we go straight and actually try to help people for a change, and it's the police who try and kill us. And I'm pretty sure what they're doing here ain't legal!"

"Where's a solicitor when you want one, eh?"

The demon banged its fists against the wall, and let out an almighty roar. Its eyes glowing a fierce red, its hideous face twisted in hungry rage, muscles rippling beneath hard, scaled, rhino-like skin.

"Right, "said Spencer. "This is Trevor, the demon we spoke to the other day, right? Let's see if we can get him to remember us."

"Erm, you remember what he ended up like after a few minutes of talking to us?" asked Bart. "A bit like he wanted to rip our heads off our bodies? A bit like now?"

"You got any better ideas?" Spencer asked him. When there

was no answer, he turned back to the demon. "Look, mate," he said, edging unsteadily towards the creature, "I don't know why you think you're here or what you think you want to do, but trust me when I say that you ain't got no quarrel with us. We're prisoners here, just like you. It's them out there you should be cross at, not us. "

The demon let out another piercing shriek and pounded its fist against the ground.

"I don't think he believes you," said Bart.

"He can't hear me over that God Almighty racket he's making," muttered Spencer. He backed off again as the monster advanced on them, fists raised, ready to strike.

They heard the sound of keys turning urgently in the lock.

Chapter Thirty

Inspector Jones stood in the hallway of Flint Hall, his hat held in front of him, clasped to his stomach like a shield. He played nervously with the brim of the hat as he spoke to a distraught Tess.

"I'm sorry, he said. "There's nothing we could have done. The demon came out of nowhere and overpowered us. I barely made it out myself."

"And they are both dead?" Tess asked. "You're sure of that?"

Jones nodded. "I'm afraid so."

Tess looked away for a moment and then straightened her back, taking a deep breath before turning to look at him. "I want to go and see the bodies. I refuse to believe it."

"I'm afraid that there's not much of their bodies for you to see," said Jones. "We will make arrangements in due course but, for the time being, you should stay here."

"I am not some shy and retiring maiden who swoons at the first sign of blood," she said.

"I do not doubt it. But the demon is still at large. We have officers out, combing the area, but until it is found and subdued I need you—and everyone else—to remain indoors."

She opened her mouth, but Inspector Jones cut her off with a raised hand. "I must insist," he said loudly.

Emilia appeared behind Tess, putting an arm around her to guide her away. "I will keep her safe, Inspector," she said. "Come now, Tess. You have had a nasty shock. Let us get some tea."

That evening, they all gathered for dinner in the dining room. The room was illuminated by candles which cast a flickering glow which reached no more than a foot or so beyond the table, the edges of the room swathed in a darkness which, in any other circumstances, would have given the occasion a cosy feel. The atmosphere was subdued, all of them glancing warily at Tess, who sat quietly, picking at her food.

"I am sorry about your loss," said Lord Beaumont. "A terrible thing."

"Although quite a poetic comeuppance, one could say, eh?" said Ralph.

They all glared at him and he stared back, wide-eyed but unapologetic. He focused back on his own plate with a shrug and a shake of his head.

"What will you do now?" Lady Beaumont asked.

Tess took a deep breath. "I do not know. They did not have any family—at least none that I am aware of—so I do not know if there is anyone to notify. The funerals will be rather a strange affair."

"Damned shame," muttered Lord Beaumont. "I mean, I know they were hardly our type of people, but no one deserves that."

Ralph coughed. "Sorry. Something stuck in my throat."

The room descended into quiet as they all focused on their food, the only sound the clink of cutlery on plate and the ticking of the clock in the corner. The Beaumonts glanced at each other, while Tess kept her focus squarely down at the table.

The stillness was disrupted by a loud roar from outside. Without a word, Tess immediately stood, her chair scraping on the wooden floor. Her face was fixed into an expression of vague concentration, focused on something unseen in the middle distance. She moved like an automaton, walking round the table and out of the room.

None of the others tried to stop her, or indeed allowed it to disturb their meal. After a few minutes, having heard the door slam shut, Ralph stood and went over to the window, pulling the curtain back and peering out into the darkness.

"There she goes," he said. "Good girl."

He sat back down and they continued to eat, each of them keeping an ear out for sounds from outside. After a few moments, they heard a cry and another roar, and then all was silent.

As one, all in the room seemed to exhale.

"Is it over?" asked Lady Beaumont.

"I think so," said her husband, putting down his knife and fork and picking up his glass. He looked up as the door opened and a dark figure stepped in, keeping to the shadows. "Well?" he addressed the newcomer. "Is that it?"

A pause, then the shadowy figure said, "Yes."

Lord Beaumont nodded and raised his glass in a salute before draining the contents. "I trust our debt is now repaid and we are free to go about our business once more."

Another pause, then the shadow again said, "Yes."

Emilia let out a sob, burying her face in her napkin.

"What is the matter with her?" asked Lord Beaumont. He turned to Ralph. "Control your fiancée, man."

"Control!" spat Emilia. "That's all you've ever done: control me. I did not want to be a part of this sordid plan. And to do such a thing to poor Tess…"

"It was necessary," said Lady Beaumont.

"No it was not! None of it was necessary! Just because your damned brother wanted us to aid him in his petty vengeance!"

"Do not speak of your uncle so," said Lady Beaumont coldly. "Show some respect."

"Why? Or he'll do to me what he did to all those other women? Oh, yes, I know all the rumours and stories. The reason why he came back here in disgrace, why he's been skulking around upstairs, plotting. Such a bitter, petty little man. And now he's dragged us all down with him!"

"He is family," said Lady Beaumont. "He is my brother, and he is a genius of a man. You would do well to hold your tongue, Emilia."

"Genius!" shouted Emilia. "How quickly you've changed

your tune. After what he did to Calvin!"

"That was an accident. He explained everything to me. It was meant to be Bart and Spencer out there that night. Your brother was stupid enough to go out into the woods without the protective amulet. He…" She stopped, suddenly surprised to feel tears rolling down her cheeks.

"You do not truly believe that, do you?" said Emilia. "I do not know what he has done, but somehow he has played with your mind. Made you stop caring, so he could carry on with his terrible plan." She turned and shouted at the figure in the corner. "Your own sister!"

"That is enough!" snapped Lord Beaumont. "The important thing is that all of this is done. We can all go back to normal, although we are not quite out of the woods yet. We need to maintain our composure when the police arrive, to investigate this latest murder. Our story is simple: we all assume that Lady Marchant retired to bed just now. She was out of sorts. We will discover the body in the morning, call Inspector Jones, be suitably distraught and appalled and then, when he has come to the realisation that there is no human hand behind any of this, we can all go back to normal." He nodded to the dark shadow. "And I assume you will be packing up and getting as far away as possible before then."

There was silence from the shadowy figure.

"Well?" asked Lord Beaumont, a nervous edge to his voice.

Instead of the deep voice from the shadowy figure, another voice spoke up. A female voice. "Do you think that is enough for you, Inspector?"

The door swung wide open to reveal, in the light from the hall outside, Tess and Inspector Jones.

The Beaumonts looked round, some starting to their feet, others rooted in shock. Ralph started for the other door, which opened to reveal two figures, one large and one rather less so.

"Where'd you think you're going?" rumbled Bart.

"Yeah," said Spencer. "Be much obliged if you'd sit back

down, mate."

Ralph boggled at them. Contrary to what they had been led to believe, both men were very much alive. And Spencer, for some reason, was wearing a dress and a bonnet.

"But... What... Emerson, what is the meaning of this?" bellowed Lord Beaumont, at the figure who was still standing stock still by the door.

"Oh, do not mind him," said Tess. "He's not really feeling himself." She held up a tubular device. "A little something I brought with me, an invention of a friend of mine. It is rather effective at ensuring someone does as they're told."

"Yeah," said Spencer. "Take it from me, it's very effective."

Lord Beaumont blinked. "I have no idea what is going on here," he blustered. "I do not know this man, and nor do I..."

"Pull the other one, sir," said Inspector Jones, walking into the centre of the room, followed by half a dozen constables, who took up positions around the table. "It's got bells on it."

"We heard everything you said after I left the room," said Tess. "And as for this man..." She turned to the shadowy figure and said, "Step forward."

The figure obeyed, walking jerkily forward until he was in the light. His eyes glared, showing that, while his body was out of his control, his mind was very keen to rebel against the control imposed on it by Tess and her device.

Tess smiled sweetly as she walked to stand next to Emerson. "You said just now you do not know him, but how could you not recognise your brother-in-law?" she asked Lord Beaumont. "The mysterious lodger in the supposedly empty upstairs room?"

"My..." started Lord Beaumont, but further words failed him and he sat back, his arms folded firm across his chest.

"That is correct, is it not?" Tess asked Lady Beaumont. "Your maiden name is Emerson."

Lady Beaumont opened and closed her mouth, but said nothing.

Emilia was looking from Tess to Spencer and Bart, and back

again. "But how did you…?"

"Manage to not get murdered by your uncle's pet demon?" asked Tess. "Glad you asked. You see, your uncle, Mr Emerson here, may be a rather ingenious individual when it comes to the paranormal, but we have something even better—our very own magician."

"Let him talk," Jones said to Tess, nodding at Emerson. "I would be interested in any responses he might have to this."

"Very well," Tess said, pressing a button on her device. "You may talk," she said to Emerson.

Emerson's mouth started moving, as though it had just been thawed out after a long freeze. A string of expletives came out, snarled with an intensity that silenced everyone in the room.

"I should add, though," said Tess, "that if you make any attempt to mesmerise anyone, I will seal your lips again."

Emerson's eyes flicked to her. "It is touching that you feel you are strong enough to resist my powers."

She shrugged. "I might not be. But he is." She nodded to the corner, and Thaddeus appeared, nodding briefly.

"You," snarled Emerson. "I made you an offer…"

"Which I declined," said Thaddeus. "I have no desire to get into business with a charlatan such as yourself."

"Charlatan! Why I—"

"This is all very entertaining," said Jones. "But I for one am keen to wrap up this evening's events. You will all, of course, be taken into custody."

"I do not understand," muttered Ralph. "They were all dead."

"Mistake number one, mate," said Spencer. "If you're going to do the dirty on someone, make sure you're there to watch. It's amazing how things can go wrong."

"Yes," said Jones. "Like when you mesmerise an officer of the law into letting a demon into a prison cell with two defenceless men. Thankfully, Thaddeus arrived in the nick of time to release me from the spell and then subdue the demon."

"How did you know?" asked Emerson.

"You were clumsy," said Thaddeus. "You mesmerised Tess on more than one occasion. Firstly when she originally met you, back in London. An occasion which you repeated many times in the lead up to when you possessed her with that demon. Tess and I had been having a number of conversations to unpick how you had managed to exert your influence over her. Initially, I had thought it was some sort of spell, but then I realised it was a lot more mundane: mesmerisation.

"The one problem with that is that, while it does not leave Aetheric residues like a magical spell would do, it does leave its imprint in the mind. And when Tess arrived here, she started to dream about you and your influence. I knew then that there was a connection."

"So did I," said Tess. "And when I saw correspondence with Lady Beaumont's maiden name on it, I knew that there was more than coincidence at play here. Of course, my suspicions were first aroused by the inconsistencies in how you all greeted us. Emilia was keen to make it clear that she had told no one we were coming. And yet Ralph let slip that you had talked about nothing but collecting us, and it was rather telling that you had the exact number of rooms ready for us."

"We entertain a lot," sniffed Lady Beaumont.

"Except you do not; not anymore. The servants told my friends as much. And it is clear from the way that this house has been kept that you have fallen on hard times."

"Tess, I…" started Emilia.

"I thought we were friends," Tess said to her, a cold edge to her voice. "But you were the one who asked me to come here. No, practically begged me. All of us. It was only as events unfolded that I started to realise: there might be a demon here, but its target was not your father, not your family. No. The real targets were me and my friends. And all because we bested you, Mr Emerson."

"You did not best me!" Emerson spat. "You are nothing to me. Nothing!"

"And yet here we are," said Spencer. "Beating you again."

As Emerson started to spew out another stream of curses, Jones nodded to the constables. "Take him away. Take them all away."

Tess instructed Emerson to go with the policemen and his body complied, while his mouth continued with its vile outpourings.

As Ralph was led past them, he sneered at Spencer. "Nice outfit," he said.

Spencer grinned, wafting his skirts. "We had to make you lot think Tess was going out into the woods," he said. "Give her time to run upstairs and catch Emerson unawares with her freezing device thingy, while he was also watching what he thought was Tess going out to the woods." He gave Ralph a little curtsy as he was led away.

"Easy, mate," muttered Bart. "You're enjoying that a bit too much, you know."

"But the demon…" said Emilia, as she was led to the door.

"Oh, that," said Jones. "That beast is safe in our cells. Thaddeus subdued it."

"Then what did we hear…?"

"Just now?" asked Bart. "Did it sound a bit like this?" He threw his head back and let out a loud roar.

"That was you? But… But that sounds nothing like the demon in days past…"

"It's close enough, though, right?" said Spencer. "And it's amazing how folk'll hear what they want to hear."

Jones turned to Thaddeus. "So you have released us all from Emerson's influences?"

"Completely," said Thaddeus. "The suggestions which made you want to see Spencer and Bart locked up with a demon are fully excised; although I suspect that the notion itself did not take too much persuasion."

Jones grinned. "No," he said, glancing at the two men. "I suspect it did not."

While Spencer and Bart started to protest, Thaddeus added, "And also the commands he placed in your head to compel you in insist on coming down to investigate this case."

"I remember when Tess questioned me about the reasons for me taking this case," said Jones. "It were as though there was a brick wall in my mind; deep down I knew it was strange, that it was so far away from my usual patch, but there was something in my head which would not allow me to question that.

"Indeed," said Thaddeus. "And the suggestions placed in Lady Marchant's head should now be largely removed. Including the compulsion he placed for this evening, intending that you would walk out to the woods and into the demon's clutches as soon as you heard its roar."

"Clever, though, eh?" said Spencer. "He nearly had us framed for something he did, then murdered before we could clear our names. And if Tess'd gone out to the demon like she was supposed to, you lot would've just thought nothing of it, blamed the demon and gone back to London, eh?"

"Yes," said Jones. "If not for Thaddeus…"

"Oh, no," said Thaddeus quickly. "I want no part of any of this. I just lifted the veil. It was Lady Marchant who realised the nature of the veil itself; indeed that there was a veil there in the first place."

"Veil?" asked Bart. "We still talking about women's' clothing?"

"Nope," said Spencer. "He means all the fancy stuff Emerson did to make everyone think stuff."

"I do wonder, though," said Jones. "What made you realise there was not just a rogue demon at play here?"

Tess smiled as all eyes turned to her. "Several things just did not add up. Firstly, why would the demon only come at certain times of the night, to a specific place, and not do much else apart from cause noise and a bit of minor damage?"

"Yeah," said Bart. "We all said it didn't look like your normal demon goings-on. They like to make a big mess, and they get bored easy."

"Correct," said Tess. "Whereas this demon returned every night to the exact same place, and disappeared shortly afterwards."

"But it could have been the curse that they contended it to be? A forewarning of the deaths to come?"

"It could," said Tess. "Except why do such a thing? If you're going to curse someone with a demonic death, why go to all the trouble of the demon manifesting before then? That sort of thing works if the curser intends to grind someone down, drive them mad with worry. But the one thing we noticed right from arriving here was that the family—and in particular Lord Beaumont, the person supposedly the focus of the curse—seemed remarkably unbothered by the demonic happenings.

"Then there was the question of why the demon confined itself to the woods, rather than coming to the house. I noticed a number of emblems around the house and also worn by every member of the household. Lady Beaumont tried to pass them off as mere curios, patterns that she liked. But we have had experience in the past of protective amulets."

"Yeah," said Spencer. "Special things that stop demons having an interest in you."

"It is more than that," said Thaddeus. "Done properly, they can actively deter a demon, cause it physical pain if it tries to do anything to the wearer, or even make the demon completely disregard them."

"So that was what you gave me, that night when I went into the woods and found Calvin's body," said Bart.

"That is right," said Tess. "And that is why the demon ran away rather than attack you. Calvin, unfortunately, was not so lucky. The original plan was for you to chase him into the woods, with him safe as he was wearing the amulet."

"Why was he not wearing it?" asked Jones.

"The argument with his parents," said Tess. "I hear him say he did not want to play a part in something; clearly that 'something' was Emerson's plans for us. Calvin was standoffish with the whole family, drinking as though he was trying to distance himself from everything. He did try to warn us a few times, but there was always a member of the family with him, so he could not elaborate. Then, after he had the row with his parents, he threw away the amulet."

"But why?" asked Jones.

"He was worked up, and probably had been drinking. I think he decided to go and have it out with his uncle."

"And instead met his uncle's pet demon."

"Yes. But he did not realise the demon would be out there."

"But we'd all heard it," said Bart. "And why go to all the trouble of the amulets if there was no demon?"

"Good question," said Tess. Bart grinned at her, proud of the complement, as she continued. "I believe that controlling a demon takes a lot of energy."

She looked to Thaddeus, who nodded in agreement.

"So," she continued, "he only deployed the demon when he really had to. As we said, the behaviour we saw—the limited damage and noise in particular—did not match what we would normally expect from a demon. The night when Mr Bishop was attacked... Well, that was not a demon."

"It was Ralph, wasn't it," said Spencer. "I knew it."

"Probably so," said Tess. "Aided by a projection by Emerson, a trick which scared Mr Bishop into believing there was a demon there. An illusion he created from his bedroom window, that looked directly down to the place where the supposed demon was appearing. That explains why my devices showed no demonic activity."

"And that's why they were smashed up the next day!" said Bart.

"Exactly! If I had proven beyond doubt there was no demon there that night, then that would have changed everything. And made Emerson's job so much more difficult. This is the key point. Emerson became far too sloppy; no doubt his desire for revenge outweighed his commonsense. But there were too many hints that there was more to this family than just the members we met when we arrived. The noises upstairs, which kept disturbing our sleep. And like all criminals, he could not resist visiting the scene of the crime."

"The little holes in the ground," said Spencer. "We said they looked like they'd been made by a walking stick!"

"That is correct," she said. "And then there was the fact that it was him who upset the maidservant."

Bart blinked. "Not Calvin?"

"No," said Tess.

"But she said the brother had upset her."

"That is right. But you assumed she meant Emilia's brother, when in fact she meant Lady Beaumont's brother!"

Bart nodded slowly and then grinned. "I knew she wouldn't try and stab me in the back!"

"Faith in humanity restored, eh?" said Spencer.

"Quite incredible to think that Emerson was behind all of this," said Jones. "I will take particular pleasure in unpicking this with them all, down at the station." He looked at Tess. "You must have greatly upset him, for him to go to such lengths."

She shrugged. "As my friends said, we beat him. Some people do not like that."

"Also," said Spencer, "You might've noticed, but me and Bart tend to get under peoples' skins a bit."

"Really," deadpanned Jones. "I had not noticed at all."

Spencer laughed and clapped him on the shoulder. "By the by, I take it this means our slate's clean here, on account of the stuff you banged us up for."

"And then banged us up with a murderous demon," said Bart. "Don't forget that."

"Yeah," said Spencer. "We'd never forget that. And I'm sure your superiors at Scotland Yard would be very interested in you doing that. Of course, if you treat us fairly, we'd see no need to do nothing but treat you fairly back, you get me?"

Jones glared at him. "I get you. And don't push it. I would ask that you all make yourselves available, just in case I have any further questions. That includes you, Mr Thaddeus…" He looked around. "Where did he go?"

Thaddeus had disappeared while they were talking.

"He does that a lot," said Spencer. "Not really the sort for getting involved in stuff."

Jones grunted. "I expect you three to not do a similar vanishing act."

"Perish the thought," said Tess.

"Yeah," said Spencer, eyeing the table, which was still ladened with food and drink. "It'd be a shame to leave this stuff here. I reckon we'll stick around for a bit."

"You do that," said Jones. He walked to the door and then stopped, one hand on the doorknob. "I'm going to regret this," he said, "but, when you get back to London, I have a problem which I think would benefit from your particular skillsets."

"You want us to work with you?" asked Spencer. "The Peelers? We're not—"

"We'd be delighted," said Tess. "We will call on you in Scotland Yard."

Jones looked at them, Spencer and Bart already shovelling food and wine into their faces, while Tess stood to the side, as inscrutable as ever. "No," he said. "I will call on you in your offices. It is better that way. Let's just say that bringing you on board may not have the blessing of my superiors." He nodded a goodbye and then left the room.

Tess turned to her friends. "I am sorry."

"For what?" Spencer asked around a mouthful of beef.

"For dragging you up here. For being distant. For not being as good a business partner as—"

"Shut up," said Bart, handing her a wine glass. "You're our Tess and that's all there is to it. And we won, didn't we?"

"I've just had a thought," said Spencer. "Do we get paid for this?"

"We've just sent our clients to jail," said Tess. "I think there's not much chance of them paying us for that."

"You reckon Jones'll pay us for that job he was just talking about?"

She grinned. "I reckon he won't have much choice, don't you?" She raised a glass in a toast. "To more great big demon hunts!"

SPENCER AND BART WILL RETURN IN
THE GREAT BIG DEMON PROTECTION AGENCY

Did You Enjoy This Book?

If so, you can make a HUGE difference.

For any author, the single most important way we have of getting our books noticed is a really simple one—and one which you can help with.

Yes, you.

Us indie authors and publishers don't have the financial muscle of the big guys to take out full-page ads in the newspaper or put posters on the subway.

But we do have something much more powerful and effective than that, and it's something that those big publishers would kill to get their hands on.

A committed and loyal bunch of readers.

Honest reviews of our books help bring them to the attention of other readers.

If you've enjoyed this book I would be really grateful if you could spend just a couple of minutes leaving a review (it can be as short as you like) on this book's page on your favourite store and website.

Acknowledgements

As always, there are so many people I want to thank, who have helped this book go from some random thoughts and musings to the more structured bunch of words you hold in your hands.

To Jess, Tom and Sam for your love, support and encouragement — I am truly blessed to have you in my life.

To Mum and Dad for your constant support, always.

To Simon Finnie — for your support, constructive thoughts and generally listening to me moan over countless beers.

To our amazing beta readers and reviewers, who took the time to let me know what you thought about the first book as well as this one. Every comment means so much, and it's thanks to you that I had the motivation to keep this series going. Yes, it's your fault: I hope you're proud of yourselves! And, if you're wondering whether it was your comments that led to Thaddeus continuing to keep popping up in these stories, yes it was you (you know who you are)…

The Agency's journey is only just beginning: Spencer, Bart and Tess (and Thaddeus, and Inspector Jones) will ride again, very soon, in The Great Big Demon Protection Agency. Sign up at peteroxleyauthor.com to be the first to be notified when it's released.

Peter Oxley
Hertfordshire, January 2024

If You Enjoyed This Book, Why Not Dive Into...

THE GREAT BIG DEMON HUNTING AGENCY

London, 1868. The streets are haunted by thieves, murderers... and demons from beyond the Aether.

Spencer and Bart are the city's most incompetent crooks, and they are in deep trouble. Hunted by both police and their fellow criminals, they are forced to consider the unthinkable —going straight.

Forming The Great Big Demon Hunting Agency, they thought their troubles were behind them, but they soon find themselves caught up in a web far more dangerous than they could ever imagine, pitched against demons, criminals and evil magicians.

Why are there so many demons roaming the London streets, and can Spencer and Bart stop them before it's too late?

Who are the mysterious Tappers, and what are they doing with the women they abduct from the streets?

Can Spencer and Bart change the habits of a lifetime and not only stay on the right side of the law, but also save the day?

The Great Big Demon Hunting Agency is the new novel from Peter Oxley, the author of the Infernal Aether series. If you like dark gothic adventures with a light-hearted twist, then you'll love The Great Big Demon Hunting Agency.

THE INFERNAL AETHER

*The Aether always held the universe together... but in the
nineteenth century, it just might tear it apart.*

London, 1865.

Betrayed by his closest friend and rapidly drinking through
his inheritance, sometime adventurer Augustus Merriwether
Potts returns home to a world being torn apart by supernatural
terrors.

A chance meeting with a mysterious stranger thrusts Augustus
and his brother into a terrifying underworld of demons, ghosts,
golems and clockwork men. An underworld controlled by a
demon known as Andras, the God of Lies.

Andras has a plan: to bring Hell on Earth using the power
of the Aether, a terrifying otherworld populated by creatures
from beyond humanity's worst nightmares. With the world's
governments in thrall to the demons, Augustus and his friends
find themselves in the front line of a battle to save humanity
against all the odds.

Dickens' London has never seemed so scary. *The Infernal
Aether* is the first book in a gothic fantasy series which has been
described as "no-holds-barred". If you like page turners with
unpredictable twists and chills then you'll love Peter Oxley's *The
Infernal Aether*.

Praise for The Infernal Aether:

"Epic, Epic, Epic, this story was so good I couldn't put it
down and was sad that I reached the last page."

—Aviar Savijon, Goodreads

"This no-holds-barred story features golems, bizarre devices,
clockwork entities, an airship, soul-suckers, and more (including
a cameo by Charles Dickens) and is told with wit and a touch
of humor."

—Kathy Burford, Amazon.com

"An awesome read. The author definitely has a handle on his art as a writer. Do yourself a favor and read it and everything he writes."

—Alan McDonald, Amazon.com

"I liked the way the story was told almost as much as the story itself."

—Tommi, Amazon.com

"Steampunk meets sci-fi fantasy horror with a great deal of magic weaving it all together in a real page-turner. With unpredictable twists and characters that I loved and loathed in equal measure it was a thoroughly enjoyable book which I devoured in one sitting. I can't wait to see what happens next."

—Alibel, amazon.co.uk

A CHRISTMAS AETHER

A Christmas Aether - a Novella from the universe of The Infernal Aether

Following the events of The Infernal Aether, surely humanity is safe at last?

The story continues in A Christmas Aether, a collection of new short stories continuing the story of Augustus, N'yotsu, Maxwell and Kate.

Find out what happens next, as Augustus finds himself beaten, bloody and helpless in London's demon-infested slums, as well as meet a terrifying new adversary in *The Ballad of William Morley*. Finally, *The Potts Demonology* provides fresh insights into the new world unleashed by the Aether, plus a sneak preview of the terrors to come in *The Demon Inside…*

THE DEMON INSIDE

How can you save the world when it's impossible to tell friend from foe?

Augustus Potts is in trouble.

The Fulcrum is fast approaching, an event that will tip the world into a new magical Dark Age and expose mankind to the full terrors of the Aether. More and more powerful demons are materialising on Earth, while neighbours and families are turning against each other thanks to the evil influence of the Witchfinder Generals.

While fighting the hell-hordes from the Aether, Augustus realises the runic sword that gives him all his supernatural powers is also turning him into the one thing he fears and despises the most: a demon.

At the same time N'yotsu, his friend and the one-time saviour of mankind, is realising that the only way he can survive is to turn back into the hated demon Andras.

When his closest friends and allies start to disappear, Augustus finds himself in a race against time to not only save the world but also himself…

In this most desperate of times, when the line between good and evil is not just blurred but torn to pieces, could his greatest enemy also be mankind's last hope?

Praise for The Demon Inside

"The Demon Inside is one tale you don't want to miss! Steam punk, touch of horror, humor, fantasy creatures, action, adventure, and just plain fun reading. I loved this book! Great plot, loads of twists and wonderful characters of all sorts, and refreshing new fantasy. I read the book out of order but it didn't seem to matter, it didn't effect the story at all. I am now going to read book one for sure! Wonderful fantasy, can't say enough about this book!"

- Montzalee Witmann, Amazon.com

"Strong captivating characters, a page turning plot: The Demon inside is an overall great read."

- Victoria Palmer, Amazon.com

"This was an amazing book. I enjoyed it's dark and intriguing atmosphere. The characters are well developed and the story is well developed. The second in this series and it seems to have gotten better with this instalment. Recommended."

- Alina Hart, Amazon.com

"I was caught up in it from the very first paragraph. There is lots of action and some surprising twists. I really enjoyed it. Definitely worth a read."

- Tommi, Amazon.com

BEYOND THE AETHER

When Satan himself comes calling, what would you do?

In the summer of 1869 evil once again threatens England from the endless darkness of the Aether, with humans and their new supernatural allies locked in a battle for survival against the malevolent Almadite forces.

When the famed demon hunter Kate Thatcher is kidnapped by the enemy, Augustus Potts and his friends must risk everything—including the safety of the entire planet—to rescue her before she is lost forever.

Their quest will take them to the very edge of existence, to distant worlds beyond their worst nightmares where they must overcome an unholy entity that could destroy everything they hold dear.

Their only chance of rescuing Kate and saving mankind lies in forming an alliance with the demon Andras. But Andras has his own plans that could lead to him holding ultimate power over all creation…

If you could cheat the laws of time and space to save the one you cared the most about, would you do so—no matter what the price?

Beyond the Aether is the third book in Peter Oxley's Infernal Aether Series, a dark gothic fantasy set in Victorian London described as "fantasy at its best", "epic" and "no holds barred". If you like electrifying action, rich characters and fantastical demonic worlds, then you'll love Beyond the Aether.

THE WEDDING SPEECH MANUAL: THE COMPLETE GUIDE TO PREPARING, WRITING AND PERFORMING YOUR WEDDING SPEECH

Now available in audiobook as well as paperback and ebook!

Do you need to do a wedding speech but have no idea how to start or what to say? Are you nervous about standing up and speaking in public?

The Wedding Speech Manual is your complete, practical, step-by-step guide to how to write and perform a personalised wedding speech: something which will be enjoyed and cherished by your loved ones, friends and family.

"Thank you very much Mr Peter Oxley, the wedding was yesterday and the speech went down a storm. This book helped me so much, everyone said I nailed it. If anyone out there has a wedding speech to do soon, then forget the rest, this book is the only one you'll need or want. Thanks again" – Robert Butler, Amazon.co.uk

This book will show you:

What you will be expected to say and do

How to master your nerves and stop them getting in the way of your successful speech

How to find loads of entertaining and amusing material to fill your speech

How to get the audience on your side right from the start

The key reasons why so many wedding speeches fail - and how you can make sure that yours doesn't

How to write and perfect your speech – a lot quicker and easier than you ever thought possible

The "dreaded wedding speech etiquette" made simple - what you should and shouldn't say on the big day

How to deliver your speech as confidently, calmly and impressively as possible

How to handle all the other stuff which can blind-side a public speaker: like using props, microphones and handling difficult audiences

The Wedding Speech Manual includes exercises to walk you through the process of writing your speech, plus a host of troubleshooting tips and techniques so that you are fully prepared for everything that could possibly happen!

This book is for all wedding speakers – not only the father of the bride, groom and best man, but also brides, mothers of the bride, bridesmaids – and will:

Give you the confidence to approach the wedding day safe in the knowledge that you have an excellent, original wedding speech which hits all the right notes

Get your wedding speech written quickly and straightforwardly – so you can focus on practising and all the other things you have to do!

Show you the tools which the professionals use to master their nerves – so you can deliver your speech confidently, coolly and calmly

Take away the stress of the dreaded wedding speech – so you can focus on enjoying the big day!

About The Author

Peter Oxley is an author, editor and coach who lives in the English Home Counties. He enjoys reading and writing in a wide range of areas but his main passions are sci-fi, fantasy, historical fiction and steampunk.

His influences include HG Wells, Charles Dickens, Neil Gaiman, KW Jeter, Scott Lynch, Clive Barker, Pat Mills and Joss Whedon.

He is the author of The Infernal Aether, A Christmas Aether and The Demon Inside.

He is also the author of the nonfiction book: The Wedding Speech Manual: The Complete Guide to Preparing, Writing and Performing Your Wedding Speech.

He lives with his wife, two young sons and a slowly growing guitar collection. Aside from writing and willingly speaking in front of large crowds of strangers, Pete spends his spare time playing music badly, supporting football teams that play badly, and writing about himself in the third person.

peteroxleyauthor.com
Twitter: @Peteoxleyauthor
Facebook: PeteOxleyAuthor
Tiktok: @peteroxleyauthor

About Burning Chair

Burning Chair is an independent publishing company based in the UK, but covering readers and authors around the globe. We are passionate about both writing and reading books and, at our core, we just want to get great books out to the world.

Our aim is to offer something exciting; something innovative; something that puts the author and their book first. From first class editing to cutting edge marketing and promotion, we provide the care and attention that makes sure every book fulfils its potential.

We are:

Different

Passionate

Nimble and cutting edge

Invested in our authors' success

If you're an author and would like to know more about our submissions requirements and receive our free guide to book publishing, visit:

www.burningchairpublishing.com

If you're a reader and are interested in hearing more about our books, being the first to hear about our new releases or great offers, or becoming a beta reader for us, again please visit:

www.burningchairpublishing.com

More From Burning Chair Publishing

Your next favourite new read is waiting for you…!

The Great Big Demon Hunting Agency, by Peter Oxley

The Infernal Aether series, by Peter Oxley
  The Infernal Aether
  A Christmas Aether
  The Demon Inside
  Beyond the Aether
  The Old Lady of the Skies: 1: Plague

The Casebook of Johnson & Boswell, by Andrew Neil Macleod
  The Fall of the House of Thomas Weir
  The Stone of Destiny

By Richard Ayre:
  Shadow of the Knife
  Point of Contact
  A Life Eternal

The Curse of Becton Manor, by Patricia Ayling

Near Death, by Richard Wall

The Haven Chronicles, by Fi Phillips

Haven Wakes
Magic Bound

Love Is Dead(ly), by Gene Kendall

Beyond, by Georgia Springate

10:59, by N R Baker

The Other Side of Trust, by Neil Robinson

The Sarah Black Series, by Lucy Hooft
    The King's Pawn
    The Head of the Snake

The Brodick Cold War Series, by John Fullerton
    Spy Game
    Spy Dragon
    Burning Bridges, by Matthew Ross

By P N Johnson:
    Killer in the Crowd
    Run to the Blue

Push Back, by James Marx

The Blue Bird Series, by Trish Finnegan
    Blue Bird
    Blue Sky
    Baby Blues

The Tom Novak series, by Neil Lancaster
    Going Dark
    Going Rogue
    Going Back

The Wedding Speech Manual, by Peter Oxley

www.burningchairpublishing.com

Printed in Dunstable, United Kingdom